HIT

P.S. Bridge

Clink
Street

London | New York

Published by Clink Street Publishing 2017

Copyright © 2017

First edition.

ISBN:
978-1-911525-86-8 - paperback
978-1-911525-87-5 - ebook

COMING SOON

Hitback

Each one of us has a Mark King inside of us. Someone who goes through something horrific, who suffers immeasurable loss, and endures momentous pain, yet manages to grow from it and come out the other side, a stronger, wiser and better person. There is a difference between accepting the path that lies before you, and choosing to walk it.

So to those who have helped me, you know who you are and I thank you. To the others, those who said it couldn't be done, or wouldn't be done, I say look, read, understand and above all, judge not the faithful and the true, for there will be a day when those you have judged, judge you.

Prologue

Syria, Three months ago

Two black Agusta A109 Grand helicopters surveyed the landscape as they hurtled towards the rendezvous point just south of their current location. They cut through the air, flying low, and kicked up clouds of smoke as they landed just opposite a stone building, one of the few still standing after the destruction of the previous few days. Seven heavily armed men got out, wearing scarfs to cover their faces against the flying dust and dirt as they hurried towards the building away from the rush and noise of the rotor blades downdraft. A young man, dressed as if ready for battle, got out wearing a scarf over his lower face, and Aviator sunglasses. He was carrying a small black Heckler & Koch MP5-K sub-machine gun, and he had a large Kabar army knife, sheathed in his belt. He checked his silver Rolex watch and looked around him to make sure they had not been intercepted or followed. The other armed men stood on guard either side of the doorway of the stone building as he marched through the doorway and into the darkness. Two guards then stood guard in the doorway, gripping their AK-47s tightly.

The convoy of yellowish brown four-by-fours kicked up clouds of dust as they rumbled through the war-torn brown landscape, destroyed by drone attacks and Syrian airstrikes.

Twenty-two months of war had transformed the once thriving town into a barren, derelict wasteland. From his window, MI6 agent Nathanial Williams scoured the ruined buildings behind a pair of Aviators in shock at the utter devastation which had been wreaked on this town, only days before.

The convoy rumbled on its dusty journey as the attaché from the National Defence Force's Government counter-insurgency force spoke in Syrian to the interpreter sat next to Agent Williams, pointing out key stronghold positions which were active only days before their arrival.

At night, it was a no-go area for anyone, with militia still trying actively to recoup lost ground. The surrounding hills, once inviting, were now foreboding and scarred where mortar shells and artillery shelling had burst upon its surface, causing it to resemble the surface of the moon.

'We capture this town two days ago. Much killing here. Syrian air force they try to drive back insurgent militia until drone strike.'

Williams turned suddenly.

'Wait, what, a drone strike did all this damage?' he asked, shocked at what the interpreter said.

The attaché, a man in his mid-forties who didn't speak English, looked confused at Williams. Williams, forgetting the need for the interpreter, apologised and turned to the interpreter, asking the same question for him to ask the attaché. He waited patiently for the response.

'Young boys used play football here. "Middle class" people meet and cook dinner, listen to music all night long. Gone now,' he relayed to Williams.

The interpreter pointed down the road and waved his arm around.

'He say cedar trees used grow along all three side,' he translated as he waited for the attaché to continue.

'No more. Taken for firewood.'

Williams shook his head in disbelief. He had worked mainly in Europe and this was his first time in a war zone.

The interpreter patted him on the arm to get his attention. Williams' attention was taken away to huts, lining the roadside, with their tin roofs stripped off, probably to be used by the swathes of refugees who either passed through here or moved from here to escape the approaching onslaught.

'He says drone strikes like this happen all of time. He said western governments, mostly Americans, they know when Al-Azidi meets his commanders and they target him two days ago.'

Agent Williams nodded and turned back to look out of the window before their driver, also with the National Defence Force, and dressed in National Defence Force uniform, motioned that they had arrived. Williams jumped out first, his weapon at the ready. The group, made up of six men, mostly from the National Defence Force and one agent, Todd Greamer, from the CIA, huddled together next to the lead vehicle, out of sight of the stone building ten feet away.

'Right, I want two at the back, two to provide cover fire and Greamer and I will go in the front,' he commanded in an authoritative, Scottish tone. Greamer nodded, and the interpreter relayed the message to their attaché. Williams rolled his eyes, frustrated with the language barrier and Greamer laughed silently, shaking his head. Williams waited until they were all clear on what to do and they crept out from behind the vehicle towards the building.

Within seconds, they were met by a volley of automatic gunfire and dived for cover, shouting instructions at each other as the bullets bounced off the dry, crumbled stone around them. There were few areas of cover out here and Williams' heart beat faster. He had been separated from his interpreter and attaché and he looked desperately around for Greamer, who had found cover alongside a pile of rock further up the road. Greamer nodded to him and Williams nodded back, motioning that he thought there were eight or more men inside.

With a keen and well trained eye, he noticed several men exit the rear of the building on foot, towards a Jeep, whose driver was already looking panicked.

'Looks like we interrupted your meeting, Azidi,' Williams said aloud as he motioned for Greamer to follow him. The two men managed only a few steps before one of those fleeing turned and opened fire on them. Williams and Greamer scattered, avoiding the bullets ripping up the ground between them. They were back on track in seconds but the Jeep was mobile and heading off among a cloud of dust and smoke. Williams could hear gunfire back at the building behind them and ran towards the lead vehicle in their convoy. He jumped in and started the engine, wheel spinning into the dust as he thundered after Azidi's vehicle.

Azidi opened fire on them vigorously from the back of the Jeep and Williams threw the steering wheel left and right, swerving to avoid the hail of automatic fire. His windscreen was hit and Williams, in the panic, flung the wheel round sharply to the left, hitting a rock, causing the four-by-four to crash over onto its side as the engine emitted plumes of smoke. There was a satisfied cheer from the Jeep as it quickly vanished out of sight toward the Lebanese mountains. The pursuing vehicles, realising Williams' plan and having given chase, screeched to a halt at the side of the overturned vehicle. The wheels were still spinning, and the engine was over-revving, smoke billowing out from the undercarriage. Williams was hurt, not badly but enough to draw blood, and he scrambled out of the passenger window which was facing the sky, covered in blood and dirt, looking beaten but OK.

Greamer grabbed his arm and helped to haul him from the wreckage and clear of the vehicle in case the fuel tank had ruptured. It was a good call from Greamer, for as they staggered away from it, the entire vehicle erupted into flames. The men threw themselves at the ground as the shock wave and heat from the fuel tank hit them like a tsunami, throwing them forward. Williams was the first to put his head up, spitting blood and dust as he checked around for everyone else. Greamer was cut but otherwise unharmed. Everyone seemed OK, breathless, but alive. Williams got up and kicked the stones in frustration.

'I HAD HIM!' he shouted to Greamer, who was walking towards him reloading his weapon and looking around for snipers.

'I bloody had him!' he cried again at Greamer. Greamer nodded as he handed Williams his water tank, which Williams drank from excessively and wiped his sweat-laden, dirty forehead.

'Don't worry man, there'll be another opportunity to get the bastard!' Greamer reassured Williams before checking the horizon to see the rush of vehicles coming towards them.

'C'mon man, we gotta get outta here,' he warned.

Williams agreed and Greamer patted Williams' back in support as the group ran back to their vehicles. Williams jumped in the front passenger seat, his weapon ready. Greamer jumped in the drivers' seat and handed his AR-15 tactical defence rifle to Williams. Williams took it and held it at the ready as Greamer wheel-spun the vehicle around and headed off back in the direction they had come. None of them were happy at getting so close to Mohammed Al-Azidi and letting him get away.

An hour later, Williams and Greamer were at a camp where they had spent most of the night before planning their assault on Azidi and gathering intelligence on where his cell would meet next. It had taken months of planning to get to this stage and Williams was angry and disappointed. He spoke quietly but firmly to his associate.

'We have to report to London immediately. I need you to go to pick up the Azidi trail and report directly when you have a confirmed sighting,' he ordered.

His associate, a younger agent, nodded and left the tent, leaving Williams to pack the rest of his gear, before heading out to the airport.

Chapter One

England, Present day

The public gallery paused with bated breath, as the prosecution stepped forward, smiling and with a plan; the young dark-haired learned man in the black robe and white wig turned around towards the jury to survey them, gathered in anticipation.

There wasn't a single person in the room who didn't know the names Mark King and Mohammed Al Azidi thanks to the coverage from the newspapers over the last few months. Public reaction over the allegations was largely one of anger and calls for tighter border controls, anti-immigration, political intervention. Surrounded by wooden pews, lined with officials, and overlooked by a packed public gallery, the prosecution's star player stepped forward and addressed the court, in his two minute opening statement.

'Age old law,' he began, raising his arms up as he looked high around the ancient courtroom, 'that pillar stone of the justice process, has bought us here together today.'

The judge removed his tiny spectacles and leaned forward across his bench, intrigued by the opening statement. High in the press gallery, a small man, a journalist with a notebook and a fringe which dangled tattily over one side of his face, narrowed his eyes towards the prosecution as the two men's eyes met. The prosecution paused for a second as both men held their stare before the journalist broke eye contact and scribbled notes in the battered-looking notebook. The prosecution smiled as he turned back to address the courtroom.

'As you well know, the prosecution has the burden of proof to prove its case,' he smiled, acknowledging the judge who was by now smiling, 'beyond ALL reasonable doubt.'

There was chatter from the public gallery as tenseness came over the court where you could almost hear a pin drop and cut the atmosphere with a knife.

'Therefore, the prosecution must present evidence which proves, beyond reasonable doubt, that the defendant...'

There was another pause as he spun around like lightning, pointing a finger directly at the defendant, causing the defendant and the courtroom to jump back and gasp.

'This man, this clearly GUILTY man, did, on February twenty-eighth of this year, commit an act of atrocity against this country, against the free world and against humanity itself!'

There was a stir again from the court as the defence sat scribbling notes; some watched this master class of a closing statement.

'Ruthlessly, he did on that fateful night whilst we were all in our beds, seemingly safe and soundly sleeping, decide on an inauspicious and tragic course of action.'

The defendant bowed his head, not wanting to face the inevitable truth that the country's best lawyer was against him and there was no way he would escape a momentously long prison sentence.

'Evidence has been presented to this court, this wondrous house of truth and justice, which is unequivocal and inescapable in its legitimacy. We must send a clear message to those who would seek to travel to our shores, bask in our hospitality, benefit from our graciousness and take from our resources, that you cannot commit these kinds of crimes and escape justice.'

The judge, on hearing this, which may be construed as interfering with sentencing legislation, sat forward and frowned.

'Mr. King,' he began but was prevented from continuing by the prosecution's Mr. King putting his hand up immediately in acknowledgement of what he had said and continued in his speech.

'Mr. Rahman, a young man who until now had led a life of peace, tranquility and hard work. Indeed we have heard testimony from many witnesses as to his character, his reputation and his deeply devout faith and, yes, indeed some may be swayed.'

Mark King had gotten quieter and quieter at this point and those who knew him best, those who had seen him in action before, knew he was building towards a dramatic crescendo.

'That this somehow exonerates him from fault?' he shouted, his voice raised louder, his climactic theatricality entertaining the entire courtroom.

Mark stopped, and turned to the jury who watched, drawn in by the theatricality and razzle dazzle of the show before them.

'Radicalisation?' he asked, slowly walking past the jury, occasionally stopping at a member of the jury sat nearest the front. 'Perhaps, but what the fundamental truth is is that no matter what the reason for the crime, the crime WAS committed.'

Mark swept across the courtroom towards the defendant, arms outstretched like a warlock about to cast a spell on an unsuspecting victim.

'BUT IT WAS MURDER!' he shouted, his hand held high as a finger pointed towards the ceiling, 'was it not, which occurred that night, MURDER, deliberate, calculated and pre-meditated murder, of an innocent civilian, all because Mr. Rahman wanted to obtain materials to build an explosive device and the victim, the innocent and ill-fated victim, a family man with children, whose wife sits in the public gallery surrounded by her friends and family, cries herself to sleep at night as she tries to explain to her children that daddy isn't coming home.'

Mark pointed to the defendant whilst facing the jury.

'This man, the defendant you see before you, is the ONLY person responsible for this heinous crime. Richard Wilkinson, the deceased, sacrificed his life to prevent mass murder, to protect the innocent from what COULD have been an atrocity, the scale of which has not been seen since the July 2007 London bombings.'

There was a deliberate pause by the prosecution as he let the jury and the courtroom soak up everything he had said as Mark returned to his desk, his glasses in his hand and one arm of the glasses in his mouth as he turned a page over in his notebook.

'Members of the jury, sadly, it is not MY decision to seek to enact justice against this man, merely to present to you the truth. Not a version of the truth decided by one party over another, but the unavoidable truth because of the facts presented herein. I ask you, this man IS guilty, search your hearts and your feelings, and you WILL come to the right decision.'

He walked towards the defendant one last time.

'The ONLY decision which should be returned,' he paused again and stared into the eyes of the defendant.

In all Mark King's years of behavioural profiling, he knew when someone was about to crack and he sensed it here, now, as he took his final breath, he felt the tension in his entire body as he slowed his breathing down, centered his balance, took one final look deep into the defendant's eyes and turned.

'GUILTY!'

The loudness of the shout made everyone in the courtroom jump and a shocked gasp from the crowd, together with the drama and theatre of Mark's statement, caused the defendant to sob and nod his head. Mark merely waved his arm towards the defendant as if he were allowing the jury to walk through a door he had held open for them. Their faces, one by one, became stern and unforgiving. Mark turned, smiled at the judge who gave a nod of acknowledgement, and returned to his seat.

'Your Honour, the prosecution rests,' he said pleasantly and glanced up towards the public gallery.

The journalist was shaking his head in anger but it wasn't Ian Hawking that Mark King was looking at, it was Mrs.

Wilkinson, the wife of the victim who smiled and mouthed the words 'thank you' to Mark. Mark smiled and nodded. Now it was down to the jury to decide.

Chapter Two

Mark King pushed his way through the huddle of journalists with cameras, microphones and notebooks as he attempted to leave the courtroom; as usual, there was one journalist in particular who reached him first, and it was Ian Hawking.

'Mr King, such an overly dramatic and unnecessary presentation of the facts in your statement, do you really think theatre and over-acting will continue to win you cases like these on this scale?'

Mark King shrugged as he deliberately made eye contact with the journalist.

'That depends, do you think a gaudy suit, tatty hair and the smell of last night's stale beer on your breath will obtain better news stories?' he said nonchalantly, continuing to walk past.

The pack of journalists Mark King hated so much erupted into laughter as a female news reporter stood next to Hawking caught a whiff of his breath and screwed up her face in disgust before backing away in a very obvious manner. Hawking looked mortally wounded, confused and angered as the rest of the pack pushed him to the back and followed Mark out towards the stone steps which lead into the court's marbled foyer. Hawking was left behind and threw his notebook on the floor in disgust.

There was a waiting mob of reporters, all set up with TV cameras on tripods, and TV news crews' vans which had been camped outside the courts since the trial began. It wasn't Mark's biggest audience, but he took the hand of Mrs. Wilkinson, whom he had led out onto the steps, surrounding by almost the entire litigation team of Lever & Sons LLP who had been instructed to prosecute Mr. Rahman. Mark smiled at Mrs. Wilkinson and winked before he held his hands up to silence the waiting mob.

Shouts came from the waiting press as each one of them wanted their question answered first.

'Mr King, did you expect a guilty verdict?' shouted one; Mark chuckled but didn't have time to respond.

'Mrs. Wilkinson, are you pleased with the result and feel you can now lay your husband to rest?' another shouted.

She glanced at Mark, who smiled and put his hand up, signalling for her not to answer.

'Do you think this case will set a precedent for the government and security services to act quicker to prevent home grown terrorism?' a voice cried from within the crowd.

Mark patted Mrs. Wilkinson on the back as she took out her folded A4 sheet of paper she had prepared a speech on. As she began, the crowds listened and, fighting back tears, she described how her family were coping with the tragic loss and how they could now finally move on after achieving justice for her husband. Quietly and stealthily, Mark King slipped further back until he was at the back of the crowd, and slipped away towards his parked car.

Had he moved moments, seconds even, earlier, he may have avoided the hounding and bitter questioning of Ian Hawking, who had eventually found his way out of the courtroom and spotted Mark tiptoeing away and followed him.

'Mr King, a word now if you please,' he squirmed, fumbling for his notebook and pencil, upsetting his case of paperwork all over the concrete as the wind swept paper up into the air.

'For God's sake man, who the hell are you anyway, can't you see I've got a home to go to?' snapped Mark as he quickened his pace to reach his car before Hawking followed.

'Always got a witty remark, haven't you, King,' Hawking snarled as he attempted to pick up the paperwork from the floor.

'Look, where do you get off on this ...' Mark couldn't remember his name and fumbled for a moment or two trying to remember, 'whatever your name is, why do you feel it necessary to harass me?'

'I just want some answers from you; you avoid me all the time, what have you got to hide?' Hawking replied sarcastically.

Mark shuddered as he reached his car and remotely unlocked it, putting his case and court papers into the boot. Hawking was quick on his feet and the two men stood, face to face. Hawking smiled a wry and sycophantic smile as he felt his anger build.

'You will fall one day, Mark King, and I will be there to catch every second of it!'

Mark watched as the pathetic little man chewed on his gum and smiled through stained teeth.

'Good luck with that Harrington,' he remarked as he got into the car and drove off, leaving Hawking stood there alone, still smiling,

'It's Hawking,' he uttered in a disgruntled voice, 'my name is Hawking,' before he turned to leave.

As Mark walked in through the doors of Levers & Sons LLP law firm, he was greeted by a joyous and triumphant welcoming party of laughing and victorious staff who patted him on the back and shook hands with him as he tried, with difficulty, to make his way towards his office.

'Well done, Mark!' a voice shouted.

'Wonderful performance!' shouted another.

'Magnificent achievement, a great victory!' another one cried as Mark reached the lift and the doors opened.

He smiled a reluctant smile and put his hand up to wave in appreciation as the lift doors closed. When he reached his floor, he was greeted by almost as celebratory a group as the one he had just left downstairs, although this one was much more reserved. As Mark walked towards his office, he could see the familiar suited, white haired, and short, trimmed bearded figure of his boss and half of the creators of the firm, Hugo Lever. Mark smiled as he stood in front of his senior partner.

'Mark, well done boy!' Hugo said his face broadening with a beaming smile, as he firmly shook Mark by the hand and slapped him on the back.

'Thank you Hugo, but I have work to do.'

'On the contrary old boy, now listen, I have just had word from my contact in the security services,' he explained as Mark rolled his eyes in wonder at how Hugo was so well connected.

'Oh really?' Mark said, feigning interest.

'He advised me thanks to your "performance" in there, they are now investigating a second "Person of Interest" higher up the chain of command of this splinter group of terrorists.'

'That's good.' Mark nodded and smiled as Hugo walked Mark towards his office with his arm firmly around Mark's shoulder.

'Now, take the rest of the day off. Why not go and have a rest, celebrate with Marie, think of it as a "thank you" for all your hard work.'

'That's very kind of you, Hugo, but I ...'

'I insist,' Hugo interrupted, his eyes narrowing into a serious frown.

Mark knew better than to argue with Hugo on matters like this, and reluctantly placed his paperwork and case down, and reached for his car keys.

'I'll see you tomorrow,' Hugo said insistently as he directed Mark towards the door.

'Thanks Hugo,' Mark uttered as he left the room.

Hugo shut the glass door behind him and walked towards his desk phone. He picked up the receiver and dialled a speed dial number, and awaited an answer.

'Yes, this is Hugo; I think we need to talk.'

Chapter Three

Within the halls of MI6 Headquarters, London UK, Counter-terrorism Division, a young agent with an impressive track record in catching international terrorists was pacing the floor looking through intelligence files.

Agent Nathanial Williams of MI6 Counter Terrorism skulked into the main operations room and various admin staff and agents turned to see the ominous figure as he made his way down to the main plasma screen in the centre of the room. The head of MI6, together with the team tasked with discovering and illuminating threats to UK security, have been tracking the movements of a known terrorist Mohammed Al Azidi. Williams was reading his file as he silently moved around the room.

Mohammed Al Azidi, the twenty-nine year-old, self-proclaimed "Jihadi" and eldest brother of three, was a well-known Person of Interest within several intelligence agencies, but none had gotten close enough to him to gain anything useful against him. Williams had a personal interest in this case; his younger brother was maimed in an explosion several years ago, with Azidi as the only viable suspect. Williams was, although he would never admit it, treating this as personal, something an MI6 agent should never do. His superiors knew of his interest in this case, and if it wasn't for his superior skill and methodology over his fellow agents, he would never have been assigned to this case. Besides, he thought if anyone could catch Azidi, it would be him. He hoped they wouldn't give him another case which would take away precious time he could spend hunting down Azidi and finding out about his terror cell, and who was funding it.

The section chief had been alerted by Williams, who had been tracking Azidi since before he encountered him in Syria three months ago.

Williams answered his mobile which caused the entire room to turn to look at him. In his thick Scottish accent, he answered in his usual dour tone,

'Williams.'

The voice from the other end of the phone was Williams' contact within Mossad, the intelligence agency for Israel. Williams was unimpressed by the news.

'NO!' he shouted down the phone angrily, 'MI6 have tracked Al Azidi to London because he plans to blow up the Houses of Parliament, and other UK targets we have intelligence about, in a systematic attack on the UK. I do not plan on sharing any intelligence until we know what we're up against.'

Williams hung up the phone and sighed, frustrated with the apparent lack of inter-agency co-operation.

Suddenly, a phone rang out of the blue and one of the other agents answered it. Williams' attention quickly turned as the room fell silent. The agent looked across at Williams and his face went white. Williams rushed over and took the phone off the agent and answered it. Williams' face also dropped when he was informed over the phone that another field agent tracking Al Azidi had been found dead, his throat cut and Azidi's whereabouts were at this time unknown.

Williams would not wait to get authorisation to enter the field. He had finely honed skills as a covert field agent and didn't want to hang around to lose this lead. During the last eight months, alongside tracking Al Azidi, Williams had also linked Azidi to a faceless and mysterious group of individuals, an organisation of professional hit men, who he believed were pulling the strings behind a multitude of terrorist organisations and probably helping to finance them. Williams was convinced there were members of this group within MI6 but he didn't have enough evidence, nor did he realise how far up this organisation went, and he was finding it difficult to wade through the murky waters of the secret service.

'How long ago did Waters check in?' Williams asked with a voice full of regret at leaving someone else in charge of watching Azidi. They had, at their disposal, the largest database of active terrorists and terrorist group profiles in the world.

Mark King appeared from the living room of his home in rural London into the kitchen to find Marie, his wife, making breakfast for them both, and his children Benjamin and Hope sat at the kitchen table, already part way through their own breakfast. He held onto the brief case and files he was carrying and grabbed a piece of toast, kissed Marie and the children goodbye and tried to rush out of the door. Marie, experienced in this early morning manoeuvre, tried to persuade him to sit down and eat.

'You need to eat before work today; it's a big day for you!' she said with her usual air of concern.

Mark smiled at her, adjusting his suit jacket and his tie in the large hallway mirror. He wanted to look his best and to look slightly menacing as it made the defence nervous. He peered into the kitchen.

'I'd love to spend the day with you guys but remember me telling you about a new case that came in a few months back? Well, today is the first day, early start!'

Marie tutted at his level of ambition but she loved that about her husband; he would do anything to make their lives better and he wanted a practice of his own soon.

'Oh excellent, sounds interesting, let me guess?' Marie responded, smiling.

There was silence before they both simultaneously chimed, 'But I can't talk about it?'

They both chuckled as the children continued to eat their breakfast, not interested in their parents' working life.

'Darling, this could be THE case which will make and define my career,' Mark pleaded excitedly.

'Don't forget, we are going away at the end of the week. I've packed all my stuff and the children's clothes too!' Marie replied distantly.

Mark had forgotten they had arranged to go away this week. He had been fighting for time off for weeks. Finally Hugo had agreed, and he winced as he imagined the villa in the south of Spain, with its warm golden sandy beaches and drinks at the bar. He imagined Marie in a swimsuit and peace and quiet but he had a feeling he would have to postpone.

'Honey, will you look for the passports for the children? I think they may be in the study in the safe?' Marie asked, thoughtfully.

Mark agreed although he wasn't listening fully. His mind was focussed on preparing the case. He had been going over and over it in his mind for most of the night and believed he could obtain a guilty verdict. He wanted to be noticed; maybe then he would get the chance to own this practice, and if not he wanted to start one of his own.

Mark rushed out of the door leaving Marie watching after him, worried. She turned to go inside to tidy up after breakfast. Ben and Hope were both plugged into MP3 players and Hope was reading a fashion magazine. Marie put the breakfast dishes in the dishwasher and grabbed her handbag and car keys, and moved some of Mark's paperwork from the side to the kitchen table. She tutted and shook her head when a half-empty packet of cigarettes fell out and onto the floor. She remembered back at university when both of them smoked, Mark more so, but only when he was stressed. She stopped and thought for a moment as she picked up the packet.

'I haven't had one in years. Should I?'

However, the feeling that Mark had hidden it from her made her slightly cross. She soon dismissed the thought as she knew he had been under serious pressure at work lately and had been responsible for prosecuting numerous criminals linked to an organised crime ring operating in the north and midlands. She smiled as she thought she'd smelt it on him the week before, but put it down to him meeting clients on the way home from work. She would have to invite Hugo Lever, Mark's boss and senior partner at Mark's law firm, and his wife over for dinner again soon, and then she could moan about the pressure he was putting Mark under.

'Hope! Benjamin!' shouted Marie as she left the front door open for them. 'Now please or you walk to school.'

The children, not being needed to be told twice, both ran past her and out to the waiting car, still attached to their MP3 players. Marie wondered how it was they heard her now, yet when she stood next to them, they could never hear a word.

She glanced around as usual, to acknowledge the neighbours but no one was around today. However, she wondered if someone had bought a new car as she noticed a Range Rover four-by-four parked across the street, blacked-out windows and a strange number plate. She'd never seen the car before. Perhaps it was a friend's or Mark's, or someone waiting to give someone a lift. She brushed it aside and got into the car herself and left to drop the children off at school.

Mark smiled as he drove to work, listening to the music in the car. He pulled out one of his 'emergency' cigarette packets from the glove box and lit it, enjoying the feeling of exhaling the nicotine as he wound the window down. His mind took him back to the halls of St Andrews University where he and Marie first met. He remembered the way they used to look at each other and listen to music while they studied together, the plans they made and how life seemed so distant from pressures, other than the pressure of getting in their dissertation on time. They had been so distracted by work and life, he felt they had forgotten how to have fun and relax. He would have loved to have gone on holiday where he had planned to do as little as possible and forget the rush of life and just relax. Mark was aware he had spent little time at home lately and he felt guilty about it, but he knew Marie was behind him even though sometimes it hurt her when they were away from each other for long periods of time, and when he WAS home, he was in his study working on active cases. She would look after the house, the children, and get herself to work. He wondered what he would do without her and how precious she really was to him. He would win this case, for her, and show her that all the sacrifice and distance was worth it.

He pulled up outside the barristers' chambers and solicitors' firm Lever & Sons LLP, the most successful legal firm in the country. Before he had the chance to enter the building, a journalist, Ian Hawking, rushed towards Mark with a notebook and dictaphone and a camera slung across his shoulder firing questions about his previous case and personal life.

'Mr King, Mr King, is it true that the police made you aware of the link between Al Azidi and the recent crime syndicate you prosecuted?' Mark, irritated by this invasion of privacy, put his hand up to Hawking's face.

'Go away. I will NOT jeopardise this case to give YOU a scoop on this. Please leave.'

Hawking persisted, paying no heed to Mark's warning. Mark spun on him.

'Who are you anyway, head of the Chigwell Gazette?' Mark mocked as Hawking looked offended.

Mark knew full well who he was. Ian Hawking, freelance journalist and bane of Mark's life, was always trying to get him to give a story and had hounded him for years, just waiting for him to trip up so he could write another one of those sick, twisted celebrity gossip smear stories. Mark was having none of it. He did the usual thing of pretending not to know who he was as he knew Hawking was insecure about his status as a reporter.

Mark rushed through the doors into his office, stopping to harmlessly flirt with Margaret La Tour (Maggie to those who knew her best), the aged secretary behind the large beech and chrome reception desk at the front of the building,

'Good morning beautiful!' Mark cheerfully chimed and winked at her as she smiled at him. 'Wow, you really look amazing this morning and I love the perfume, very seductive!'

'Oh go on you,' she replied playfully but secretly grateful for the compliment, 'or I'll tell your wife.'

'Oh, she already knows I'm madly in love with you and I plan to leave her for you and run off into the sunset!' Mark laughed as Maggie turned bright red.

Mark dearly loved Maggie and always welcomed seeing her sitting behind the front desk, in front of a sign which read 'welcome' in hundreds of different languages against a white background. Mark always made a point of picking one out each week to learn it throughout the week and Maggie would regularly give him pointers on how to pronounce it.

He was about to continue when he was met by his young and attractive PA Penny, who gave Mark a rundown of his diary for the day and handed him a coffee.

'Oh Mr King, your two-thirty has requested a rescheduling as they cannot make it, those case files you requested have arrived and are on your desk, I've filed your expenses claim and I've emailed you that client list you asked me to provide for you,' she panted, smiling proudly.

Mark smiled at her and valued her efforts hugely.

'Oh and don't forget to buy a present for Benjamin, call your mother-in-law and don't forget your one pm lunch appointment at Carlo's restaurant with Mr Ling.'

Penny was about to turn away when she remembered one last detail.

'Before you do any of that, Mr King, Mr Lever needs to see you urgently in his office.'

Mark nodded and kissed her on the cheek gently. In another life, he may well have got together with her but they were more like brother and sister. He laid down his case, notes and jacket on his desk and walked into Hugo's office to face a serious looking Hugo.

'Close the door,' Hugo grimaced, which Mark thought was highly unusual but obeyed his boss.

'Mark, I need you to clear your diary for the next three weeks, ensure Penny sees to it right away.'

'Three weeks!?' Mark exclaimed loudly. Hugo lifted papers from his desk and handed them to Mark.

'It seems your popularity, no thanks in large to Ian Hawking, has earned you particular acclaim.' Mark read through the papers that Hugo handed to him and narrowed his eyes before his eyes scanned across the part which described that Mark had been specifically requested.

'Hugo, this is insane, I've got other cases to work on, Marie has booked a holiday which I am supposed to go on, and incidentally, have been looking forward to, at the end of this week,' Mark argued, handing the papers back to Hugo. Hugo shook his head. 'Can't you give it to a senior partner?'

'Mark, I hate to be the bearer of bad news, but you are doing this and that's the end of it!'

'No can do Hugo, I've told you, I haven't had a holiday in three years and this time Friday, I shall be on a beach in the south of Spain, enjoying a well-earned rest!'

Hugo glared at Mark and slapped the papers on the table.

'You'll have your holiday Mark, but you are working this case.' Once again, Mark tried to argue but Hugo threw the case notes on the desk in front of Mark and his tone changed to a sterner, commanding tone. 'Downing Street is watching this one closely,'

Mark was worried and intrigued.

'Why me?' he asked nervously, almost afraid to hear the answer. 'What's wrong with the Crown prosecuting?'

Hugo turned and sighed.

'Mark, as you know, the CPS can instruct external counsel in private practice and, because of your higher court advocacy qualifications and experience, they have requested us or rather YOU, to prosecute on behalf of the CPS.'

Mark reluctantly agreed and Hugo summoned Penny in via the internal phone line. Mark stood reading the file and his well-trained eye found the section which described what the case was all about. He placed the case notes down and stared in disbelief at Hugo, watching the sly grin grow on his white bearded face. Penny entered the room with her usual flounce and her notebook and Mark kept staring at Hugo. In a scared, serious but slightly excited tone, Mark gave her instructions.

'Penny, clear my diary of everything for the next three weeks at least. Meetings, client visits, conference calls, emails, everything.' Penny stopped scribbling and stared at Mark.

'Everything? But Mr King …' she questioned, slightly stunned and confused but was cut off mid-sentence.

'Everything,' Mark confirmed. 'At all costs.'

Penny looked at Hugo for inspiration and further details. Hugo smiled and nodded at her to do as he said. She looked at him and, with uncertainty, nodded back and left the room. Mark then pulled out his mobile, all without his eyes leaving Hugo, dialled Marie's mobile his wife and advised her that the holiday was off, and then hung up.

Mark had been given the opportunity to prosecute on the Al Azidi case.

Chapter Four

Over the weeks that proceeded Mark and Hugo's conversation Mark had spent long hours preparing the case, ensuring every single small detail had been accounted for. If it was true what Hugo told him about Downing Street paying specific attention to the case, he couldn't afford to jeopardise it.

It was nearing the end of the day when Mark was addressing the judge and jury in a fantastic speech about points of law and the evidence against Al Azidi. The legal counsel behind him was watching in awe as Mark presented his points one after another in quick fire, leaving the judge to agree and congratulate him on his points. Mark took a deep breath and addressed the judge once more.

'Nothing further, Your Honour,' he smiled, turning to the jury.

'I am satisfied, Mr King. Court will be adjourned for the remainder of the day,' the judge announced.

As everyone filed out of the courtroom, Mark was greeted by his team. They all seemed excited and congratulated him on how wonderfully he was doing and agreed to all meet up back at the office.

Mark, carrying his case and papers, skipped down the steps of the ancient courts and hadn't noticed the large crowd which had gathered outside. It was no surprise that Ian Hawking had to be at the centre of it all, flanked by a large crowd of reporters,

TV camera crew and journalists. He thrust a dictaphone once again under Mark's nose, attempting to accost Mark and get information out of him.

'Naturally,' thought Mark to himself, 'Hawking is focussing on the negatives, such as will this case end his career if he doesn't win, is it true Downing Street specifically requested him, a reckless and rebellious legal representative, and generally being nasty.'

Hawking's dingy brown suede suit jacket and messy hair made Mark's skin crawl and he wondered how he dared go out dressed like that. He wished this snake of a man would just go away and never come back, perhaps into hiding. Mark often wondered, although not seriously, if he could offer a deal to any hitmen he prosecuted over the years, that if they assassinated Ian Hawking, he would represent them for free during a retrial. Mark never had any intention to do this, but it was fun thinking about it. Mark groaned as Hawking came at him again and immediately switched to the usual façade.

'Ahh a "News of The World' reporter!' he remarked to Hawking, pushing his dictaphone out of his hand and then his hand up in front of the newspaper camera.

Hawking was insulted beyond belief. All the other reporters and journalists fell about laughing at this quick wit of Mark's. Mark laughed and confidently approached the masses of press in front of him.

'Ladies and gentlemen of the press,' he announced as the entire crowd fell silent.

Mark hated the press, and made no secret of it. He found them invasive and hated the way they influenced the public in cases. He always worried the judges and juries would bow down to public pressure when it came to deciding a verdict. He was known for his loathing of all things media and the media, although Mark believed the press didn't like him, couldn't fault his brilliant legal mind or his ability to win them over, case after case. Mark was also renowned for NEVER giving any interviews, TV or newspaper and NEVER giving the press anything to tarnish his reputation. He valued his career far too much for that and he knew it could have detrimental effect on ANY case he was working on. He courted them when it suited his needs, mostly of course to ridicule Hawking whenever he got the chance, but perhaps it wasn't the press who Mark believed didn't like him, and perhaps it was just Ian Hawking.

Mark smiled as he watched the crowd fall silent. He opened his mouth as if to make a huge speech and each reporter was poised to record, verbatim, every single word he said.

'Ladies and gentlemen of the press,' he repeated as the noise died down, 'I request to be favourably excused. I have a home to go to.'

And with that, Mark walked off without another word. The media were dumbfounded and there were groans and insults and words of disappointment that the mighty Mark King, had left got the better of them all. As he walked away, Mark smiled to himself, feeling very satisfied with his achievement against the press. He muttered, but not loud enough for them to hear, 'Vultures.'

By the time Mark had arrived home from work, Marie was watching TV. Mark checked the clock in his Audi convertible and groaned when he saw the time, it was about nine PM. The children were asleep upstairs as he walked into the hallway and Marie was sat watching the news where, earlier that day, Mark had been accosted by Ian Hawking. Hawking has been made to look like a fool in front of the entire country. Marie got up to meet Mark in the hallway and waved the cigarette packet at him she found earlier that morning. With a disapproving look on her face, she chastised Mark for being late and for cancelling their holiday and wanted answers.

'First you cancel the holiday we have spent months planning, and where the hell have you been today? You promised to be in at six thirty! It's now just after nine!'

Mark kissed her forehead and held her in a hug she began not to want, but then relinquished and hugged him tight. She was still mad at him though. He put his hands up in defence and explained, trying his best to placate her.

'I ran into the press,' he explained and Marie rolled her eyes and beckoned him into the living room.

'I saw,' she revealed. 'You really shouldn't tease them like that,' she complained, pointing at the TV screen, which was paused, showing the moment Mark walked away from the press. Mark studied the screen carefully and scrutinised the angry and disappointed faces of the press. He also noted the glare of Ian Hawking and smiled as he remembered how he made Hawking feel like that.

'That idiot should learn to leave me alone. Perhaps this will teach him,' he scoffed, rising from the sofa to go to the kitchen to pour himself a coffee from the Tassimo machine. Marie followed him, trying to make him see the error of his ways.

'That poor man is just trying to do his job and, perhaps it may show you in a better light if you just, give him what he's after.' Mark was angry at this comment and glared at Marie before his glare turned into a smile.

Hawking was renowned for a strange obsession with the King family. He seemed, in Mark's eyes, to be always out to 'get' him and try to force him to say something which could affect his career, or misquote him in a report which nearly always ended up rebounding on Hawking and making him look stupid. For years, it seemed, the man just would not give up trying to make Mark look bad, but Mark couldn't understand why. He used to wind Hawking up most of the time and perhaps that was the issue, but only when he was provoked. Mark sighed.

'Perhaps you are right my love,' he conceded.

'Oh PERHAPS?' she exclaimed at his cheek and sarcasm. Mark grinned.

'Well the silly idiot needs to learn to leave me alone. Don't you remember the Johnson case? He sat outside our house for WEEKS and the children were in a terrible state, trying his best to get a scoop from me about the trial, hoping I'd fail. Well, I DIDN'T!'

'I don't need reminding of that. Felt like a prisoner in my own home,' she replied, remembering how bad Ian Hawking had made her feel, pursuing Mark whenever he they were out and about, even with the children and virtually being camped out on her lawn for duration of the case in the vain hope that Mark would spill the beans about the progress of the case, as if he had a secret he wasn't telling anyone.

But she agreed, and she didn't like Hawking any more than Mark did. But she worried Mark would make an enemy of himself in the eyes of the media if he didn't act more approachable. Mark remembered that Hawking had been sacked from that newspaper for that.

Disappointed and angry about the holiday, Marie backed his decision to take on the case.

'It was still cruel for you to act that way to that reporter,' she advised, 'but for some reason, there is something familiar about him. I just can't put my finger on it.'

Mark laughed. 'What, you mean familiar as in taking up residence in our garden. What did you do, invite him in for tea and biscuits!'

Marie gave him a playful slap and then put her arms around him. He held her tight and sighed. He left his wife to go upstairs to kiss his children goodnight. Marie's fingers lingered in Marks as he made his way upstairs.

'You ARE a GOOD father, Mark King,' she called out after him. He turned and smiled at her. Mark pushed open the door of the children's bedrooms and found them both sound asleep. He kissed them both on the forehead. Before he left the room, he turned and promised in a whisper, 'Life will change soon. Things won't always be like this. We will spend so much time together soon I promise. One day we will move to New York to be with Granny in her big house. One day, when I've started my own practice I will be able to stay home all day and play with you because I'll be able to have holidays when I like.'

Marie looked on quietly from the end of the corridor after following him upstairs. She hugged him from behind and he hugged her back, pulling her arms around him.

'Oh, before I forget, there was a strange car parked outside today.'

'Oh yeah? What kind of strange?'

'I don't know,' she whispered, concerned by Mark's questioning. 'I hadn't seen it round here before. Looked expensive, a Range Rover I think?'

'A Range Rover eh. Bet it was a Vogue too.' Marie was amazed at how Mark did that. He seemed to instinctively know, from just a few details, what she was thinking.

'It was black, with smoked windows. Looked brand new.' Mark thought this was curious.

'Is today the first time you've seen it?'

'No, it's been there nearly every day these past few weeks.'

Mark thought for a while, trying to think of anyone, maybe he knew. He shrugged.

'Probably a reporter waiting to "get a scoop" on me before the others because of the Azidi trial,' he joked.

Marie smiled and shrugged it off in front of him as he closed his study door. She waited for a moment thoughtfully and worried, 'The press didn't know the morning you were given the case until you knew at Chambers,' she said aloud. Mark didn't hear and called to her to ask her what she said.

'Nothing darling, just me thinking out loud,' Marie replied so as not to worry him before making her way back to the kitchen.

Mark turned on his desk lamp in his study and poured himself a small Glenfiddich Scotch. Sitting at his table in his favourite black reclining office chair, he glanced at the file on his desk. It was the Al Azidi file containing statements, photographs and mug shots along with intelligence files relating to Al Azidi and photographs of evidence. His concentration was broken by the sound of his study phone and he answered it, confused who would call at this time of night. A low muffled voice at the other end of the phone spoke in short and sharp sentences.

'Mr King. I trust I have got your attention?'

'Who is this?' Mark asked, his eyes narrowing.

'Drop the case or there will be "repercussions".'

'Hello? How dare you tell me ...'

The dead line tone ringing in Mark's ear before he had time

to speak revealed the caller had hung up. He didn't recognise the voice and chuckled to himself. He was to expect this in his line of work, but was concerned that someone had gotten hold of his study phone number. He shrugged and sipped his Glenfiddich, feeling the warmth of Scotch ease his harsh throat.

Chapter Five

The following day the same morning routine occurred with Mark being, as usual, last into breakfast in the King household. However, this time, Mark was on the phone to the police and then to Hugo advising him of the mysterious calls. Hugo told Mark the office have been fielding the same calls and that the police were aware and were trying to trace the caller ID, but to not let it deter him and shift his attention away from the case.

Mark made his way to his car after kissing Marie and the children goodbye. Marie watched him go from behind the curtain in the hallway window, concerned about his phone conversation. Mark strode down the small garden path, sandwiched between two small lawns, past the large double garage and towards the car parked on the drive. He stopped suddenly and rolled his eyes as he caught sight of Ian Hawking, who was waiting for Mark again and chased after Mark to his car to get a statement from him. Mark noticed the black Range Rover and turned to Hawking.

'You, thing, whatever your name is, wait here,' Mark said sharply. Surprised and taken aback, Hawking did as he was told and watched as Mark marched over towards the Range Rover and knocked on the window. It rolled down to reveal a man with sunglasses on. The man stared at him without saying a word.

'Yeah, er, hi. What are you doing waiting out here day after day?' Mark enquired. There was silence from the man as he continued to stare at Mark. Mark tried again.

'Why are you here? What do you want?' This time, the man answered in a low, basic English but with a thick foreign accent; Mark thought it to be Russian or Ukrainian, possibly Albanian.

'What do you want?' the man grunted.

'What do I want? What do YOU want?' Mark replied indignantly, shocked at the man's attitude.

'Gardener. Municipal services. We mow grass, cut weed.' Mark was surprised and felt slightly silly approaching a stranger like this.

He looked into the back of the Range Rover and noted rakes, garden spades, green garden bags and a black plastic rubbish bin. Mark nodded and apologised. The stranger asked Mark again what he wanted, and that was when Mark caught sight of the revolver in his lap and the ID badge clipped to the man's chest.

'Roman Vose,' he said to himself quietly, he would remember that name.

Sensing danger to himself or to someone, Mark tried to take a swing at Vose through the semi open window of the Range Rover. Vose opened the door on Mark and knocked him over before slamming the door and instantly started the engine and tried to drive off. Before he did so, an accomplice in the passenger seat punched Vose violently in the face. Mark saw Vose reach for a knuckle duster and, before he could remove his hand from the open window, Vose had smacked Mark's knuckles with it before Mark withdrew his hand. Mark winced in pain but wouldn't give the driver the satisfaction of hearing him make a sound.

Vose got out, and by this time, Hawking was busy snapping photographs like his life depended on it, and Vose was covered in blood. Vose and his accomplice were dressed in gardener's overalls and played up to Hawking, knowing he was watching, indicating Vose had been assaulted and threatening to press charges. This is just what Hawking had been waiting for and took pictures and statements for them for the papers.

Mark, looking troubled and winded, turned to Hawking and pleaded with him.

'I swear I didn't touch him! He had a gun! You gotta believe me!'

'All I saw,' Hawking replied whilst writing furiously, 'was you throwing punches through the window and then the driver got out covered in blood!'

People were rushing about answering phones and Hugo Lever was in his office behind the glass windows with the door shut on the phone having what looked like a very angry and heated conversation when Mark arrived for work, oblivious to the onslaught about to hit him. He stormed past Maggie the receptionist and ignored his PA Penny, who tried her best to prevent Mark from barging into Hugo's office while he is on the phone. Hugo motioned Penny to stop when she tried explaining to him she couldn't stop Mark from coming in and Hugo directed his anger first at Penny.

'Penny, COFFEE!' he shouted.

Penny dashed out of the room holding back tears of fear. She was non-confrontational and hated arguments, which was ironic considering her profession. She went to make the coffee, whimpering as she went. Various others tried to comfort her as she sobbed and pointed towards Hugo's office. Hugo finished his telephone conversation, staring at Mark with anger and disappointment. Mark stared back, angry at whoever had made Penny upset. He didn't care who it was, NO ONE upset Penny.

'What the devil did you think you were doing?!' Hugo shouted as Mark desperately searched for answers.

'This is NOT what it's been made to look like Hugo, you know the press!'

'Yes I do, I've spent forty years dealing with the press and you played right into their hands like a bloody fool!'

'I never touched him Hugo, I swear, he had a gun!'

'If it wasn't for your hand Mark, I'd believe you but we all know evidence does not lie,' he snapped, looking terrified and not knowing what to do next. He was red in the face and his fists were clenched.

'The passenger thumped him to make it look like I did it and then the driver, this Vose guy, wrapped my knuckles with a knuckle duster to make it look like I hit him!' Mark insisted.

'I think you are suffering from stress as a result of this case Mark, it happens to all of us.'

'Hugo, which hand do I write with?'

Hugo failed to see the relevance of this question and reacted angrily to Mark's question, shaking his head in disbelief.

'That's not relevant to what we do next.'

'HUGO! Answer the question,' Mark shouted, getting Hugo's attention.

'I don't know, the left.'

'Exactly!' exclaimed Mark triumphantly 'and the bruised knuckles are on my RIGHT hand, I'm LEFT handed.'

'I don't care!' Hugo argued. Mark's blood pressure was rising.

'Damn it Hugo LISTEN TO ME!' Mark screamed, banging his fist down on the table, virtually nose to nose with Hugo. Hugo stared at Mark, terrified at his behaviour. Slowly he backed away towards the other side of the office, not taking his eyes off Mark. He buzzed for security.

'Maggie, get security to escort Mr King off the premises.'

Mark couldn't believe what he was hearing as he desperately thought of ways to get out of this. It couldn't be happening, not now, not on THIS case. Hugo turned to Mark and spoke slowly.

'You are suspended on full pay pending an investigation. If the CPS takes action against you, I am afraid there will be no more I can do for you. You've always had an issue with authority which would explain why you were removed from Sandhurst!'

'But the Azidi case! My clients!' Mark protested, his blood boiling. Hugo took a file from his filing cabinet.

'I have assigned the case to a new representative until we can somehow manage the fallout from this. You may well have ruined the case, Mark. In the meantime, I will make an appointment with a friend of mine, a counsellor in anger management.'

Mark went dizzy with the thought of it. The case of his career, and he KNEW Azidi was guilty. He simply couldn't believe it. He left the room looking helplessly at Hugo.

Breathing heavily and sweating, Mark closed the door of Hugo's office and made his way through all the staff that were still standing silently, staring at him. An office junior who got in Mark's way froze in fear as Mark walked towards him. The office junior moved silently out of the way, scared that Mark might assault him as he walked towards the exit. Penny rushed up to Mark, and he smiled at her, clasping her face in his hand he kissed her on the cheek.

'Everything will be OK. I promise.'

Hugo sat down at his desk looking like he hadn't slept all night and reached for some tablets in his top drawer and the glass of water on his desk. Penny arrived with a tray of coffee and put it down on Hugo's desk nervously. She attempted to talk to Hugo about the day's diary when just a look from Hugo silenced her instantly. She left the room apologising, taking a loving, lasting look at Mark on the way out.

The hustle and bustle returned as people took calls, panicked and worried, trying to field calls from the press and news agencies about Mark's assault on the gardener.

At reception, Maggie the aged receptionist spotted Mark and sternly stared at him. Mark knew to be wary of this, as he had known her a long time and saw their relationship like a teacher/favourite pupil understanding. He had a lot of love for Maggie and she, him. She tried to be angry at him but she couldn't keep it up and instead embraced him. She reminded Mark a lot of Professor McGonagall from the Harry Potter films Mark saw with the children recently.

'You can't dictate to him like that, you know, Mark,' she said softly. Her wisdom always helped Mark when he was in a tight spot.

'I did nothing wrong, Maggie!' he pleaded, like a child to a disciplining parent.

'I'm sure you didn't, but they don't know that, and they want blood,' she said pointing outside to the swathes of reporters and TV crews outside the offices. Mark sighed and shrugged as Maggie took him by the hand.

'Go home to Marie and explain everything,' she suggested.

'I'm sure she'll understand?'

Mark nodded and smiled at her. He had a lot of love for Maggie; she had been there since the beginning and went back along way with Hugo. If anyone could make him see sense, it was her.

'Can YOU talk to him Maggie, make him see sense?' he asked, desperate for Hugo to see he was being manipulated by the media. Maggie sighed not looking hopeful.

'I will try my best my dear. You know, you were his prize student,' she explained, picking up a photograph from the reception desk of Mark and Hugo when Mark was presented with his practice licence.

'He is very proud of you,' she chuckled, holding back a tear.

'He has high hopes of handing the firm over to you soon.'

Her remarks didn't make Mark feel any better. In fact, it made him feel worse. He didn't look hopeful.

'Hugo is a stubborn man, Mark; I remember when he was in your shoes once. However, he has a daily battle, not just with the Justice Department, but with politicians, especially when it comes to cases like this.'

Maggie looked at Mark and he spotted tears in her eyes. She knew how hard it was to come back from an event like this and she really felt for Mark. They hugged tightly and Mark left the offices not sure when, if ever, he would return.

Outside the office swathes of reporters and media, TV crews and newspapers gathered, all trying to question Mark about the "assault". Naturally, Ian Hawking was right at the front of the queue with a smug look on his face as he mocked Mark.

'Not such a hot shot now are we, Mr King? Could you tell me how you feel now you've been removed from the Azidi case? Do you feel that your actions have put the case in jeopardy?'

Mark ignored him, but inside his blood was boiling over. If anyone would be hit, it would be Hawking. He lit a cigarette and wound the window down, exhaling the smoke out and breathing deeply. He sat back in the driver's seat and closed his eyes, wishing he could go back and change his reaction the day before. His phone buzzed repeatedly, and he checked it to see if it was Marie that had seen the media fall out and called him. It was an unknown number, so it was probably the media as his office line was still on divert to his mobile phone. He shut it off and put it in the inside pocket of his jacket before taking another lung full of cigarette smoke. He felt terrible and, as he looked in his interior mirror to adjust his tie, he looked as bad as he felt. What was he going to do now, wait and see what happened, sitting at home, with this hanging over his head? He couldn't bear the thought of that. He HAD to do something, even if it wasn't work related.

He decided he was going to the shooting range. As far as he remembered, his membership was still valid. He usually drove there after work to let off steam. Before he started the engine, he attempted to call Marie. It went straight to voicemail, so he left a message saying he was leaving work early and would be home around six.

A short drive later, Mark arrived at the shooting club and had calmed down slightly but was still red faced. He reached for his 'emergency' packet of cigarettes in the glove box and lit another one up as he walked from the car to the main entrance. Once inside, he requested his personal sniper rifle which he had used here since he had left Sandhurst Military Academy when he was in his twenties. Mark was an expert marksman and still held the record for the country's best shot.

He entered the club and walked down the lavish, red carpeted hallway to the dark mahogany desk and security gate at the far end. Adorning the walls either side were glass cabinets filled with trophies for various competitions and Mark's trophy stood, as always, in pride of place along with a picture of him with his target and rifle, next to Reynolds, the manager. He stopped and smiled at it, remembering fondly the day he won the title for the best shot in the country. It was the only thing that made him feel good about himself all day and he wondered if he should enter this year's contest. He was an exceptional marksman and would enjoy the competition. His mind wandered back to Sandhurst and his sniper training days. It was intense, but he enjoyed it. It challenged him mentally and physically and he had put everything he had into it. He was on his way to leading a unit of eight other snipers and advising his commander where they could be put to best use on the battlefield.

He had undergone weapons training on nearly every single firearm and had been comfortable with any weapon, especially a rifle. As one member of his unit had said, if he was armed with a rifle, no one was safe. He could lie still for hours at a time and his sight was excellent, using a multitude of methods to disguise him, while he scoped his target. It took a special and specific mental capacity to be a sniper, to accept that, just by pulling the trigger, you can end someone's life without them ever knowing where the bullet came from. Not all of his battalion could do that and many dropped out partway through their training. Mark, however, stayed the distance because he was disciplined and when he put his mind to it, nothing would stop him. Perhaps that's why he was a good lawyer, he thought to himself as he slowly made his way along the rows of trophy cabinets towards the reception desk.

He gave a nod to the familiar face that greeted him.

'Mr King, what a pleasure to see you again,' said Reynolds, the manager, a well-spoken ex-army Major who had known Mark for several years.

'Nice to see you, sir,' he replied, instantly standing to attention as the two men shook hands.

'Now Mr King, I have told you to stop calling me sir,' he smiled whilst Mark looked around, avoiding eye contact.

'I know sir but it's a hard habit to break,' he replied. Reynolds laughed but then looked concerned.

'Mr King, I couldn't help but notice the news. Is everything OK?'

Mark pulled him to one side and whispered, 'Not really, Reynolds. Do you have a range free for me this afternoon? I need something to take my anger out on.'

He entered the seventy-five-yard indoor target range with his rifle and small sidearm. He liked to keep up with the hobby. It had been drilled into him at Sandhurst that he should always take any opportunity to hone his skills. He hooked up the paper target and watched it wind away from him. He picked up his rifle, loaded it and pulled back the hammer, watching through the telescopic sight as his target got further and further away. Once the mechanism had stopped, he slowed down his breathing and lined up his cross hairs, aiming at the head of the black and white torso hung on the hook. He relaxed his body and cleared his mind of everything except the target. He could hear the voice of his commanding officer in his ear talking him through each assessment he had at Sandhurst.

Gently, he squeezed the trigger and hit the shoulder.

'Damn,' he cursed, thinking the sight must be off. He adjusted it and calmed himself down.

He lifted the rifle and, again, aimed at the centre of the head. Caressing the trigger until his breathing had slowed down further, he pulled the trigger.

Chapter Six

Mark pulled up on the driveway expecting to see his wife waiting for him after getting the phone call earlier. He had also texted her a few times to say he was at the club and wouldn't be long. Normally, Marie knew if he'd been to the shooting club after work, he had a particularly bad day and would usually wait at the door for him to come home. She worried about him driving in that frame of mind. The curtains were still closed and the morning paper was still on the doorstep. Mark noticed the black Range Rover speeding off round the corner and, angry that it was worrying Marie, he gave chase, shouting and swearing at it until it was out of sight.

He walked towards the front door and, noticing it was slightly ajar, dropped his things and ran into the house calling for Marie over and over. He panicked because he knew something wasn't right and there were signs of a struggle. The house was dark and there was a cold chill as he cautiously made his way into the darkness. Looking all around to allow his eyes to adjust to the darkness, he tentatively stepped forward, noticing he was treading on broken plants, crockery and papers as he tried desperately not to make a noise. He peered into the study and instantly spotted her lifeless body lying on the study floor surrounded by paperwork thrown all over the place and broken ornaments and glass, scattered around.

The room had been ransacked. Papers were littered everywhere and drawers were emptied. Pictures half hung off the walls and the mirror in the hallway was shattered. There was a breeze blowing in from the kitchen direction which Mark believed was due to a broken window or conservatory door. It was semi-darkness but Mark could make out something dark lying in the hallway. He looked upstairs and called for his children.

'Hope. Benjamin,' he called. There was no response. 'It's dad. Are you OK?'

There was still no response as he cautiously edges along the hallway to where he could see whatever it was laying there. Initially he thought it might have been the body of whoever had broken in.

'Damn drug addicts and thugs,' he thought, remembering the black Range Rover. He knew there was something off about those two. He thought perhaps they had been watching the house, as they were due to go away; perhaps someone in the neighbourhood had mentioned to someone they were going away. It looked like something had disturbed them, possibly the neighbours. He thought it strange that the burglar alarm hadn't been triggered and looked at the wall at the smashed control panel.

'Guess that's why,' he said to himself, nearing the dark object further up the hall. He glanced around as he stealthily crept up the hallway. If that was the burglar lying there, there may be others and if he could just get to his weapon, he would feel a lot more confident.

He had studied unarmed combat at Sandhurst and could more than handle himself in a fight. But if they were armed, it would be a totally different story. As he put his foot down, something crunched beneath his feet. He slowly bent down to see what it was. It was Marie's locket, and it was stained with blood. He wondered if the burglar had dropped it on his way out, tripped and fallen in the hallway, knocking himself out on something.

Frozen to the spot, he stared in disbelief at the sight before him as the dark object he had spotted, came into the light. It was at that moment that his life stopped. His eyes darted backwards and forwards as if searching for some alternative outcome to the one before him. His bottom lip began to quiver as his hate rate sky rocketed and he felt like it would burst out of his chest.

Slowly he knelt down and fumbled in the dark towards the body which lay before him. Leaning over the body, covering himself in blood in the process, he sobbed and hyperventilated as cradled his wife's body.

'Marie darling, I'm … I'm home,' he sobbed, rocking backwards and forwards with her head in his lap. 'I'm sorry I'm late.' He trembled.

Tears streamed down his face as he gripped her cold, bloodstained hands in his and lifted her head up, cheek to cheek with him and sobbed even harder as he rocked her gently.

He had lost track of how long he'd been sat on the floor, but his legs felt numb. He kissed her forehead, smearing yet more blood over his face. His suit was covered in blood as he gently laid her back down.

He saw the bullet wound to the head and realised she was dead. Stricken with grief once again, he fell to his knees, picking up her locket and holding it in his hands as he rocked again, cradling her to him as images of their younger days, wedding day, birth of their children and happiest moments flashed before him. He cried and screamed until he had no voice left.

Time stood still for Mark as the strange, hazy blur reduced enough for him to see his neighbour who, upon hearing the noise, had come to investigate. They appeared in the doorway of the study seeing Mark cradling his wife's lifeless body. The neighbour reached for his mobile and called 999, trembling as he dialled.

'Hi yes, umm, Police please. I need to report a murder.'

Mark suddenly came to, hearing the neighbour report the address to the police, and shouted about the children.

'My children, Hope and Ben, where are they?!' he screamed. 'Please, I must find my children! Hope! Ben!'

The neighbour put a finger to his ear so he could hear what the police control room were saying.

He reached for his desk cordless phone and tried to dial a number but the line appeared to have been cut and Mark realised there was no electric to the house either. He reached in his back pocket for his mobile and called the children's school.

The secretary in the office answered and Mark, voice trembling and trying to sound normal, asked who collected the children from school.

'I am sorry, Mr King,' the secretary explained. 'But the children didn't show up today.'

Mark was silent. The secretary continued, 'Your wife called to explain she was taking them out of school to New York as their grandmother was sick and it was a last minute emergency.'

Mark dropped the phone in shock. He could hear the voice at the other end of the phone speaking, but it sounded so distant to him.

'I hope everything is OK with your mother-in-law.'

Mark reached down and pressed the cancel button to end the call.

Thinking they may have been kidnapped by the same people who shot Marie, he called Benjamin's mobile but there was no answer. He then received a text of a picture of Benjamin and Hope on a plane with a text:

'Hi Dad. Mum says we are going to see Granny and mum's friend Julia (Marie's school friend) is taking us.

Love you B & H.'

Mark concluded the text had been sent by Hope. Mark felt the vibration of his phone and pulled it out of his pocket, smearing blood over the screen. He received a missed call notification from Julia with a voicemail from her telling Mark she was taking the children to New York. Mark would have to tell them and Marie's mother in person. He couldn't bear the thought of doing it over the phone.

Mark looked up in horror at the figure stood at the door, motionless and staring down at the fateful scene. There were no words. All Mark could do was cry silently and sit still holding his wife's hand as blue flashing lights illuminated the hallway and study. The sound of the siren and footsteps echoed and seemed to get more and more distant to Mark and he put his hands up as the police motioned for him, almost in slow motion, to come towards them and asked him if he was armed. He shook his head but made no sound. He felt the cold hard steel of police handcuffs on his wrists and put up no resistance as more and more police appeared to rush into the house. He allowed the police to lead him out to their car and he stared blankly at the rows of neighbours coming out of their houses to see what the police were doing there. Police activity in the neighbourhood was rare. Any police activity sent the area into a frenzied flutter of curtains and rumours. Mark shielded his face as the familiar flash of the media's cameras hurt his eyes. What he didn't see, was the confused face of Ian Hawking, lurking behind the other photographers as the police officer read Mark the caution. He nodded in acknowledgement, not uttering a word as questions were fired at him. He looked out of the police car window to see the forensic team tape off the front of the house as Crime Scene Investigators in white overalls entered and exited the house. One younger officer rushed out of the front door and threw up on the lawn outside. Everything was a daze, like it was in slow motion and had been smudged by a white light preventing Mark from making out details. He wasn't sure if his eyes were closing or if he was hallucinating.

Mark didn't remember the journey to the police station. Nor did he remember coming into the interview room or having his clothes taken from him for forensic analysis. He didn't remember getting into the jogging trousers and hoodie provided for him by the station. All he knew was that he was suddenly giving a statement to two CID officers sat before him across a wooden table. He was in an interview room and his hands were placed, palms down, on the table while a cold cup of coffee sat in a white polystyrene cup. He sat silently at the table while the police read back his statement to him. Hugo entered the room, as he had elected himself as Mark's legal representative.

'My client will say nothing further to you until he has had the chance to consult with me.'

The two CID officers got up from the table, replacing all the paperwork from their file and looked down in silent judgement at Mark, then at Hugo.

'As you know, officers, I would like to speak to my client alone so if you could please leave the room.'

The female CID officer sighed and shook her head before following her colleague out of the room. Hugo looked at the mess which sat before him, head bowed and wearing white forensic overalls. The man before him was a total mess.

The two interviewing officers, having obeyed Hugo and left the room immediately, stood outside the room talking to what appeared to be their superior. Hugo looked down upon Mark, who was staring ahead, not moving, and not saying anything. There was sympathy for Mark as Hugo's eyes narrowed. He questioned Mark.

'What in the world happened?'

Mark shrugged and continued to stare blankly ahead. Then he spoke.

'I went shooting after leaving you. I got home, and she was …' Mark could feel the tears flow again as Hugo's hand gripped his shoulder firmly and supportively, 'shot execution-style. I was too late.'

Hugo, visibly shocked, shook his head and sat down across from Mark.

'Don't worry my boy,' Hugo reassured him, trying to comfort Mark and reassure him everything would be OK.

'I will provide Lever & Sons' FULL support and resources to find out what happened. Now let's get you home.'

He spoke softly but confidentially to Mark, who was now in clothes provided by the police.

'It's obvious from the evidence from the scene that suspicion is initially on you Mark, especially as the police are taking into account your assault on the "gardener" yesterday.'

Mark's voice trembled. 'Marie was shot. It must be connected to the black Range Rover that has been parked outside our house every day for weeks.'

They were interrupted by a knock at the door. It opened, and a well-suited man walked in. Hugo immediately spoke.

'I require time with my client,' he snapped but he was interrupted by the flash of an MI6 ID badge reading 'Agent Nathanial Williams'. Hugo backed down and Agent Williams looked solemnly down at Mark.

'I think you and I need to have a "little chat".'

The office within the villa was cool and quiet, with its white marble floor and dark wooden doors. The CCTV cameras were strategically placed throughout the villa, flashed their red movement sensors while a cool breeze rustled the light net curtains and leaves of the various yucca plants that were placed in ornate but modern vases either side of most of the doors that led off to the multitude of different rooms. The breeze eased the stifling heat common in the Mediterranean. Tropical and secluded, this paradise was off the radar, as were other 'properties' belonging to the organisation. It was perfect for business such as this to be carried out. The villa was built at the top of a remote hill, meaning it was away from prying eyes. Armed men stood at the main entrance, carrying Uzi 9mm weapons and bowie knives in their belts. The large balcony facing the sea was occupied by a bamboo patio table and chairs and a few sun loungers. An older man was seated on a sun lounger reading a newspaper.

The headline in the newspaper described lawyer Mark King's 'assault' on gardener/hitman Roman Vose in his Range Rover and alongside it was another headline showing Mark being arrested after his wife was murdered in a shooting. The old man read that the story tried to implicate Mark as a distressed madman who assaulted an innocent person, was fired from his job and in a fit of rage, went home and shot his wife in the head, killing her. This old man smiled as he read further that Mark was witnessed going to a shooting range before returning home to 'kill' his wife. The article continues with the theory about Marie, Mark's wife, having an affair and Mark catching the couple in the act or suspecting her and finally snapping, taking her life out of jealous rage. Either way, it didn't look good for Mark. The old man was Thomas Theodore Lundon, and this was his villa, and he had been watching Mark for some time. Quietly and from the shadows was how he operated. Thomas Lundon was responsible for ensuring that problematic people and situations were 'taken care of' and a great deal of responsibility rested on his shoulders from higher up in the organisation, to make sure he handled this threat with tact and without exposure. This organisation had flourished for decades by always being in the shadows, never revealing itself to anyone or letting anyone who had seen their operations, live to describe what they had seen.

This game was a game Lundon enjoyed. He was a busy man and had many areas of responsibility and his time was precious. He could not afford a problem such as this, to disrupt their main objective. Usually, Lundon's solution to a problem was to throw as much money as it took at it, to make it go away. Most people he encountered could be bought, or at least, bought into the fold of their organisation. He had killed people along the way, those who would not be turned or could not be bought or those who simply got in the way so much as to warrant killing. He had always thought of killing people as a necessary evil, an evil he had become accustomed to. However, at his age, he didn't feel the need for killing so much, unless it was necessary. With Mark King however, Lundon was more than happy to pull the trigger.

It wasn't that Lundon didn't like Mark King. They shared a very similar outlook and goals. Lundon wanted to be at the top of the 'food chain' and Mark King was a lawyer who revelled in the power of putting criminals in prison. To Lundon, the process was the same. What had slowed Lundon down throughout his career and driven his thirst for all things powerful was his severe diagnosis, when he was in his twenties, of epilepsy. He found this particularly difficult when socialising among his peers, as when he was young, this illness was not commonplace and people could be cruel. Prior to his membership induction, he remembered one particular acquaintance mocking him relentlessly for his condition so much that he shut himself away for months, totally cut off from the outside world, embarrassed and alone. When he finally resurfaced, he was angry, bitter and vengeful. The doctors had reminded him on numerous occasions throughout his life that the longer his fits went on, the more pressure they would put on the brain and the more he would find it difficult to rationalise and make decisions in his life. Several months ago, he had a seizure which nearly killed him and it was after this that a member of his organisation had introduced him to a contact in Syria whom Lundon thought may be of use to him.

Lundon laughed at the headline before answering a call on his mobile. On the other end of the phone, Lundon recognised Roman Vose who always addressed Lundon as 'Boss' in an accent which could have been Russian or Albanian. Lundon didn't care, and it didn't matter anyway. He was a hired thug, a spare part that could be switched out and replaced whenever required. The conversation was quick and direct.

'Boss, phase one is completed. Target one has been eliminated.'

'Good,' Lundon replied in his usual short, sharp way before hanging up the phone. He pointed his fingers like a gun whilst smiling satisfactorily that his plan was finally coming together.

'Gotcha. Now the game REALLY begins.'

The sun shone down upon Oak Park Cemetery in the Oxford countryside whilst the mourners filed into the large country church Marie used to spend nearly every childhood Sunday. The line of mourners seemed to go on forever as black suit upon black dress filed into the medieval stone church.

The air was cool inside, and the organist was seated while the funeral bell tolled its mournful song.

Mark's mother-in-law Wendy, flanked by Benjamin and Hope, had flown back from New York to lead the procession into the picturesque village church. It moved silently past a vast array of people from Mark and Marie's life. Mark had considered being a pall bearer, but he needed to support the children, so the six men, Marie's brothers and friends, carried her on her final journey. The agreement with Wendy was straightforward. She was to take care of Hope and Ben for a while until Mark was back on his feet and could take care of them himself. The agreement had been made prior to the funeral, and many believed it was the best course of action. It was a hard day for all and Mark, with his Aviators and perfect black suit, white shirt and black tie, sat with his head bowed on the front pew of the church whilst the service was conducted. The minister, a friend of Marie's, conducted the service and addressed mostly Wendy, Mark and the children.

All the relatives made a fuss of the children, Wendy and Mark as they made their way from the funeral back to the waiting cars to take them to the wake. Mark carried his single white rose to the graveside as the grave was half filled with earth. He knelt at the graveside and, before throwing the rose onto the coffin and pile of earth, made a vow to Marie.

'I'm sorry I was late again, my darling. I guess you were used to that. But I swear by my own blood, that I will find those responsible and do what I have always done, punish them and avenge you.'

He stood up and sprinkled the earth onto the coffin and looked up into the sky.

'The sun shines on the righteous, my love,' he muttered and Hope held onto his hand tightly, resting her head on his arm. He held onto her and felt a tear drop onto his hand. This made his own tears flow more freely as he struggled to hold them back for the sake of the children.

Mark stood up, and the minister began the committal. Mark shuddered at the sound of the earth hitting the coffin.

He had attended many funerals in his life and had always hated that sound. To him, it sounded almost final.

Mark, the children and Wendy were the last to leave. People stood around, hugging and shaking hands whilst women wept into tissues and handkerchiefs. Men solemnly comforted them and shook hands with one another. Hugo Lever waited at the path for Mark and patted him on the back.

Ian Hawking lurked behind a tree, away and out of sight of the family and mourners. He wasn't attending as a journalist but as a mourner, and silently wept from his hiding place. Hawking, too, carried a single white rose. He waited until the family had left the graveside and into the waiting line of black cars before he shuffled towards the graveside. He knelt, as Mark had done, and dropped the rose onto the earth covered coffin as the minister put a hand on his shoulder.

'My son, there is no need to hide from God.'

Hawking looked up, surprised that the vicar had spotted him.

'I don't hide from God,' he replied, 'but sometimes, one can be more effective hiding from people.'

The minister patted his shoulder before blessing him and walking back towards the church. Hawking rose to his feet and backed away from the grave. On the way past one of the flower bins, he took his notebook and pen and dropped them into the bin and headed across the cemetery, back towards where he had parked his car so as not to be noticed by anyone.

Back at the house, the mourners shuffled about holding plates filled with buffet food and drink. People commented on the new carpet Mark had fitted recently. Mark had also had his study, where Marie was killed, renovated and the smell of fresh paint and varnish were still hanging in the air above the smell of lilies. When he arrived, someone has collected all the post received that day and placed it on Mark's desk. Mark noticed a large yellow Jiffy bag cellotaped up with a handwritten address label on it which had been written in black marker. 'FAO Mark King' was written in bold but he couldn't bring himself to deal with that right now as he had people to look out for at the wake. Mark's children both appeared behind him and they embraced him, sobbing as they fired questions at Mark about what life would be like now. Mark tried hard to manage a smile.

'Don't worry you two,' he reassured them, 'Daddy will sort it all out and once I've done that, I will come to New York and be with you.'

They both looked up at him, managing half-hearted smiles.

'Go and speak to Granny about what time your flight leaves for New York, there's good little angels.'

Both children ran towards the living room where Wendy was being comforted by two or three others as she cried helplessly into her handkerchief.

Several people approached Mark, shaking hands to pay their respects, but Mark wasn't really focussed on them. However, one which got his focus was Hugo Lever.

'This is all a set-up, Hugo,' Mark whispered angrily, holding back tears of rage. Hugo sighed and tried his best to be supportive without being insensitive.

'You have to believe me. You fired me over a set-up.'

Hugo looked sympathetically at Mark but inside, Hugo was frustrated and pleaded with Mark.

'Mark, please. This is not the time to discuss this. Think of your guests and your lovely children. They need you now more than ever.'

'What they NEED, Hugo,' replied Mark angrily, his voice rising as he spoke, 'is the truth, answers, justice?'

'Revenge?' Hugo warned. Mark looked at him wide eyed. 'If you are thinking that this is somehow related to Azidi, and that his group targeted you because you are prosecuting him, I would tread very carefully. I researched this thoroughly and there was no record of any calls being received to your phone of this nature.'

Mark sighed.

'I HAVE to know what's going on. There is more to this, I know it. I have a particular skill set which can help.'

Hugo looked gravely at Mark.

'Walk away from this, Mark. Move to New York, be with your children and live a peaceful happy life. I have an estate agent in LA who deals with property in New York. I'll give him a call and get him to give you a good deal. If money is an issue, I can help with that, for Marie's sake. Leave this behind and move on. It won't end well,' he warned before finishing the last mouthful of his wine and patting Mark on the back.

'C'mon Hugo, you know me better than that. It's a se ...'

'Enough!' Hugo angrily interrupted, before softening his tone, regretting his harsh manner towards a grieving man. Mourners looked nervously to where the raised voices were coming from. Hugo looked round nervously. Mark stayed silent as Hugo squeezed his shoulder and walked towards the front door.

'You are grieving and desperate for answers. What happened to Marie was tragic, but you mustn't blame yourself or go looking for revenge. These people are clearly dangerous, whoever they are.'

Mark wasn't focussed on any idea of walking away from this now and, although it was tempting, something was telling him to stay. Hugo's 'cruel to be kind' approach fell on deaf ears but made Mark wonder why he was behaving like that. Once in his car, being driven by a young chauffeur, Hugo picked up his mobile and pressed the speed dial button.

'We may have more of a problem than we thought.' Hugo hung up the call and beckoned his driver to drive. Gradually, mourners left the wake, much to Mark's relief. It was early evening and the last of the mourners left Wendy, Mark and the children at home. Mark put them to bed and kissed them goodnight.

'Hey, you know you can both talk to me about anything. Especially Mum, OK?'

They both nodded, and he kissed them again, tiptoeing out and gently closing the bedroom door behind him. He faced Wendy in the hallway.

'Talk about Marie? Mark, it's the day of her funeral!'

Mark put his hand on her shoulder and she put her hand on his and cried again.

'I've called the airport, the flight is tomorrow. It's best for everyone for a while. I need to tidy up,' she said, trying to find things to do so she didn't think about Marie too much. Mark pulled her back.

'You need to go to bed. I'll deal with all the stuff downstairs,' Mark ordered as they both reached the bottom of the stairs. Wendy followed Mark into the living room to collect her handbag and stopped as she passed him at the living room door. She smiled and nodded reluctantly.

Mark was alone in the living room, surrounded by flowers and cards from mourners and friends and family. Suddenly he remembered the post in the study and walked to retrieve the yellow Jiffy bag from his desk, stopping in the hallway to look at his and Marie's wedding photos in their shiny black and silver frames that adorned the hallway. He ran his hand over the image of a smiling Marie as he walked.

He took the yellow Jiffy bag into the living room and, with a Glenfiddich in his hand and a cigarette in an ashtray, opened the Jiffy bag slowly. In it he found copies of the police evidence, photographs, forensic evidence and crime scene images, and information and statements from everyone including the neighbour who found Mark with the lifeless Marie. He was about to put it all back when he discovered a handwritten note in handwriting he didn't recognise. He read the note and realised it was attached to a smaller envelope. He opened it and in it, Mark found copies of notes taken from someone who seemed to have asked the neighbours about the black Range Rover. No one in the area had booked gardeners that month, so why were they there?

Intrigued by this, Mark made a decision. It wouldn't be easy; it could probably get him killed or a prison sentence or worse. Mark's old life flashed before his eyes as he remembered Sandhurst Military Academy, where he had been trained as a sniper and prepped for the SAS. He was hardened and realised that he had gotten soft as he got older. Gradually, Mark's grief turned to anger. He remembered back to Al Azidi in court, the black four-by-four outside, the fact there was no phone line or electricity in the house when he found Marie and held the forensic report out in front of him, which concluded Marie was killed from a single gunshot to the head from a high calibre long distance sniper rifle. Mark read that the police concluded there were no signs of any broken windows or forced entry into the house, which meant Marie must have been at the front door when she was shot then dragged into the study. Mark knew he tested negative for gunshot residue so they were clear he hadn't fired a weapon except for at the shooting club, where they wore gloves. CCTV placed him there at the same time as the coroner's estimated time of death and the CCTV also confirmed that Mark did not remove any gloves from the shooting club before returning home.

Mark's flashbacks became more intense and confused. He wrestled with the idea that Marie's death was pre-meditated, more than just a 'burglary gone wrong'. He also remembered an MI6 agent speaking to him at the police station; it was strange for them to be involved if it was a case of domestic murder or a robbery gone wrong, but he didn't think about it at the time as he was in shock.

Suddenly he jumped as if from a dream. His Glenfiddich was empty and his cigarette had burnt down without him smoking it. He could hear the patter of rain on the UPVC window frames; it was raining outside and there was a thunderstorm overhead. He thought he was dreaming and that the thunder and lightning woke him up. There was a figure in the doorway and Mark jumped to his feet, but then realised it was Wendy. She had come to check on him and could smell the cigarette smoke. She gave him a disapproving look as she walked towards him.

'Well I don't know how THAT will help!' Mark looked sheepish, as if he had been caught by his mother smoking when he was young. Wendy came into the living room, sat down beside him and lit her own cigarette up. Mark glared at her and she gave a wry smile.

'What? You don't think I didn't used to do it too. I gave up when Marie was born but, after today, I could really do with one.'

They sat in silence, smoking for a while. Mark could see Wendy really felt affection towards him and they were both grieving. Mark stubbed the last of his cigarette out before turning to Wendy, her hands in his.

'Promise to take care of the children in New York?'

She smiled and nodded and Mark got up, made his way towards a cabinet and retrieved his old army bag. In it, he put the files from the Jiffy bag and dashed upstairs to collect clothes, a few pairs of jeans, shirts, jumpers and shoes. He returned to the living room to a worried Wendy.

'What ARE you doing?'

Mark went over to the large grandfather clock which had been stood in the back of the room since before Hope was born, and opened it to reveal a keypad. He punched a number in and pulled the back of the clock open to reveal a small gun cupboard. In it was his old Sandhurst kit and his sniper rifle.

'Don't worry; I took the liberty of keeping this from the police. It's not been fired in years,' he explained, a faraway look in his eye as he remembered the last time he picked it up. Wendy looked terrified and wide-eyed as she watched in horror as Mark zipped it into its carry case.

He gathered his kit and passport which had been returned to him the day before by the police, car keys, two mobile phones and other belongings: wallet, credit cards and files, put it into his kit bag and turned to Wendy.

'I know Marie was murdered I think I know where to start in locating her killers.'

Wendy looked disappointed at him.

'And what will you do when you find them, kill them? That won't bring her back, Mark,' she said, lighting another cigarette up.

'What I've always done,' Mark growled quietly. I'm going to bring them to justice but my kind of "justice" doesn't involve a courtroom!'

'MARK, you can't do this, this is madness!' Wendy pleaded, her voice getting louder. 'You are already still under suspicion as it is, don't make it worse for yourself. Think of the children?'

Mark shouted, 'Marie's death was a professional HIT! Can't you SEE?!'

Wendy broke down in tears.

'I know that. I just don't want to admit it; that anyone would want my beautiful daughter dead.'

'Which is why,' Mark assured her, 'I am going after whoever carried out the hit then the person who ordered it.'

Wendy's face turned serious as she looked up at him through tear soaked eyes. Mark noticed her eyes were not sad anymore, and the sparkle he always looked for had gone. It had been replaced with pure anger.

'Nothing I say will change your mind?'

Mark dropped his shoulders and shook his head. As he turned to leave, she called after him.

'Mark, will you do me one favour?'

He turned and nodded.

'Find them, get them to confess, and kill them.'

He rushed towards her and kissed her on the cheek. On the way out the front door, he took a picture of Marie and placed it in his bag.

Mark walked out to his car with his bag over his shoulder, stopped and looked up at his children's bedrooms with their little lights illuminating the windows. He looked lovingly up and whispered softly, 'I love you and I'll be back soon,' as he turned and his expression changed instantly. It was now serious and determined. He got into his car. 'Right after I find the bastards that killed mummy.'

He started the ignition, revved the engine, and wheel-spun out of the driveway.

Chapter Seven

Mark pulled his car into a warehouse carpark behind the Travelodge off the M4 towards Swindon where he stayed in the night before. He turned off the ignition and sat in the car with a notebook and pencil. Inside, Mark had written a list of names; most were crossed out. He used pencil in case he was caught and could dispose of anything incriminating. Working as a lawyer, Mark kept detailed notes on the ways criminals used techniques to evade the chain of evidence. Mark checked all his mirrors and the windows before crossing a name off the list. He was waiting for a contact he prosecuted years ago for possession of weapons, whom the police used for information. Mark made the call shortly after leaving home and had advised the 'contact' that he had gone rogue and wanted some paid help and had provided the contact with a list of items and where to get them. Mark had also advised his contact how to get them and where to get them from, and delivered money to him in cash so as not to arouse suspicion from the authorities.

Mark sighed and checked his watch. His contact was late. Then, he spotted a hooded individual walking towards the car, hands in his grey hoodie and face concealed. The contact tapped on the window and Mark wound it down. The rough, street slang which came from under the hood was familiar to Mark.

'I only got a hand-gun and some ammo innit.'

Mark nodded and, as promised, paid him. He talked in a low voice and explained his plan. The contact listened and occasionally nodded in agreement.

'Man, I'm still pissed at you for putting me away though innit.'

Mark laughed and nodded, smiling.

'Yeah well it was my job. I have another vocation now.'

'Well, if someone offed my missus, mate, I'd bang 'em straight out too, ya know?'

Mark nodded and thanked him before the contact wandered off. Mark opened the small black military box to reveal a Glock 22 pistol and silencer, plus one hundred rounds of ammunition. He nodded, satisfied that it would do the trick and closed the box, putting it in his kit back. When he tuned in the radio on his hire car, having ditched his own to prevent him from being tracked by anyone, he reached for the box again, opened it up to inspect the Glock further. Alongside the magazine clips, he discovered a hand written note with a telephone number, address and time written on it from the contact. Smiling but curious, Mark returned to his hotel room to pack his things, before checking out and heading to the new 'rendezvous' named on the piece of paper.

Night had fallen as Mark rolled his hire car up to a set of wire mesh gates on a dockside. He had the note in his hand as he drove and the Glock 22, loaded and in his holster. He checked the time on his watch and got out of the car, locking it remotely. Noting there seemed to be no one around, he proceeded through the wire mesh gates and through an alley to a metal roll-up garage door. He checked all around it and gave a glance around, failing to notice the four men; armed with Uzi 9mm weapons silently surround him, weapons trained on him. Mark quickly assessed the situation, working out which one of the four men may be the best shot and who was the weakest before taking the safety lock off his holster without being seen.

He was just about to respond when he felt the warmth of a red laser sight on his neck, followed by a second on his forehead. Realising that he was outnumbered, he re-holstered his weapon and put up his hands, deciding to see how the situation played out. Suddenly, he heard laughing and chuckles for the men to 'stand down'. Relaxing a little, a short fat Italian man in a suit strode out of the shadows laughing at Mark. He clapped his hands around Mark's shoulders, patting them vigorously, momentarily causing Mark to cough. Mark spoke

'Russo,' he said with a sigh. Russo was a local gangland leader and explained himself in a heavy Italian accent.

'A "mutual friend" advised me you require some assistance?'

'You could say that,' replied Mark. 'But I was hoping for a more confidential arrangement?'

Russo laughed and again patted Mark on the shoulder.

'Our "friend" advised me the mighty Mark King had gone rouge so I said, "Russo, you need to see this for yourself". So here I am.'

Russo leant in to Mark and whispered, 'I decide to do this for free, in aid of Mrs King, god rest her soul,' in a serious tone as he marked himself with the sign of the cross.

Russo led Mark into the Garage which, to Mark's amazement, was actually a huge warehouse full of equipment, mostly military surplus supplies. He was led to a rail of black combat clothing such as combats, Kevlar vests, flak vests, boots and other combat clothing. Next to this was a table with the biggest collection of weaponry Mark had ever seen. Suddenly, thinking back to an old case he handled early in his career, Mark remembered what he was looking at and was completely in awe of what he saw.

'Impressive, no?' Russo chuckled, breathing a sigh of regret.

Mark could only nod as Russo explained, 'I am a son of a Mafia Godfather. Must have been when you first started your career, my friend.'

Mark remembered the case early in his legal career and that he had tried to have Russo put away several times for running drugs and weapons. However, Russo always admired Mark's resilience and cunning legal mind.

'I give you some supplies to aid your mission?' Russo chuckled as he slapped Mark's back before waddling towards the table laden with weapons. 'The contact you met is my nephew and will one day hope to take over from me, but the guys you are dealing with, people behind Marie's death, are bigger than us and so we are cutting our losses and relocating to South America, eh boys?'

Mark was astounded and lost for words. He'd spent years trying to get a conviction to stick; now he was helping him! The armed men milling about the warehouse cheered, much preferring somewhere warmer to work in.

'Before we go, we would like to offer you as much kit as you can carry. You have one hour before it is collected to be shipped to another location.'

Mark smiled as he surveyed everything in front of him.

'Hey Marky, la mia casa è la tua casa, huh!'

Mark's understanding of Italian was good enough to know this meant 'my house is your house' and followed Russo to an office to talk privately. Once there, Russo poured two Spanish whiskies and handed one to Mark.

'Tell me, what can I do for you my friend? You want I should give to you? Logistics, safe refuge, fake passports, new identities for you and your good children, what, you tell?'

Mark smiled, grateful at the kindness being offered to him by someone he pursued relentlessly.

'I am overwhelmed Russo. I didn't expect this.'

Russo tutted at him, 'There is a one condition. You no tell no one it me?'

Mark shook Russo's hand.

'Agreed,' Mark smiled, shaking hands vigorously, 'I will repay you, Russo, as soon as this is all over.'

Russo smiled at him, raising a glass.

'I am a just 'appy we are both now on same side. The only repayment you give me is that you kill all of these bad guys.'

Mark looked serious as did Russo. Russo sighed, looking forlorn.

'All the gangs and syndicates are now exposed. Everyone moving out, these guys mean business. We just cannot keep up.'

Russo made a toast. 'To Marie.'

'Marie?' Mark questioned. Russo put down his glass and leant forward towards Mark.

'We have been watching you covertly over the last year because you been in the press a lot, and I always liked Marie. She was kind and gentle and didn't ask for any of this.'

Mark was shocked but also secretly relieved that Russo is now on HIS side. Mark asked Russo if he could be excused.

'I'm going to need more than a hire car to shift this lot to where I'm going!'

Russo smiled and wagged his finger at Mark.

'Ah, Russo is full of surprises. You want I show you, come, come.'

Russo beckoned Mark to follow him and called in Italian for one of his guards who arrived with an Uzi and wearing a balaclava. He promptly muttered something to him and dismissed him before motioning Mark to follow him. Down in the warehouse, under some tarpaulin, was a black Mercedes Vito van equipped with bullet proof glass, bomb proof undercarriage and a large supply of different number plates.

'So this is how Russo used to smuggle weapons across Europe,' Mark said to himself quietly, smiling at the ingenuity of Russo's vehicle. It was used as much for protection as he moved around the country, as it was for criminal activity but it didn't matter now, the fact was it belonged to Mark and it would come in use.

'Now Mark,' whispered Russo confidentially to Mark. Mark listened intently. 'You do not put a single scratch on it or it will void my insurance!'

Mark nodded as Russo winked at him, noting the huge irony of a criminal having insurance on this vehicle. Mark shook his head in disbelief; he really had seen it all now and was exposed to a world he knew little about, but he was determined and driven by anger, not grief; there would be time to grieve later.

Mark and some of Russo's henchmen loaded the vehicle and Russo pulled Mark to one side to a special table. He explained that he had set aside the more "specialist" weapons which he thought Mark may appreciate. On the table was a selection of up to date and not yet on the market sniper rifles, concealed weapons and ammunition. Mark made his selection and loaded them into the van. Mark and Russo shook hands before Russo shouted to his team, 'Friends, we must wind this activity up.'

This order encouraged a mass rush of people packing up whatever Mark didn't take with him. Mark got into the Vito van and pulled away towards the warehouse door but stopped before the door and called over Russo. He handed him the paperwork for the hire car.

'Deliver this back to the hire company, without a scratch.'

Mark threw him the keys. Russo laughed and promised not to mark it at all. Mark then drove out of the garage and Russo winced as he heard Mark wheel-spin out in the yard. Russo rushed after him and Mark spotted him in the rear-view mirror.

'Just getting used to it,' Mark said aloud, laughing.

Chapter Eight

The traffic noises outside the eighth floor window echoed around the empty office building as lights flickered on and off in the apartments and offices up and down the inner London City street. Inside, only the faint sound of a hoover pushed around the floor by an elderly dark haired man in a black cleaning company branded polo shirt and dark blue workman's trousers, occasionally shunting the steel foot of a table, bothered the darkened figure hunched over a laptop in the corner of the open plan office.

Crumpled bits of paper, empty coffee cups and sandwich wrappers littered the desk and over flowing waste paper bin down by the side of the desk, much to the annoyance of the elderly cleaner, who periodically shot irritated glances towards the sound of furious tapping on a laptop keyboard. Shaking his head, the elderly cleaner resumed his hoovering, unable to comprehend the need for young people to work such late hours having no life. It wasn't like that in HIS day, when he buzzed around the halls of this vibrant and decorated newspaper and media company, which had covered most of the major breaking news stories of this century. The old man's mind wandered back to the times when he wore the snappy, expensive suit and ran through these corridors he now hoovered, helped by his glamorous and attractive assistant as he worked hard to break the latest news stories.

The figure, outlined only by the lights shining in from the large window which looked down eight floors and onto the hustling, bustling street below as late night shoppers, yuppie drinkers and police patrol cars, leant back in his new black reclining ergonomic office chair, and stretched his arms high above his head, groaning as he felt the soreness in his back, shoulders and head increase. He turned to his second screen and adjusted the large double black monitor arm, to which were fixed two Pro Display computer monitors, and used his black wireless mouse to scroll through volumes of high-resolution black and white images of a man loading a car with suspiciously large military bags.

Ian Hawking stretched again as he got up from his desk and wandered over towards the small roof terrace adjacent to his desk. He swiped his Cryptag ID across the small black panel on the wall and waited for the LED to turn green before sliding the large patio door open and closing his eyes, feeling momentary comfort from the cool breeze which engulfed his face. He pulled a semi-crushed packet of Marlborough Red cigarettes from his pocket and lit one up, exhaling extensively before sliding one hand into his pocket and walking casually over to the edge of the roof terrace wall to gaze down at the traffic below.

He thought it unfair that life around him should just carry on, regardless of his pain and the fact that his world had all but stopped. For the last week he had been on annual leave, drunk and living off take-away food while he resigned himself to his living room sofa, in a deep and pitiful cavern of self-pity and grief. All he could think about at first was his own sorrow, merging into jealousy, back to sorrow again, unable to muster any other form of emotion. He was void from caring about work or deadlines or news stories. He refused to watch the news because news, as he knew all too well, moved on quickly but he didn't want to move on. He didn't want to see what would happen tomorrow, he wanted to remain in this moment, this turmoil and grief because it focussed his mind on the one thing which was the reason for the grief in the first place; the unnecessary, untimely and ultimately unfair death, of Marie King.

Weeks had passed and, once he had emerged from his pit of self-destruction, he had changed. He was no longer the bumbling, clumsy and annoying idiot journalist he realised people saw him as. Now he was focussed, driven and determined. He wanted nothing of other news stories, breaking news, or the new spot at 'Sky News at Six' he had been working towards and always dreamed of. He refused any other assignments passed his way, and had turned off and destroyed his freelance business mobile. All he could see now was one man, the man HE claimed was responsible for Marie King's death. One man who, whether deliberately or accidentally, caused the death of his wife because of his own, selfish, childish and antagonistic actions which had put her in the direct line of fire for any repercussions which may be visited upon Mark.

Ian Hawking didn't care anymore that Mark King didn't even recognise who he was. He didn't care about the laughter, the jokes, the humiliation Mark visited on him every time they met. He didn't care what he had to say to the public and to Mark's superiors when he made an official statement to Hugo Lever, claiming Mark was mentally unstable, and providing evidence, photographic evidence 'proving' Mark was the antagonist against the two gardeners innocently sat outside his home every morning before beginning work. He had given up caring about the fact that he had provided them with photographs to prove that the two individuals Mark got into a fight with in the black four-by-four were simply going about their daily work schedule, nor about the legitimacy of their employment with Government Municipal Services, or the copy of the contract he had gotten hold of and had verified to prove their employment status; all this whilst he had sat a few inches away from where Mark King had worked and became the architect of Marie's death and Hawking's destruction. He didn't care any longer that Mark had the welfare and security of the entire country on his shoulders when he was prosecuting

Azidi, nor the fact that Mark didn't seem to acknowledge the responsibility of putting this man away for life before he could kill, maim and destroy countless other lives and had fluffed it.

All Ian Hawking cared about now was Mark King. And he was going to make him pay for what he had done. The only thing that mattered to him now was getting Mark King, in any way that he could. Wherever Mark King went, he would be there to witness it and, when the moment was right, he would strike at the very heart of the man who had robbed him of the only thing he really held dear in his life since university. And he was going to enjoy it.

Chapter Nine

Lying on a sun lounger dressed in white trousers and a blue button up shirt and drinking something alcoholic, Thomas Lundon sat reading a newspaper, his laptop and mobile phone beside him on a small patio table. The phone rang and he put down his paper, irritated at the interruption.

'Yes, what is it?' the old man answered it sharply.

'Mark King has vanished and we are unable to locate him. There is no trace on his bank records or credit cards and his hire car was found burned out by a canal in London' said the voice, clearly panicked and stressed.

'I see,' said Lundon slowly. 'I trust your men are on it?'

There was silence for a moment or two before the answer came.

'A man came into the hire company and purchased the car beforehand but left no details and no trace.'

Lundon's tone changed to a more serious tone as he explained, 'We simply cannot allow this individual to evade elimination. Put more resources to the task.'

Lundon hung up the call and motioned for one of his attendants. A tall man in black wearing sunglasses stepped forward.

'Go to London and pick up the trail of where Mark King would likely have gone, starting with his co-workers,' growled

Lundon. He then dismissed the man and turned the laptop towards him. The screensaver of the Invictus Advoca logo bounced around the screen before Lundon logged on and bought up another screen logging into an offshore bank account. While he was doing this he picked up his mobile phone and dialled using the speed dial. A voice answered.

'Yes, I am wiring you sufficient funds to allow the search for Mark King to continue.'

Mark King arrived at the metal wire mesh gates at the entrance to an old abandoned government continuity facility in a densely wooded area somewhere in the UK. He had heard about this place from various cases he had dealt with over the years and often wondered if it would ever come in use by anyone.

'Now seems as good a time as any to make use of it,' Mark said to himself aloud, for what he had planned.

He walked round to the back of the borrowed Mercedes van to get the bolt croppers Russo had provided for him. Mark smiled at the sound of birdsong and the feeling of the drops of rain from the trees due to the downpour about half hour before Mark arrived. Mark looked around, satisfied he would not be disturbed here while he carried out his plans away from prying eyes. Using the hefty bolt croppers to cut off the huge padlock from the gates, he swung them open; he took a short walk inside the compound before driving the van up the barely visible dusted track that lead to the hardened facility.

Mark had been informed that this building had been sold to private developers during the nineties after the Gulf War after the government sold off many of its nuclear assets. Even with the rise if ISIS, he doubted it would be needed. The current owner now resided in Sunning Dale Nursing Home and was one of Mark's most valued clients so it seemed obvious that, if he needed a hideout, this was the perfect place.

Nial Atkinson was a multi-millionaire who had come to Mark for a defence against tax evasion charges six years ago. Reminding Mark of his late father, he had taken him almost to heart and they had become firm friends. It was only when Mark was driving away with Russo's van, did he realise he had little or no idea where he was going, so took a detour to Sunning Dale Nursing home to speak to Nial Atkinson about potentially borrowing his land. Naturally Nial agreed and provided him with the computer access codes for the main blast doors and blast chamber which served as a barrier against a nuclear blast. Nial had also provided Mark with plans of how to get the place up and running again.

Once Mark had driven the van into the compound, he re-bolted the gate with a new padlock he had purchased and parked the Mercedes van out of sight. He approached the first set of blast doors which were set into the ground and slightly overgrown.

Built in 1954, this command centre was intended to be the NATO nerve centre for the combined Western-European air forces and aerial defences. As such, it coordinated exercises preparing for the worst case scenario of a nuclear strike by the USSR.

The last exercise involving this command centre took place in 1995. Up to 1995, the site was continuously guarded, even though only a select few knew of its existence. Only handpicked men at key positions in the military hierarchy were allowed access, as were the six hundred men earmarked to run the base in case of emergency. Once the MoD had no further use for it, Atkinson bought it and, as he was formerly a Major in the SAS, it was sold at a knock-down price.

At the core of the bunker was the Operation Room, taking up two levels. The walls were covered with massive maps, and symbols to indicate the military positions and the movements of troops. On the upper level, the room was surrounded by offices for the joint staffs, while on the ground floor level, in direct contact with the communication equipment, a theatre was built to act as a media platform.

Mark took a thorough inspection of the facility, making a list of everything he needed to acquire to restore it to working order. However, after venturing down to the lower levels, he found a store room with brand new equipment including rolls of electrified fencing, CCTV cameras, various computer systems, and a cache of standard issue weapons such as handguns, grenades, semi-automatic weapons, and ammunition. Mark also discovered some flares and wireless radios and transmitters. Ascended back up to ground level to collect the van and locate the electricity supply, which he found just down a protected reinforced concrete hallway a few yards inside the blast doors.

After a day of rewiring, connecting and rigging of CCTV and hidden cameras located in the trees which surround the complex, Mark had rigged up various 'Nests' in the trees to act as sniper points and had created an indoor rifle firing range deep below ground and set up a rather luxurious bedroom suite with shower, gym, sauna and escape hatch up to the vehicle parking area located a few floors above him. Most of this was already present when he arrived. He also painted the grey blast doors in camouflage colours, as he had the rest of the complex to disguise it from prying eyes. Lastly, he walked into the woods until he found a field where he had lifted all the grass turf from the field to be placed over the top of the facility to cover it from the air. The reason he did this and did not buy new turf was because it occurred to him that new turf is a different colour green to that of already growing grass in the locality, and Mark wanted it to blend in as much as possible.

Mark erected a 'Wanted' wall together with photographs of people he knew were involved as well as blank spaces for potential targets. Down the corridor from what used to be the 'Map Room' was an office filled with filing cabinets and desks. Mark had used his time wisely, getting as much information as he could about his wife's murder and storing it in the cabinets. He had also rigged each floor to explode if he triggered the explosives should anyone after him, gain access to the facility, as well as this, he had disguised all the secret exits to look like part of the walls so that only HE knew how to get out in a hurry.

In the main conference room, he had managed to fix the giant TV screen in the centre of the room and wire it up to the internet and computer system, together with slightly smaller ones around the room, all showing different news channels, and CCTV views and maps of local areas. Also he had replaced the batteries in all the world clocks on one wall so that he knew every time zone time around the world in one glance. He built a steel balcony with steps and walkway overlooking this conference facility so he could see everything at once.

Outside the complex, Mark had rewired and repaired the electric fencing, rigged up hidden cameras covering all entrances and exits to the facility and completely camouflaged it from any unwanted visitors. He had also rigged up a second ring of fencing further outside the complex to which he had also added laser sensors, electrified fencing and delayed timer landmines, a map of which is also rigged up in the security room. This room contained screens with every single camera and map of the complex in one place. The door to this room was disguised as part of the wall and it had a blast proof door manufactured from the same material as the main blast doors, meaning it was impenetrable. In this he had also erected a bed, weapons store, toilet and food, along with the main food supply and independent water storage and treatment system already built into the facility. In essence, this place was built to withstand a nuclear war and subsequent thirty year nuclear fallout.

Mark wandered through this vast underground facility He walked into the main operations / conference room to survey the various cameras and maps and approached a map table with a huge map of London on it. On a second table to his right, stood a steel table complete with hand gun, sniper rifle, bag and accessories including multiple scopes, laser sites and magazines, Kevlar vest and guile suit hung up next to it. Next to that was hung Marks new black combat trousers and jacket. He looked around and smiled to himself, satisfied his he had something to show for his hard work. As he lights up a cigarette, placing it in the ashtray on the map table, he took a file from the table next to him and flicked through it. In it were pictures and descriptions and police evidence files of the two men in the black Range Rover parked outside his house in the lead up to his wife's murder. He gazed at the map

'Ok,' said Mark, staring intently at the map, 'let's scope em!'

Armed with his first targets, the two men in the Range Rover, present in the lead up to his wife's murder, Mark King had marked his men. He had ascertained through various intelligence sources that his targets regularly visit an office building in the centre of London. He had identified them both the first as: Roman Vose: A forty-two year old professional Hitman & Bodyguard, former CIA agent, defected to Russia and now worked for anyone who would hire him, whose guise is a professional businessman who deals in exotic weapons, the same man Mark King punched in the Range Rover outside his home the day before his wife was murdered.

The second was Hix Lomas: a thirty something year old, former Chechnyan army soldier, professional Hitman and the person Mark believed was physically responsible for Marie King's death. What troubled Mark was HOW he was going to get into London without being recognised .Ian Hawking seemed to have a very irritating knack of finding Mark wherever he went. The other guys, including Vose and Lomas, wanted him dead. At this point, Mark wasn't sure whether he was the hunter or the hunted and had to work out some sort of plan of action. Mark realised his aunt, who was a theatre make-up artist, had taught him how to use make up to change a person's appearance and he remembered he was particularly interested and skilled in prosthetics. Mark decided he was going to take a trip to his aunt's storage unit outside of London and use some of her props to disguise himself.

Mark drove to his aunt's storage facility and, on the drive; he remembered how much his aunt had taught him that, up until this point, he had forgotten about. He smiled with fondness at the memories. He checked his watch which was set to US time as well as UK time and thought of Hope and Benjamin. He missed them so decided to call them (using an untraceable pre-paid cell phone) in the US to find out how they were settling into their new school. Wendy answered, putting him on speaker, giving everyone a chance to talk.

Mark smiled as the questioned were fired at him,

'When are you coming back Daddy?' they asked innocently.

'Very soon Kiddo's' Mark replied, trying not to sound upset, 'but Daddy has to take care of some business first.'

Mark grinned and fought back a tear as he told him how they were getting on, the friends they have made and Benjamin jumped in saying Hope was saying she had a 'boyfriend' at her new school. This scared Mark as he actually despaired at the thought of his little girl growing up too fast without his protection. He truthfully feared that, more than the prospect of facing his wife's killers and ridding the world of their entire network.

Mark finished the phone call and cancelled his hands free connection, being careful to wipe any record of the call before arriving at the storage unit. He got out of the van and wandered around inside, using his pocket mag light to light his way. It was a relative warehouse full of costumes and props from the theatre as well as an entire section dedicated to make-up and prosthetics. He looked around and began to load a few boxes into his Mercedes van. He loaded it up with as much as he could carry, including an old dressing room mirror, and, upon leaving, paid the security guard at reception for allowing him in without any record. The last thing Mark wanted was to be traced here.

It was nearly dark as Mark drove back to his bunker but he decided to do a quick drive-by of the office building where his intelligence revealed Lomas and Hix visited regularly. No sooner had he parked up out of sight, he saw a team of cleaning staff all stood at the side entrance of the building, presumably on a smoke break before their evening shift. He took out his small camera and proceeded to take photographs of them for reference. He made a note of the time their shift started and pictures of the whole team, including their ID badges they wore around their necks. He also took photographs of the security desk inside the building Conveniently, the security guard was studying a rota on the desk in front of him which showed what appeared to be the shifts for the next month and the staff names on the list. Mark took a picture of this and counted himself lucky he managed to find such a powerful camera. Putting the camera back in his kit back, he then looked around the area for a vantage point and decided on the roof of the building opposite: perfect sniper position.

Back at the facility, Mark had erected a long table with the equally long mirror he borrowed from the storage facility. He took out some magazines he acquired along the way and flicked through the various pictures of random people until he settled on a version of Keanu Reeves, post Matrix, with a beard. Over the next few hours, Mark practised until he had perfected the look and used some of the prosthetics, applied to his face, completely changing his appearance. From the electronics he acquired and the stores of gadgets already at the facility when he 'moved in', he managed to rig up two small cameras which beamed a pre-recorded moving image of him, which he had filmed earlier. He rummaged through the sack loads of costumes and realised one of them virtually matched the uniform the cleaners were wearing earlier. He grabbed it and began to hang each costume up on a rail. Once he had finished, he had costumes ranging from airmen to cowboys all lined up neatly on the rails. He smiled.

'This will definitely be useful,' he said to himself as he let his hand run across the rows of costumes.

He sat at the small metal table in the corner of the room and took a picture of himself on his digital camera. Using the internet and social media, Mark researched the names of the security employees, researching details of their lives, noting them down, and did the same for the cleaning team. Using a "Magicard Pronto ID Card Printer" he purchased on the way, he pasted his own picture onto several ID badges before printing off a copy of the rota. He placed the rota on a large glass writing board and, using red string, drew a line on a map of the area from the building he had selected as a target, to the outside of the map. He wrote all the names of the security guards and cleaning crew and placed them at various locations and times around the building. Reaching across the table, he pulled out blueprints he found online and building plans showing the exact layout of the two buildings.

Using a phone, he used an anti-trace device to prevent anyone tracing the call, and then made a call to the building he picked out as a vantage point, speaking to the Building Services Manager to advise them of the need for some overnight works to wiring on the ninth floor of this sixteen-storey building. He provided a 'contact' number, being another untraceable pre-paid cell phone which was then connected to the landline facility number, and requested that building services call his boss to confirm the works. Mark awaited a call back from Building Services. Within ten minutes, the phone rang, and it was Building Services. Putting on his best fake voice, Mark answered and confirmed the works to be carried out, providing a fake name and details for an 'employee' of Mark's imaginary company and told them to expect him. Mark then printed out another fake ID badge and details. Next he went online and created a website and details about the fake firm he made up including testimonials taken from other websites of similar companies. Luckily for Mark, the internet connection was untraceable as it belonged to the MoD and in the event of World War Three, the MoD wouldn't want anyone to hack into their systems to get their location.

Mark pulled out parts of different costumes and put them together to look like an electrician specialist. He put them in a bag along with his sniper rifle, handgun, mini cameras and remote control, ammunition, a zip wire clamp and a grappling hook gun, hard wired belt and harness set including Kevlar-plated leather security gloves. He then went to have a shower, shaving all of his body hair off and washing his hair thoroughly in a non-odour body wash. He also ensured he hadn't smoked for at least twenty-four hours beforehand so the smell of tobacco would be cleaned from him. After his shower, Mark applied the prosthetic mask, using the body glue and base foundation. He commented that even HE didn't recognise himself in the mirror.

He dressed in the same uniform as a cleaner and took his bag and equipment to the van. Before he got into the van, he swapped the plates for foreign number plates and clipped a timed explosive to the under-carriage of the vehicle in case he had to abandon it. He had images on his phone of all the maps, plans and photos of the people he needed, including his targets.

Mark parked up in the next street in an alley and blocked it using large restaurant wheeled bins so as not to be disturbed. He waited until he smelled the cigarette smoke of one of the staff, a student in his late twenties who Mark believed was doing this job to pay his student loan.

'Probably never good enough to get laid in the evenings,' Mark tutted and whispered to himself, 'or not popular enough to be out partying.'

He covered his face with a balaclava and put on his Kevlar gloves and, jumped out of the van, closing the door quietly. Just as the unsuspecting student turned the corner, Mark grabbed him.

'Sorry buddy,' he apologised before hitting him on the head, knocking him unconscious. Mark dragged him behind the bins knowing, apart from a sore head, there would be no lasting damage. Mark took the student's ID tag, took a picture of it and noted the name.

'Well, Stuart,' Mark said, standing up, 'you won't need this for a while!'

He reached into his back pocket and pulled out four five pound notes and folded them neatly as he took Stuart's wallet. He placed the notes nearly into his wallet and wrote a small note on an old piece of paper he found in the bin. Mark spoke aloud as he wrote.

'Sorry about the head, now go and get a new job!'

Before replacing Stuart's wallet, he removed his balaclava

and gloves and moved to fall in line with the other workers as they filed into the side entrance of the building. Mark had to think on his feet and noticed a black bin liner and plastic litter picker stood up against the wall. He quickly reached for it to use as a prop. Mark felt nervous as the security guard noticed he wasn't Stuart. As Mark got closer, the guard put his hand up to stop Mark.

'You aren't Stuart?' observed the guard. Mark smiled.

'Nope,' he replied jovially. 'Stu is out getting drunk or laid or some shit like that?'

The guard did not share Mark's jovial and comical act and continued to frown at Mark.

'I'm a mate of his. I offered to do his shift for him tonight. Please don't get him sacked; he'll never speak to me again!'

The security guard smiled, remembering his own student days, and patted Mark on the back, waving him off towards the lift. Once inside, Mark slyly took a picture of the empty lift from underneath the camera, using the guise of polishing it with a rag, pressed floors five and fifteen, and waited until the lift was on floor five. He pressed the button to stop the lift. The lights went out, including the security camera. Out of his bag, Mark grabbed the zip wire harness and hook, and a small photo printer, no bigger than a standard camera. He quickly printed off the picture of the lift and stuck it to the camera carefully, facing the lens. He looked up at the ceiling and was just able to reach up to lift a ceiling tile. He breathed a sigh of relief as it lifted with ease and he pulled himself up into the lift shaft. Using the zip wire hook, he attached it to the lift cables and to his belt; he then used the grappling hook to fire up to the floor above and launched himself to the lift doors above. He prised them open with a crow bar and jammed the lift doors open. Looking around, he found a fake yucca plant and placed one of his tiny cameras in the leaves, hiding it from sight, and turned it on. He repeated this on the top floor and climbed back into the lift shaft. Putting everything back into his bag he sent the lift back down to the ground floor. Upon passing security, he waved a packet of Stuart's cigarettes to the security guard who shook his head and tutted disapprovingly, buzzing him out to have a cigarette. Mark returned Stuart's cigarettes, while he was still unconscious, before getting into the back of his van. Changing his uniform, he changed equipment and crossed the road and broke into the rear of the second building opposite.

Approaching the security desk he flashed his badge and explained who he was. It was the same person he spoke to earlier who was waiting for him before doing his rounds of the building. Again, Mark entered the lift, pressed one floor and pulled the switch to stop the lift and used his zip wire harness to climb the cables to the top floor. Once on the roof, he set up his sniper rifle and laser sight through a hole in the wall overlooking the fifteen-floor drop to the street below. He then activated the remote control cameras and waited for Vose and Hix to arrive.

Within half an hour Mark spotted a black Mercedes arrive and two individuals get out and enter the building opposite. Using his sniper telescopic sight, Mark could see them speak to the guard and approach the lift. He flipped up a small notebook laptop, and it showed a split screen display of both hidden cameras and the projection of him running. The cameras beamed an image of Mark running, the same one he filmed at his bunker earlier on, and Mark watched the camera until they spotted his image. They drew their weapons and tried to shoot at him. Just as planned, Mark's image ran in the opposite direction and down a corridor. Vose and Hix gave chase and split up. Mark directed the image to the stairwell and Vose headed back to the lift whilst Hix chased Mark's image up the stairs. Mark breathed slow and deep, thinking his plan was going well so far.

He had hoped to get them both on the rooftop simultaneously so it would have been an easier shot and reduce the risk of the plan being discovered, but it didn't matter. Hix burst out onto the roof and walked towards the edge, glancing over. He wandered round beside an air conditioning housing unit and paused; Mark was already at his rifle and scope. It all seemed to happen in slow motion. Images of Marie and the murder scene ran through Mark's mind and his hands shook. Sweat soaked into the balaclava. Mark's eyes went hazy for a moment as he fought to readjust his sight, praying Hix was still stood in the same place he was seconds ago. Luckily he was. Mark shook his head and relaxed his breathing once again, feeling the trigger on his finger tighten a little. He closed his eyes for a second and lined the crosshairs up to the side of Hix head. Mark felt the hairs on the back of his neck stand up as he adjusted the trajectory to account for a slight breeze; however, he *was* on a rooftop. He held his breath and squeezed the trigger and whispered to Hix, as if Hix might hear Mark at this point.

'This is for Marie.'

Mark felt the trigger pull under the control of his finger and the rifle slightly pull back as the bullet let fly, making a sharp but dull thud as the barrel fired the bullet at what seemed like a million miles an hour towards its target. At Sandhurst, Mark was taught once you have fired, you move so the enemy cannot get a fix on your location, but Mark had to see this through. He HAD to see Hix fall. He kept his eye firmly on the telescopic sight and saw the bullet impact the side of Hix's head. He watched as blood spattered out from the wound and Hix dropped like a stone, blood quickly seeping out of the wound and onto the floor. Mark moved to duck behind the wall and finally remembered to breathe. He was panting, but he knew there was still a target to take down. He pulled himself together and moved silently along the wall to his second vantage point. He used his telescopic sight to get a fix on Vose, who was still running around corridors and was trying desperately to call someone. Mark turned to his notebook and switched on the second projector, beaming the image of him onto the wall opposite where Vose was stood. Mark's image turned and ran and Vose gave chase but not in the direction Mark wanted him to go, towards the roof. Instead, Vose seemed to have lost Mark's image and had instead moved himself into what appeared to be a meeting room. Mark knew he'd never get another chance like this and took aim, realising that the bullet would make it easily through the toughened glass and straight into Vose's skull where it belonged. Mark took aim through the window and fired at Vose's head.

As Mark steadied himself, something seemed to have spooked Vose. HAD he spotted Mark, or did he realise he was being played? Whatever it was, it caused him to shift his weight from one side to the other and lift his hand to his ear with his phone in it. This was just enough for Mark's perfectly aimed shot to have sped past Vose's ear and embedded itself into the wall behind him, but it didn't. Instead, it hit Vose on the hand, obliterating the phone he was holding. Vose hit the ground behind a desk and Mark took two more shots at the desk, hoping to hit Vose, but the window and the wooden desk took the speed and direction out of the bullet and all Mark could do was watch as the door opened, revealing that Vose had crawled out of the room on his stomach. Watching the building he saw Vose running out of the main reception and into the car parked outside before speeding off. Mark had missed.

However, realising that he still needed to clear up, he again changed costume in his van before making one last trip to the building to retrieve his bullet. The last thing he wanted was forensics linking the bullets to his weapon. He inspected Hix's lifeless body on the roof before discovering that the bullet had gone clean through and into a piece of metal Hix was stood in front of. Mark used sharp pliers to pull out the bullet and put it in his pocket before searching Hix and retrieving a passport and some money, some other paperwork and an electronic pass key and a car key. Mark made his way to the room where he tried to shoot Vose and pulled the bullets out of a framed picture on the wall before smashing the window so the police couldn't get an impression of the bullet from the holes it made. Back in his van, Mark was about to drive home when he spotted another car which had pulled up close by the building. The black Audi A4 sat there, no one getting in, no one getting out. Mark could make out the outline of someone through the smoked windows, so turned off his ignition and stepped out.

'Who are you waiting for?' Mark whispered to himself, leaning flat against the walls, and edged round to a large set of white industrial bins near the rear of the car.

Taking out his silenced pistol he waited in the shadows, silently, still and waiting.

Chapter Ten

Time seemed to pass slowly as Mark perched uncomfortably between the two sets of bins as he waited to see who the car was there to pick up. His patience paid off as moments later, Roman Vose walked towards the car and used his weapon to tap on the window. It rolled down, and he was passed and hand full of papers. Vose looked at them and nodded, walking back towards the building again. The window wound back up again, and the car remained parked. Mark's mind was racing as his body tensed. Who was the driver and what did they give Vose? Mark waited until Vose was out of sight and, checking the road both ways for witnesses, crept silently towards the car. He tapped on the window and waited. It wound down and Mark jumped up from behind the door, pointing his pistol at the leather jacket-clad driver. Instantly, hands were raised and Mark got in the passenger side. Once inside he sat, gun pointed at the driver.

'Who are you and why are you meeting Roman Vose here?' Mark quizzed him.

The small, weedy looking man trembled and stuttered as he stared at Mark's pistol.

'I'm just the hired driver,' he said in a Cockney accent. Mark chuckled.

'What's your job? Who do you drive for?'

'I drive for all of 'em, mate,' he replied, surprised at Mark's lack of knowledge.

'All of 'em?' Mark mocked, taking on his accent. The driver didn't look amused.

He passed Mark a list on a crumpled piece of paper and Mark took it, staring at it. It was a list of names, times, locations and instructions. Mark folded it and put it in his pocket, staring at the driver.

'If you want to live,' Mark threatened, his voice menacing and threatening, 'you will say NOTHING of this and forget you ever saw me.'

The driver nodded as his shaking increased, and Mark tightened his grip on his silenced pistol.

'Or I will come looking for you and I will kill you, do you understand?'

The man nodded again, still shaking. Mark got out of the car and jogged back to his van, excited about his find. He wasn't too worried about Vose getting away for now. He would catch up to him again soon. For now, he had enough information to process as he started the ignition, reversing back down the alley and speeding off into the night.

He pulled over into a dark dirt track which led to some woods and turned off his lights and ignition. Undoing the window to light a cigarette, Mark got out the piece of paper and examined it closer. It was a list of meeting times and places which the driver was supposed to attend, to pick up what appeared to be members of Vose's crew.

'Naturally,' Mark thought aloud, 'without a crew to operate with, Vose is now vulnerable.'

Mark would leave him until last. He continued reading until he settled upon a meeting at a railway station. There were train arrival and departure times and it looked as though the driver was due to hand over a package to the subject before they boarded a train.

'So he is a "delivery driver" as well as a "chauffeur"?' thought Mark, realising this would suit his need well.

He would need to get hold of a car the same as the black Audi A4 that the driver used. He would also need to get rid of the driver, so as not to have two of them driving around.

'Perfect,' Mark said to himself as he finished his cigarette. The meeting was two days from now at Richmond Train Station. He read that the time for the train to leave Waterloo was twelve thirty-nine and it would reach Richmond Station at twelve fifty-nine, giving Mark just twenty minutes to target the subject. Mark traced his finger down to the name on the list: Marco Salvatore.

Back at Mark's hideout, he pored over the map of the London Overground and Underground as he planned his next hit. The driver was due to arrive at Richmond at twelve fifteen and would wait to be contacted by Salvatore, and he would be there to intercept. Mark planned that he would pose as the driver and hand over the 'package', a small black case, so he knew who his mark was. Once he had a decent depiction, it would be the ideal opportunity for Mark to take him out. He couldn't use the traditional method of shooting him outside the car, it would attract far too much attention and he would be spotted. It also wouldn't guarantee a successful hit, so he had to think of another method. At that time of day, the station would be busy with passengers getting on and off the trains, so although this would provide Mark with sufficient cover, it also increased the risk of being spotted and of innocent people being hit in the crossfire. Mark needed to ensure it was a perfect shot. He reached over for his laptop and searched for images of the station, to see if he could find the best spot for a sniper attack.

After an hour of searching, Mark realised that a public hit such as this, with plenty of potential witnesses, was too risky and there were only a few places he could conceal himself and get a decent shot from his rifle from a safe enough distance. He was an incredible shot, but he wasn't THAT good. It would require more than this to bring down Salvatore. Mark knew nothing about Salvatore, except that he worked for Vose and so needed to be taken down. Then Mark remembered a case he had researched from the 1970s concerning poisoning of a victim using thallium. Mark looked up thallium poisoning on the internet and remembered the victim absorbed it through the skin in quantities of fifteen to twenty milligrams. It was perfect; he could lace the handles of the briefcase with a lethal dose of thallium and vanish, out of the way of suspicion as the symptoms don't show until two to three days after coming into contact with a lethal dosage. Mark smiled to himself but then realised he would need to get access to thallium, and they didn't just give it out at the local Boots. He considered all his options before researching local laboratories which held thallium and within seconds, he was reviewing the results. He found one close to his target area and decided he would pay them a visit.

The view from the rooftop across the road from the research laboratory was good enough that Mark could use his telescopic scope to get a good view of the cameras that covered the exterior and interior of the building. He decided that the best way to avoid the majority of the cameras was to enter via the roof, and he had spotted a skylight which was almost inaccessible; almost. Reaching into his kit bag, Mark pulled out the grappling hook gun he acquired and, checking no one was on the ground below him, aimed it towards the concrete roof near the skylight and squeezed the trigger. He smiled as he heard the sound of it burying itself into the concrete as the hook found its mark, and gave it a tug to make sure it was safe. Satisfied, he anchored the other end to the door handle of the fire escape ladder he had used to climb up to the roof, and attached his belt to it. He would need to be quick across the rope, so he anchored it higher than his head, to ensure he could quickly manoeuvre down the wire to the other side.

Pushing away using his legs, Mark inched his way silently across to the opposite roof, quickly unclipping his belt harness and crawling flat on the ground towards the skylight. He peered in and everything was silent and still underneath him. Equipped with an adjustable spanner to unscrew the skylight, being careful to ensure he left no trace of having been there, Mark unscrewed the bolts which held the skylight in place.

The last bolt caused Mark some frustration. Time was vital and he couldn't afford any hold ups, but at last, he felt the bolt move and turned the bolt head quicker and quicker. Laying the skylight next to him, he dropped his black military grade rope into the moonlit laboratory below. Inch by inch he lowered himself down until he felt his feet on the ground. Looking around him, he followed the signs to the 'Hazardous Chemical' storage where the thallium was stored.

He saw the rows and rows of small clear bottles, all embellished with the Hazardous Chemical emblem, and, pulling out his syringe, taking care not to spill a drop, Mark reached in and took them, one at a time, using his syringe to extract the contents of the bottles. Ensuring he was careful not to cause any spillage, he squirted the contents into his own bottles he had brought with him. Next he replaced the bottles in his small string bag and took out his large bottle of water. He took the syringe and replaced the thallium with water, taking care to reseal the bottles and close the glass cabinet doors quietly. He darted back to his rope and expertly climbed back up to the rooftop, pulling the rope back up once he had reached the top. The next ten minutes were spent carefully replacing the bolts on the skylight window and ensuring it was fixed back into place, stopping whenever he heard footsteps and voices on the street below.

Removing the grappling hook from where it had embedded itself in the concrete rooftop and left it lying on the concrete ready to pull away, Mark attached one end of his rope to the grappling hook and dropped the other end down the side of the building and took a deep breath as he abseiled down to the ground below. Racing across the road in the shadows, he climbed back up the fire escape and pulled the grappling hook back towards him with the rope still attached. He packed everything back in his kitbag and secured it over his shoulders, making his way back down the fire escape and into the night towards his waiting van.

The following morning, Mark put on his suit and tie, ready to meet Salvatore's train at Richmond. He had a long drive ahead of him and had to store his car somewhere safe as he planned on using the driver's car from now on. Having visited the outskirts of Richmond before, he knew, if he left the car there for long enough, it would be stolen, driven around for a while, and then burned out on the waste ground. It was the perfect place to abandon the vehicle, preventing the need for counter forensic measures later on. After packing his kit into his car, Mark headed out on the drive to Richmond, putting his Aviators on to shield his eyes from the morning sun. It was an unusually warm morning and Mark enjoyed the drive to Richmond, listening to some of his favourite songs on the way and smoking as he drove, with the window down and a pleasant breeze to keep him cool. He patted his black Jasper Conran Crombie coat on the passenger seat, concealing his kit bag, thinking he wouldn't need it today, but it was a good coat for concealing weapons, such as his newly selected Remington R51 with its new AAC 9mm suppressor. He had planned the hit down to the tiniest detail, even including a cover story. Mark lifted the Crombie to ensure he knew where to place the thallium, and gripped the steering wheel tighter with his black leather gloves. It was hot, but he had the air-conditioning on which kept his hands from sweating and he thought it was handy that he had a heated and cooled steering wheel in this car, although he had never used it to cool his hands before.

Arriving at the edge of the waste ground, Mark noticed there was already a gang of hooded teenagers on push bikes circling round. He got out of the car and left it unlocked, before pulling out his case, small bag and Crombie, shutting the door and walking down the road towards the station. He knew that within half an hour of him being out of sight, his car would be stolen and he was sorry to see it go. However, what he had to do next required no trace, and a stolen car, should he be questioned, was a perfect alibi. He rounded a corner and spotted the black Audi A4 just as he had hoped, with the smoked windows and no one around. He tapped on the window and it rolled down, as it did before, and the driver rolled his eyes before looking terrified. After all, Mark had threatened to kill him if he saw him again. Two hands rose from the steering wheel as Mark glared at him from behind his Aviators.

'Follow me,' he said gruffly. 'I have some important information for you.'

The driver got out and Mark went around to the passenger side and placed his bag, coat and case on the passenger seat before the driver locked the door and followed Mark. Mark led him to a quiet street he had picked out beforehand, with no witnesses, and down the side of the back of a restaurant. Mark smiled at the driver, putting him at ease.

'Look over there,' said Mark, pointing to the other end of the street.

The driver did as he was told and didn't see the hard metallic object Mark had concealed, which made contact with his head, rendering him unconscious. He hauled the limp body up and pulled the key from the hand of the driver, before lifting him into one of the large restaurant refuse bins and rolling him over the edge, shutting the bin lid tight.

In a matter of minutes, Mark was sat in the driver's seat of the Audi A4 and taking full advantage of the smoked windows. He checked his watch; it was twelve thirty.

'Great. Nine minutes until the train arrives,' he said to himself, breathing calmly to get his breath back.

Mark pulled the case onto his lap and reached for his cotton wool buds and syringe. He laid a cloth over his lap and slowly filled the syringe with thallium, then gradually dripped it on the handle of the briefcase. He hoped to God Salvatore wasn't wearing gloves today but figured, because of the temperature, he wouldn't be. Mark used the cotton wool buds to spread the thallium all around the handle and edges of the case, ensuring he put it into the two locks. He was wearing hospital surgical gloves under his black leather gloves to make certain he didn't poison himself, and he stood the case upright on the seat. He sat, and he waited for the familiar knock on the window.

Chapter Eleven

Thomas Lundon had been asleep for around two hours when he was woken suddenly by the vibrating noise of his personal mobile phone, which lay on the ornate wooden carved bedside table beneath an antique chandelier bedside lamp, the jewels glistening in the moonlight of the otherwise darkened room. A wrinkled hand slowly emerged from the silk covers and reached fruitlessly at first, for the phone, but eventually his hand contacted with the vibrating phone and he pulled it towards the white hair which poked out, just above the edge of the silk sheet.

Without opening his eyes, Lundon spoke in a half asleep, irritated and husky voice.

'Yes, what is it?' he croaked.

He didn't know who would call him at this time of night; only a select few people had the privilege of being given his personal number. The voice on the other end of the phone also sounded tired, but serious, as Lundon froze in bed before rubbing one eye and deciding this phone call required significantly more attention than he had first realised.

'It's me,' came the familiar voice of Lundon's contact in the UK. 'I have some more information for you concerning our "mutual friend",' it whispered surreptitiously.

Lundon was very skilled at making contacts anywhere in the world, and it would have been no surprise to him that a call should come in for him this late at night. However, THIS contact had sought HIM out and Lundon didn't altogether trust that. Not that he wasn't appreciative of such endeavours, far from it; it made him suspicious that people would volunteer to be of service to him, without fully appreciating what he did to people who let him down. However, this contact didn't care and was only concerned with the ruin of one man. It happened Lundon also sought the ruin of the same man and was prepared to give the benefit of the doubt until the individual had been eliminated, then he would deal with anything secondary.

'Go on,' Lundon croaked, sitting up in bed, his face illuminated by the light of a full moon shining through the thin cotton curtains which rustled in the breeze and allowed the relaxing sound of crashing waves to serenade Lundon soothingly to sleep at night.

'I have sent you the images by secure, encrypted email,' the voice instructed, as if almost rehearsed. 'It seems we may have more of a problem with our Mr King than first thought of.'

'Really,' Lundon said discontentedly as he reached for his glasses and the laptop he had secured in a hidden drawer beneath his bed.

'Mr Lundon,' the voice replied, irritated at his lack of care, 'I had hoped we would become, how should I put it, mutually beneficial partners in this affair, and that you held Mr King and his demise as your highest priority? Please do not show me the same lack of concern you may have shown others in the past. It would be a pity for our "professional relationship" to suffer an irrevocable difference of opinion.'

Lundon seethed as best he could in his half asleep state of mind that anyone would DARE to speak to him in such a tone. If this bastard had been in front of him, he would have shot him himself for his insolence. However, Lundon had relied on this source of information for some time now and so far, he had provided exceptional intelligence on Mark King's movements. The voice continued.

'I would hate to think that this secure information should fall into hands other than yours,' it said sarcastically.

Thomas Lundon, though seething, put on his best sympathetic and grateful voice to appease this nameless individual. He would find him after Mark King was dead and put a bullet in him PERSONALLY.

'Forgive my rather rash response, I, er, have been unwell and have not been sleeping,' he begged.

'Better,' the voice at the other end of the phone replied after a pause, 'I was beginning to think you no longer required my services.'

Thomas Lundon feigned a chuckle and rubbed his forehead angrily as he felt his blood pressure rise and the colour in his face turned redder by the minute.

'On the contrary, my mysterious friend, it is you who I hold in the highest regard as a source of accurate and valuable information!'

'Shut up and listen, we'll forget the false pleasantries for the moment,' the voice replied and Lundon felt stupid at his waste of effort, which made him even more angry as he reached for his glass of water. 'Mark King has been sighted collecting a large amount of equipment from Russo's site. It appears our Mr King isn't taking this situation lying down. Make peace with whatever demons are still unaccounted for and do your best to take him out before he gets to you.'

Lundon was about to respond when he heard the dialling tone at the other end of the phone confirm that the source had hung up. In a temper, he threw the phone down towards the other end of the massive dark wooden four poster sleigh bed, irritated it didn't hit the wooden foot board and smash. Lundon knew it was too quick a call to confirm a trace and that it was made from a burn phone anyway, which means the caller had either memorised his number or was working off the grid. Either way, it made tracing the individual impossible.

Lundon spun around as his bedroom door flew open and a young man in a dark blue polo shirt with a wireless telephone headset on his head stood in the door, realising he forgot his manners.

'Sir, I, er, I'm sorry for the intrusion Sir,' he trembled, noting Lundon's furious expression and red face, 'er, unfortunately sir we could not get a trace on the latest call to come in to your private cell, we're still working on the recording now, sir.'

'GET OUT!' Lundon spat as he threw whatever was nearest to hand at the poor young IT assistant who quickly exited the room, closing the door and thanking God it was only a pillow Lundon had thrown this time.

In the corridor, the villa was bustling with people in the semi-darkness, some with clip boards, some with headsets on, moving quickly from one room to another once the silent alarm was triggered, which indicated that someone was calling Lundon on his private cell phone. Protocol stated that a trace was to be made on every single call, email, text message and communication going in or out of the villa, especially during the night, and it involved a trusted few whom Lundon personally had recruited for security reasons to manage this when he was asleep.

Inside his room, Lundon dropped back down onto the remaining billows and puffed out excess air, frustrated and annoyed at the lack of respect shown to him after waking him up at this hour; also at Mark King for causing so many problems when the man just wouldn't die.

In the darkened office building in central London, a pre-paid mobile phone stood on an abandoned desk, strapped to a speaker and facing another pre-paid mobile phone, taped with electrical tape, to a coffee mug. On the rooftop across the street sat a small, black news reporter's antenna pointing east and making a barely audible beeping noise as it rotated around and around.

Down on the street below, a hooded figure hung up the receiver in the phone box on the corner of a council estate. As he moved away from the phone box, his attention turned to the man he was holding by the throat who had been inside the phone box before he made his call, dropping him unconscious to the floor. Turning to go with an evil grimace on his face, and a few new scares on his forehead and cheek, he reached into the pocket of the hoodie, and pulled out a packet of Marlborough Red cigarettes. He lit one up, paused and looked around before making his way to an old dark blue Ford Focus parked half on the verge, and half on the road.

As he walked at a determined and victorious pace, only his eyes and lower face were visible underneath the hoodie as he breathed out one lung full of cigarette smoke after another. The place was quiet, and he knew it well from his childhood. It was the perfect spot to make an untraceable phone call with no witnesses, save one who wouldn't be worrying about anything he may have witnessed or overheard.

The night air was cool, compared to the office blocks of the inner city business districts, and few people ventured this far for fear of being mugged by the swathes of gangland members who wandered these streets. The sound of yobbish chants and the bassline from someone's loud music echoed through the deserted streets, along with the sound of breaking glass, screaming dogs barking and the sound of a siren, encouraged Ian Hawking to quickly flick his cigarette and jump into the focus. He pulled out a third pre-pay burn phone from the pocket of his dark blue jeans and opened the screen, pressing the only number programmed into the speed dial, and waited for the other end to pick up.

'It's me, we're on,' he said and hung up the phone, before wheel-spinning around, sending stones, dirt and wet grass up into the air, and speeding off down the road.

His brakes screeched as he stopped right next to a large bin at the side of the road. He took out the phone he had just used and dismantled it, removing the sim card, battery, and snapping the memory board in half, before dropping it into the bin, lighting another cigarette, and speeding off into the night, the faint flashing red and blue lights of a police car summoned to investigate the sound of breaking glass and screaming he had heard moments beforehand.

Chapter Twelve

Two taps on the driver window brought Mark back from his distant thoughts with a jump, realising that it was time to work. He wound it down a little and stared at the face of Marco Salvatore, who grinned at him, breathing alcohol into the car. Mark's nose wrinkled as the waft of stale alcohol and cigars floated in through the window. Mark gave Salvatore a nod and picked up the case, winding the electric window down far enough to pass the case through. Salvatore nodded and smiled again, passing a yellow envelope back through to Mark. He figured it was probably cash and he would check that later. Mark checked Salvatore's hands, and he breathed a sigh of relief as he saw Salvatore was not wearing gloves.

Mark figured it would take two to three days for the effects of the thallium to take hold and judging by Salvatore's breath and apparent lack of personal hygiene, it would aid in the coroner ruling an accidental death. Mark checked the yellow envelope and saw it was cash. Then a thought occurred to him: if the drop was sooner than two to three days away, what would whoever was supposed to receive the contents of the case say when they realised the case was empty? He called after Salvatore hastily.

'Eh, Salvatore,' he called, waving a handful of notes at him from the open window.

Salvatore chuckled before walking back towards the car.

'Boss says you been working overtime lately and deserve a little "treat" for loyalty. Take this and have yourself a few days rest before delivering the package,' Mark whispered, passing him the money.

Salvatore smiled and nodded his head, looking thrilled at the offer. He shook Mark's leather-gloved hand through the window and walked off toward the station with a skip in his step. Mark chuckled to himself, thinking about the fact that Salvatore would blow all of that money on bad food and alcohol before he handed the case in to whoever it was supposed to go to. He started the ignition and felt the powerful S-line three litre turbo diesel 272PS engine roar into life. He wasn't expecting such power under the hood and he realised, with amazement, he needed to be careful with this car; it was much more powerful than he thought it would be. He flicked on the radio and auto-tuned it to his favourite station and reversed out of the parking space, looking for somewhere away from prying eyes.

After about an hour, Mark pulled over near a roadside café and pulled out his list of remaining targets. He used a pencil to cross off Salvatore's name from the list and wondered who the other people were. He sat quietly, flicking the yellow envelope full of bank notes over in his hands until his eyes rested on something: the franking stamp on the back of the envelope. It was a haulage company in London. Mark took out his camera and took a picture of it, replacing it and thinking nothing more on it. He looked at the next name on the list; he smiled at some of the codenames and settled on the next one, Daniel Swiftlock. He saw notes scribbled in the margin under this name and held it up to the light to see. He was due to be delivered a piece of equipment for a job and it was in the boot, in pieces which Swiftlock would have to re-assemble. Curious, Mark got out of the car and went to the boot, remotely unlocking it. There was a large black cloth covering what appeared to be a long, thin case with two clips at either end. Mark opened the clips and lifted the hinged lid to reveal an extremely powerful long range Israeli-made DAN .338 rifle, magazines, an infrared telescopic scope, wireless earpiece and a burn phone. Mark knew his weapons, and this was currently the world's most powerful sniper rifle. He remembered someone once telling him that one round from this rifle could stop a car by splitting the engine block in two. It had the potential to disable aircraft, vehicles and offered a very high kill ratio. Mark shuddered, putting his hand on the weapon, and felt relieved that it wasn't hot so had not recently been fired. He also noticed a small corner of a piece of paper which was hidden under the foam lining. He lifted it up and revealed it was a large invoice for a shipping company and freight haulage company. Mark couldn't make out much of the wording as it was so faded, but he read the name of the person who administered the invoice: Mr M Underhill.

'Wherever this is headed, it will be bad news for someone,' he said to himself aloud, 'I can't allow this to fall into the wrong hands.'

He closely inspected his newly acquired DAN .338 rifle in its case, looking as deadly as it was intended to look. Mark noted, for an instrument made purely for the purpose of killing, it looked strangely beautiful and, with no ammunition in it, may have looked almost harmless to anyone else. He paced back and forwards in front of it a few times and stared at it intently, thinking it would be just as easy to keep it. No, he thought, far too dangerous. He slammed the boot and walked back to the driver's seat, lighting a cigarette as he did so. The hot sun had now vanished, and it was getting chilly, with a wind that had picked up, making it feel colder. Mark thought to himself for a minute. 'If this weapon is going to be used soon, it would be largely dependent on the weather and how the cross-wind affected the trajectory of the bullet,' he said out loud, remembering the gruelling hours and days of training in all weathers on both moving and stationary targets.

As he exhaled, he thought about the calibre of weapon he had in the boot. If it was true that it was capable of stopping a car by splitting the engine block in two, was it possible that THIS was what it was destined to be used for by Swiftlock? Mark considered the name 'Swiftlock' and guessed it was not his real name, but he had acquired it because of his skill with a rifle. Mark got back in the car and flicked his cigarette into the dust. It was time for him to pay Mr Swiftlock a little visit.

After a short drive back to the bunker he was 'leasing' from Nial Atkinson, Mark had turned his attention to looking through all of Hix's belongings he had taken. He discovered that he did not have just ONE passport, but several, all in different names, but couldn't work out what the electronic pass key was for. Was it a hotel, a security gate or door, a safe deposit box? He didn't know, but searched the internet for the various names of all those aliases Hix was using. After a while, he came up with a list of results and filtered through them until he connected an alias to a freight company. Using Google to locate the offices, Mark decided he would pay them a visit and find out what link this had to Hix and whether he could track Vose there too. His search results bought up a website, address and pictures of freight with a client list. Mark also located the building plans and blueprints for the company's freight yard, complete with information and a suitable guise as an estate agent wanting to ship some 'fine art' abroad.

However, before he could investigate this lead, he had a few things to take care of, such as Daniel Swiftlock. He stared again at the rifle he had removed from the boot of the Audi A4 and studied it carefully, having put it together once he was shielded from anyone curious enough to take a look. It was beautifully crafted and was light, but sensitive to being knocked, so required careful handling. Mark spun around in his chair to his laptop and typed in the name 'Daniel Swiftlock' into Google. The results took a while to load but when they did, several results looked promising, including a mobile cleaning service run by a D Swiftlock.

'A cleaning service?' murmured Mark to himself. 'I suppose that is a good enough guise for a hitman!'

Mark pondered several things that worried him about luring out a professional hitman. Firstly, he would be obsessively careful when meeting anyone, so the chances of a rooftop sniper round to the head in a fake meet-up would be out of the question. If this guy was as good as he was or better, he would likely scope out the area of their 'meet', long before Mark got there. There was the potential to arrange for him to use a double to play the part of Swiftlock. Mark was despairing, but realised that he had answered his own question. He needed to check the list again as Swiftlock was expecting the rifle to be delivered to him for a job. Mark spun around and looked at the rifle, his eyes widening with an idea.

If the rifle made it safely to its owner, there would be no problem. Mark examined every single empty section of the rifle. He could pack it with explosives, rigged to go off at a predetermined time with a remote detonator. Mark stared at the rifle and a menacing grin grew on his face. He was formulating a plan.

He found a large quantity of explosives hidden in the bunker, in the form of C4, administered by way of a tube through a nozzle. He ran back to his table and filled the barrel, chamber, magazines and under the case with C4 explosive and added a source of ignition. He rigged the wireless ignition detonator to be set off by calling the burn phone, which was already fully charged, switched on and in the case.

He replaced the rifle, in its individual components, in its case and clipped down the locking mechanism, before replacing it in the boot of the Audi and returning to his desk. He checked the piece of paper and noted that he was to deliver the rifle at midnight tonight; he had time to spare so headed for the same routine before every hit, a shower using non-fragrant soaps so he could not be detected by anyone, a shave to prevent any hair fibres being recovered, and to relax his mind before another kill. He was relentless and merciless. These people had to die.

The sound of a distant dog barking and sirens melted away into what was otherwise a peaceful night as Mark checked his watch again. He had re-conned the area obsessively in the run up to choosing it as a location to meet Swiftlock, so he knew where all of the places were that a sniper would likely position themselves. It was one forty-five and the streets were deserted as the streetlights glistened and threw shadows around the carpark behind 'Gecko's' nightclub. The place was closed up during the week so it was the perfect spot. Also there were no cameras covering the rear of the carpark, so there would be no evidence.

'The ultimate aim of this,' Mark thought, 'is to be totally untraceable and unseen.'

It was OK for the target to see their killer, because they would be dead so it wouldn't matter. However, he was working his way through a hit list and, sooner or later, those who paid these men would eventually put the pieces together and figure out Mark's plan. However, now was not the time to worry about what MIGHT happen. All Mark was concerned about was causing as much pain as possible to this organisation which had orchestrated his wife's murder.

It occurred to Mark to target those at the top of the chain of command primarily, but that would be suicide because he didn't know enough about them yet, or how far their reach was, or, HIS role and where HE fitted into it all. Marie's death was not random, or a bungled burglary gone wrong. It wasn't purely connected to the Azidi case or a revenge attack for his involvement; he was merely doing his job. It ran much, much deeper than that, and if he killed whoever ordered the hit, it would get him no answers at all. He wanted whoever was in charge to suffer like he was suffering. He wanted them to watch as, layer by layer, their protection was stripped away until they were completely exposed, exactly the same way as they had done to him.

It was now eleven fifteen and nearly time for his target to turn up. He got out and, buttoning up his long leather jacket, he lit a cigarette, exhaling the smoke and watching it drift its way upwards towards a cloudy sky, illuminated by a street light. He THOUGHT he saw movement in a window above him so wandered around to see if he could get a better angle on the window. He slowly meandered around the carpark, taking the occasional look up at the window and, after a few moments, returned to the car and leant against the driver's door. Out of the corner of his eye, he spotted it again. Despite the lack of a light in the window, he could definitely make out a shape moving backwards and forwards in the window. The hairs on the back of his neck stood up, and he knew *something* was amiss. He made out he was wandering towards the wall to shield his lighter from the wind to light another cigarette, and when he reached the blind spot under the window where he couldn't be seen, silently climbed up the metal fire escape ladder towards the broken wooden door which led to the room. He peered through the slats in the wood and saw the outline of a well-built man, crouched in the deserted room that Mark guessed used to be a kitchen of some sort. Drawing his pistol, he carefully reached for the handle on the door and pushed it open, praying it didn't have rusty hinges to give away his position. It swung open without a sound and he stepped in, allowing his eyes to adjust to the light. He paused, but the man didn't move, so he crept on, weapon drawn and pointing at what Mark could make out was the man's head. He was a foot away when the figure turned round, staying crouched, to face Mark. Mark froze and held his breath, checking to see if the man was armed. He wasn't, but Mark could make out the shape of a case, similar to that in the boot of his stolen Audi A4, underneath the window. It must be a shooter, Mark thought to himself quickly as he worked out his next move. He spoke into the shadow at the figure.

'You armed?' he said quietly. The outline of two arms rose up as the figure began to stand, showing Mark he was unarmed.

'What are you doing here?' Mark quizzed the man. He stepped forward and Mark tightened the grip on his pistol, finger poised on the trigger.

'I am here for you,' he replied. Mark looked confused, but not surprised Swiftlock didn't come alone.

'You're with Swiftlock?' Mark exclaimed, his muscles tense and ready for the man to make trouble for Mark. The man nodded.

116

'He paid you?' Mark asked. Again the man nodded. The pair stood silently, staring into the darkness at each other, neither one of them making a move.

'And your job was to kill me once I'd handed over my package?' Mark questioned, already knowing the answer. Mark saw the man nod and his mind was racing a million miles a minute. The longer he stayed here, the more risk there was of him not meeting Swiftlock downstairs.

It was at that moment that the man suddenly lunged for the rifle laid out in the case under the window. Two muffled shots rang out in the dark and the man in the shadows fell dead over the rifle case, two bullets lodged in the side of his head. Blood poured out over the case and Mark quickly grabbed the rifle and stripped it of ammunition and put it into its separate pieces. Putting it back in its case, he looked around for something flammable. He found white spirit in what was left of a kitchen cupboard and carefully poured it into the room. He heard the sound of a distant car engine so put away his pistol and dashed out of the room and back down the metal fire escape ladder towards his car. He took a cigarette out and lit it, looking calm and relaxed, leaning against the driver door of the Audi as the headlights temporarily blinded him. A good tactic, Mark thought to himself. That way, if Mark was to reach for his weapon, his vision would be impaired by the headlight glare and he wouldn't be able to get a clear shot, costing him valuable seconds if it was gun vs gun. The car slowly crept towards him before the engine fell silent. The door opened, revealing a man whose eyes were constantly on Mark.

He was well built, about six foot, wearing dark jeans and a black jumper with a biker style leather jacket, zipped up to the next. He was blond-haired and wore black leather gloves, identical to Mark's. Mark nodded and received an acknowledging nod back.

'You're early,' Swiftlock pointed out, surprised. Mark nodded and smiled sarcastically.

'Hey, in this line of work, sometimes it pays to be early,' Mark replied, risking a glance up towards the window and walking towards Swiftlock to meet him in the middle of the carpark.

'That's far enough,' Swiftlock warned Mark, who took absolutely no notice of him. Swiftlock looked surprised by this, but respected the man's guts. Mark put his arms up to show he was unarmed.

'You have something that belongs to me,' Swiftlock grunted, unzipping his jacket. Mark felt his pistol in his holster inside his jacket. Swiftlock took out an envelope which Mark presumed was cash for the drop off. Mark reached for the key to the car and unlocked it remotely.

The boot lifted open and Swiftlock smiled, walking past Mark, round him towards the boot. Mark's eyes followed him and he turned round to see Swiftlock haul out the large case and walk towards his own car, putting it in the boot and slamming it down loudly. Mark caught the sealed envelope that Swiftlock threw at him, which was just enough time for Swiftlock to pull his own silenced pistol out of his jacket and aim it at Mark.

'Now then, turn around,' Swiftlock ordered. Mark did as he was told and Swiftlock reached for some cable ties in his back pocket. Just as Mark leaned over the car ready to be cuffed, he threw his head back at Swiftlock which caught him square in the jaw. The shock caused Swiftlock to drop his weapon and, like lightning, Mark spun around and picked it up, aiming it at Swiftlock as he propped himself up from the floor on his elbow, touching his bloodied nose and wiping it with his jacket sleeve and glaring at Mark.

'Get back in your car and disappear, before I put a bullet in you!' Mark seethed as he motioned for Swiftlock to get up. He did as he was told and Mark waved towards Swiftlock's car with his pistol.

As Mark stood at the open passenger window, he took out the ammunition from the pistol, unscrewed the silencer and threw the pieces into the passenger seat. Swiftlock looked angered at Mark for his insolence but confused at his actions. Mark noticed this.

'Well,' Mark said, shrugging his shoulders. 'We all have a job to do.'

Swiftlock started the engine and reversed his car before slowly creeping out of the carpark. Mark dashed to his car to get the detonator, not sure what kind of range it had.

He picked up his burn phone and dialled the number of the phone in the case. In the car, Swiftlock was sweating and trying to stem the blood flowing from his nose as he hit the steering wheel in anger. Then he heard the mobile phone from the back seat. He reached over with his spare hand and unclipped the case, pulling it open and fumbling around for the phone. As he pressed the answer button, the entire car erupted into a massive fireball, sending pieces of the car skywards and in all directions. The car flipped onto its roof from the force of the blast, before the fuel tank ruptured, causing a second massive explosion.

Mark's car was gone from the carpark. He was driving in the opposite direction and had left seconds after Swiftlock had; he smiled as he heard the explosion and, in his rear-view mirror, saw the flames reaching for the sky a few miles behind him. Other cars on the road screeched and skidded to avoid the oncoming fireball as it tumbled down the road before crashing into a roadside barrier, causing the metal to buckle and scorch from the heat. People got out of their cars and rushed towards the wreckage, beaten back by the flames and intense heat. Some of them were on their phones to the emergency services, others just stood and stared in horror at the sight before them.

Mark smiled as he rested his list on the steering wheel. With the other hand, he crossed Swiftlock's name off the list and replaced it back in his pocket. Satisfied, he lit up another cigarette and turned on the radio to Classic FM. Vivaldi made him smile as he drove deeper and deeper into the night.

Chapter Thirteen

Thomas Lundon was sat in front of a huge luxurious office desk in his study, surrounded by books and ornaments and a large glass globe. On the desk were paper files, a crystal decanter and some brandy and two crystal brandy glasses and an ashtray with a cigar in it, smoking silently. Lundon was filtering through papers when he received a call on his mobile phone. Few words were exchanged but Lundon was extremely angry, silently, at what he had been told. He hung up the call, took a drag of the cigar and slammed his fist down on the table in anger. A guard dressed in black and white camouflage combats and carrying a sub-machine gun on a sling around his neck entered at the sound of the slamming of the desk.

'Everything alright, Sir?' the guard asked inquisitively.

'Fine. Just fine,' snapped Lundon. 'Send Vose in after the Doctor has patched him up,' Lundon growled, motioning for the guard to leave the room.

He rose from the desk while the guard exited and moved towards a window looking out on to the warm, blue tropical waters outside. A thin white net curtain blew slightly in the breeze and Lundon silently smoked his cigar. He reached for the desk and poured a brandy before returning to the window. He drank it down in one and put the glass down on the desk. As he raised his cigar to his lips he sighed deeply, the look of concern growing ever present, his brow wrinkled and red. Lundon picked up his cell and dialled a number, speaking in a low, hushed tone.

'I don't know what happened or who murdered Hix but someone has taken out one of my best men. This makes me nervous.'

The voice at the other end of the phone merely chuckled, which angered Lundon even further.

'I want the police files relating to the incident, on my desk by eleven AM tomorrow!' Lundon sighed and hung up the phone before returning to stare out of the window. The guard outside the door winced at the noises coming from the other side of the door.

'Damn!!!!' yelled Lundon, throwing his mobile phone against a wall.

Inside the room, Lundon had thrown the phone across the room, hitting an antique leather chesterfield sofa sat in front of a huge floor-to-ceiling oil painting in a gilt golden frame. The picture revealed a circle of people standing around a stone symbol set into the floor. All the people in the picture were looking down at the logo etched into this stone. Lundon sighed again and sat at his desk and resumed flicking through the files.

Mark was showering, just stood there, letting the water fall over him as he stared blankly into the past. Visions of Marie, Hix, Salvatore and Swiftlock ran before him in slow motion and normal speed, like a film being played out over and over. He recalled every single second and replayed the moment Hix died over and over and over. His thoughts then switched to his wedding day, the birth of his children and the many nights he spent with Marie. Mark realised he was shaking. It was the first time he'd killed anyone, and the effects were showing in a delayed reaction. Thinking to himself that he MUST get a hold of himself or he would not be able to carry on, he tried to pull himself together. 'Yes, OK, there's one down but there are many more responsible. This sort of crime doesn't just take one man a few days alone to plan; it is something more sinister and more organised than it appears,' he thought. Bringing himself back to reality, he turned off the shower and grabbed a towel from the rail behind him. He did a good job of refitting the shower with little else to do to get over Marie's death. Much as he got a hell of a lot done with the bunker to fit it up ready for use, it removed none of the feelings he had surrounding Marie's death. However, what he also noted as interesting was that killing Hix only partly eased the feelings he had, and that Vose got away meant he didn't allow for a well-structured contingency plan. Also could it have been that Vose had spotted him? He certainly knew *something* spooked him but he wasn't sure what.

Mark walked from the shower room into the ops room and sunk into the corner sofa in front of a large flat-screen TV he had erected in a living room area. His wandering eyes came to rest on the camera he had used, and he remembered that he still had the footage of the kill so picked up his notebook to view it. Flicking through the files he realised he hadn't properly analysed his methods from the hit, so decided it was best to do this after every hit. He found the file and loaded it on Movie Player and connected it to the flat screen TV in front of him. Frame by frame Mark analysed the scene until, just as he was about to give up, he spotted it, but not right away. He had to look over it multiple times before he was certain that what he had seen was genuine. As Vose was stood in the meeting room, Mark had been aiming through toughened glass, which, even at night, had certain reflectivity. He cursed himself when he saw it, a slight flash in the reflection of the window which moved over Vose's eyeline, causing him to move slightly to avoid it shining in his eyes and preventing him from seeing anything. At that point Mark knew exactly what it was: it was the telescopic sight cover which hung on a cord away from the lens when not in use. It was black on the outside but plastic Perspex on the inside to protect the glass in the sight. Somehow, it had caught a light, either from one of the building windows or a street light or sign, and had temporarily blinded Vose. Mark realised that he was not dealing with amateurs here. Vose had realised at that point that someone was firing from the rooftop opposite and taken evasive action after the light blinded him for a second or two.

'The problem,' Mark thought aloud, 'is that in this game, a second is all it takes in a life or death scenario.'

Mark was angry. Now THEY knew someone was after them, but luckily they didn't know who. At least for the time being, he had the element of surprise.

Back at the site of the Mark's first hit, two men entered the building. One of them was Vose; the other was a bodyguard. They made their way up to the roof and examined the scene of the shooting. Vose took several long hard looks across the rooftop at the building opposite, remembering what he THOUGHT he saw, but not being 100% sure. He surveyed the skyline until he was sure he was right.

'Stay here,' Vose ordered. 'I'm going to check out the roof opposite.'

Vose made his way downstairs to the meeting room and stood himself exactly where he was stood a few nights previous. He looked behind him and discovered the bullet holes in the picture on the wall. Taking a torch and a pair of pliers, he searched for the bullet in the holes but to his disappointment, there were none. He turned and smiled a frustrated but also admiring smile. Whoever the shooter was, they were professional because they took their ammo with them. Kicking a desk chair in frustration, Vose left the room and made his way to the roof of the building opposite. Within minutes he was up on the roof and at the exact spot Mark shot at him from. After a few moments of searching, he found the hole in the wall and reached for a laser from his pocket while reaching for his cell phone; he dialled the number of his companion, still in the building across the road.

'Do me a favour, go and stand in the office I was in when he shot at me, and wait there.'

The companion followed Vose's instructions and waited for him to get into position. Shining the laser across from building to building, he confirmed what he thought, that THIS was the spot where the shooter was hiding. Back in reception, Vose demanded all CCTV footage from the twenty-four-hour period before making another phone call.

'Borin. Hack into the street CCTV and pull the images from that night.'

The jovial, sarcastic voice at the other end of the phone angered Vose.

'Ohh, I take it our "guest" is evading you?'

Vose snarled, wishing the little dirt bag was in front of him right now so he could strangle him.

'Shut up, Borin, before I kill you, fool!' Borin backed down, knowing Vose could, and would, snap his neck in a heartbeat.

'Why you have to get all ratty on me? Jeeze man, I'll send it to your cell and computer for analysis as soon as I have it.'

Vose returned the phone to his pocket and was angry but also felt a sense of accomplishment. 'Get ready,' he snarled, looking around him. Vose crossed the street to his car. 'We're coming up right behind you.'

Once inside he used the wireless hands-free kit to dial a secure number direct to Thomas Lundon.

'Boss, we still don't know WHO they are dealing with, but we are close and will know once the CCTV is analysed. I have found the sniper's nest across the street. No bullets though, looks like whoever it was took them with them. Must be professional!'

'Send someone to assess the damage from the car bomb,' growled Lundon menacingly.

Lundon was not alone. He had several intelligence agents on his payroll and they were just about to arrive at his location. He hung up the phone to Vose and placed it in his jacket, nervously awaiting his guests.

The view from the rooftop was awesome as Mark laid his trap for the unsuspecting Tim Durrant, the next name on Mark's hit list. Mark opened the legs on his bipod and set the rifle on the edge of the flat, moonlit rooftop. Lying down, he looked through the sight and levelled his crosshairs, focussed the lens until he was happy with the view, and loaded the magazine.

He checked the list and his watch to ensure he was early. He was on a rooftop overlooking the London Underground entrance to New Chanel Station and all was quiet. The last train that ran from that station at this time of night never carried many passengers and, when Mark had checked with the Underground, his research had uncovered that it was only used at night to transport trains back to their overnight yards as it linked with the Piccadilly Line. This made Mark stop and think.

'Why would anyone want to use the station at this time of night?' Mark thought, 'moving across the vast expanse of the city of London unseen would be hard enough as it is, but it is stations like this that enable professional hitmen to move undetected across the city to avoid being spotted.'

The tunnels underneath London also allowed for multiple escape routes and hideouts if anyone knew where to find them. Mark looked through his telescopic sight again and swept the area for movement. There was the odd car driving past, the occasional black cab, but none of them stopped. Durrant apparently was a stickler for timing and routine, which, for an assassin, was a dangerous habit because it meant he could be easily followed and lead to predictability. Mark realised his survival depended on being unpredictable. He gathered his thoughts together and, just when he was considering moving to a better spot, he noticed movement down on the street below.

Mark could see someone sat in the coffee shop across the road from the station, drinking coffee and sat on a stool in the window. He noticed how this person didn't seem to fit in to his surroundings; there was something about him that caused him to stand out.

'This must be my guy,' Mark whispered to himself, adjusting his crosshairs for a better look. The man had a long black coat on and was carrying a small, laptop style bag over his shoulder which he seemed intent on keeping as close to him as possible.

'I wonder what's in there you don't want anyone to see?' Mark whispered, before assessing the rest of Durrant.

He was drinking his coffee black, which fit Mark's profile of him, and had his hair slicked back and it looked greasy. Mark tried to get a good look at Durrant's skin to see if he was tanned or clean. He had stubble and light-ish skin which Mark safely assumed was due to having not washed or shaved for a few days.

'Not currently on a job then, my friend?' Mark joked. But he was right.

Timothy Durrant hadn't worked for some time now; the job was getting to him too much and he had made himself enough money to slip out of the country unnoticed and live a peaceful and quiet life.

Durrant sipped his coffee, burning his lips as he lifted the cup too quickly, spilling the hot liquid over his mouth and into his lap. He flicked the hot coffee off his hands and looked around helplessly for a paper towel. He found one on the seat next to his and mopped the spillage up. Mark tutted to himself; probably a lack of food causing the shakes, he thought as he kept his eye trained on Durrant. He got a good look around the late night coffee shop and there were a few customers in, mostly night shift workers and young student staff busily cleaning tables and emptying bins.

'No,' Mark thought, 'this isn't the right setting for a head shot.' It would scar the customers and staff for life and there would be chaos. It would be clean, concise and out of sight of ANY witnesses. Mark checked his watch again and remembered what the train schedule had said; Durrant's train would be along any moment.

Mark only had a split second shot according to his recon and planning. Half way down the stairs to the Underground, Mark had noticed a blind spot where no one from any direction could see anyone stood there. This meant that he could take a clean headshot and no one would notice, until the security staff picked up his body when they locked the gates, and Mark would be long gone by then. Mark shifted his gaze back to Durrant, who had now ordered a chocolate 'tiffin' and another coffee.

'Great. Now I'll be here all bloody night!' he hissed, irritated at the delay.

Unless Durrant wanted to miss his train, he'd better get a move on. Durrant, meanwhile, smiled sleazily at the young blonde haired waitress as she carried his coffee and tiffin over to where he was sat. He put his greasy, unwashed hand onto hers as she set the plate down and she looked uncomfortable, but in the interests of customer service seemed happy to go along with it, smiling nervously as he heaped compliments on her. She tried several times to pull her hand away but each time, Durrant kept hold of it tightly, until the saving grace came when a customer walked towards the till and she had to return to serve them. Durrant turned back towards the window, a creepy grin on his unshaven, dirty looking face.

'Slimy bastard,' Mark said, shaking his head in disgust, now even more eager to put a bullet in him as he settled down to a long wait.

Chapter Fourteen

'One guy poisoned, another had his car stolen outside Richmond Train Station two days ago and the dead guy was seen speaking to someone in the same car, and we have NO leads?' Williams ranted as he paced up and down the floor, file papers flying off the desk of his office as he did so.

Everyone around him looked at the ground, including the head of the Metropolitan Police, who had no CCTV of the driver of the black Audi A4 and none of the witnesses at the station recalled seeing the face of the driver, or even hearing his voice. Williams was livid.

'I don't understand, so you are telling me this is a one off or that there may be more out there?' he demanded. The Police Commissioner lifted his head.

'We don't know. We have nothing conclusive until, IF or WHEN, another body turns up.'

'Right, I want everything we have on this guy. His job, his employer, what he was doing there that day, the contents of the missing case, who he saw, what he ate, everything. Go!' Williams ordered.

Everyone left the room. Williams looked like he had been awake all night and was pouring himself another coffee. He sipped at it, relaxing at the satisfying taste of caffeine. He wandered the empty room, talking aloud as he did so.

'A hitman is found dead on a rooftop, bullet holes in the office, then another hitman turns up dead a few days later?' He mused until he was interrupted by a young female assistant.

'No results on the car, sir,' she nervously announced. He spun around, nearly spilling his coffee all over the place.

'No,' he said, a theory suddenly formulating in his mind, 'of course there won't be, because our guy is too careful, he won't risk being caught.'

'You think you know who he is, sir?' she asked shyly.

'Not exactly, but I think I do. He's working to a hit list, which puts him in the psychology of a "mission oriented killer".'

The assistant looked worried.

'He won't stop, you know, not until he has completed his list. No matter what you do, he won't stop,' she acknowledged with a worried tone in her voice. Williams glared at her, silently agreeing that she was right.

Mark had been waiting on the rooftop for an additional hour; the train he expected Durrant to catch had long gone and now he wasn't on it, Mark was unsure of what to do next. If he didn't go towards the Underground, Mark wouldn't be able to take the shot and would have to change position and risk taking Durrant out in the street. That wasn't what he wanted, and his mind was a whir of ideas and possible scenarios of how this could go down. One thing was certain; Mark was not taking any chances with his target. If one of his targets got away, they could warn the others and then they would all disperse and Mark would have no way to track them. It HAD to be tonight, and it HAD to be a kill-shot.

Durrant stepped off his stool and put the tissue he had just used to wipe the chocolate from his face flat on the plate and drank down the rest of his coffee. He had written something on some paper and, as he walked towards the till, he passed it to the young blonde waitress who smiled and, out of politeness, took it from him and put it in her apron, before watching Durrant leave the coffee shop. After he had gone, she took it out of her apron pocket and Mark watched her tear it up before sprinkling the torn up pieces of paper into the bin under the counter. Mark smiled, impressed at the young waitress's composure and professionalism but cringing at Durrant's pathetic attempt at getting laid.

Mark's crosshairs followed Durrant towards the Underground entrance and he breathed a sigh of relief that Durrant was going where Mark wanted him to go. He eased his finger on the trigger as Durrant took the first two steps down the concrete steps, and squeezed the trigger. He wasn't sure what happened, or why it didn't happen the way he had planned, but Mark's shot ricocheted off the ornate black railings and caused Durrant to hit the deck like a stone. Mark cursed and dropped his rifle, realising there would be no second shot, and ran to the rooftop entrance and pounded down the staircase to the street below, taking two stairs, sometimes three at a time. As he ran, he took out his silenced pistol and, holding it against his thigh as he ran, jumped the railings of the Underground, expecting to land on top of a shaken Tim Durrant. Instead, Mark felt the shock-wave of pain shoot up his legs as his feet contacted with solid concrete.

Hearing the footsteps ahead of him, it confirmed that Durrant was on the move but had only just got himself to his feet. As Mark ran down the staircase, he noticed there was a bloodied handprint on the railing and noted he MUST have hit Durrant somehow, perhaps in the deflection of Mark's bullet. The white bricked tunnel of the Underground was hot and the further down he went, the thinner the air became, exactly why Mark didn't enjoy taking the Underground across London and preferred to drive. Mark considered himself very lucky that this station was old enough and not used often enough to warrant installing CCTV anywhere. He burst onto the platform and felt the rush of air down the tunnel as trains moved around in the darkness up and down the Piccadilly line this station connected to a few miles up the track.

Mark's eyes darted all around the empty platform, looking for any signs of movement, weapon at the ready. He stopped and held his breath, listening for the shuffle of feet or the loading sound of a gun. Nothing came. Leaning over the platform edge, looking both ways through the darkness of the electrified line, Mark listened. Unsure if it was the distant sound of trains, or his imagination, he swore he heard the sound of shoes on gravel in the tunnel but was distracted by a sound behind him. Mark turned to find a rough sleeper, drunk and wrapped in a dirty blanket, lying against the wall of the station. This man was elderly and had a very dishevelled beard and brown coat and beanie hat, and was laughing through multiple missing and stained teeth as he pointed down the tunnel. Mark nodded and smiled at him before carefully climbing down the edge of the platform and tentatively stepping into the dark. Reaching for his trusted Maglite, he illuminated the track ahead of him to avoid stepping on the electric line. His light shone left and right as the odd rat ran under his feet, until it rested on the figure of a man running away from him into the darkness ahead. Mark pointed his weapon and, aiming high to avoid hitting anything important which would turn the tunnel into a mass fireball, let off two shots in quick succession towards the figure. They missed but several shots were returned to him, causing Mark to drop to the floor, inches away from the electrified line. Mark blew out a relieved breath and pushed himself upright, thankful for his physical fitness and all those push-ups he forced himself to do whilst in the bunker. It had served him well, and he reminded himself next time he was pushing himself to do fifty more push ups, never to complain about doing them again as he shone his torch in the direction Durrant had run in.

Mark stepped onto the foot-wide pathway which skirted around either side of the line used by workmen to access the rails for maintenance work. His torchlight darted off the walls as he pursued Durrant down the line, as he wondered how long it would be before Durrant reached the next station along the line, worried that if Durrant wasn't taken out down here, if he got to the station ahead of Mark, he would get away and Mark would probably never see him again. However, his fears were allayed as two more shots rang out, echoing down the tunnel towards Mark as sparks flew off the brickwork near to Mark's head.

'Shit, this guy's good,' Mark panted, throwing himself flat against the wall to avoid being directly in Durrant's sights. He jumped down onto the track again and, using his torch to light his path, let off two shots in the same direction as the shots came from. There was silence. Had Mark hit Durrant or not? He couldn't work it out. The sudden rush of air down the tunnel quickly confirmed why Mark didn't hear movement ahead of him; there was a train coming, and Mark desperately looked around for somewhere to move to, to avoid being made part of this goddam tunnel. He spied a small door, probably a plant or maintenance room, and hopped over the line, one leg at a time towards the door, his panic made worse because he was suddenly bathed in light from the headlights of the oncoming train. His eyes widened as he tried to quicken his pace, terrified he would be hit by the train. The horn from the train only served as further encouragement for Mark to jump for the edge of the narrow path he was on a few moments earlier. He threw himself towards it, arms outstretched and reaching for the stained red brickwork to haul himself up. He shoulder-barged the small wooden door with such force that it broke away from its flimsy hinges and sent Mark careering into the small engineer's room on top of the door just as the rush of the train flew through the tunnel at breakneck speed, the sound of the brakes screeching down both ends of the tunnel. Mark spun his head round as the silver of the train flashed passed him. He waited until it had passed before checking the tunnel and inching his way out onto the narrow brick path again. He heard laughter in front of him and realised that he was closer than he thought to Durrant, who Mark guessed was clearly out of shape.

'What do you want with me, you crazy bastard?' Durrant shouted at Mark, his voice echoing around them both, making it difficult for Mark to understand what he said.

Mark didn't reply, but instead, realising that it was a delaying tactic for Durrant to buy himself time to think of an escape plan, Mark continued to inch his way along the path until he was confronted by Durrant, weapon drawn, but unable to see Mark clearly in the darkness.

'One of your guys was responsible for killing my wife!' Mark growled, feeling a build-up of hatred and blood pressure inside him as he gripped his pistol and his finger moved to the trigger.

'Bugger off, mate,' Durrant replied, confused. 'I didn't kill nobody's wife, you got the wrong guy!' he pleaded. Mark took a step closer and Durrant jumped onto the track, coming into the light and seeing Mark for the first time.

'So that was YOU what shot at me earlier then?' he said, pointing at Mark angrily.

Mark gritted his teeth.

'Uh huh,' Mark replied, nodding.

Durrant chuckled, unimpressed by Mark's marksmanship. Mark didn't blame him, it was a lousy shot.

'Look mate, I dunno what your beef is, but I didn't kill no one's wife, I'm lookin' to get out of this game yeah?' he pleaded again. Mark wasn't convinced.

'If that's true,' Mark responded nonchalantly, 'why do you still have your weapon drawn?'

'You shot at me, you crazy freak, what you expect me to do?' He laughed.

Mark felt the same rush of air down the tunnel as he felt moments earlier and realised that another train was coming, but he couldn't work out the direction it was coming from. Durrant stood motionless, looking amazed that anyone would be crazy enough to follow him down here like this. He had to hand it to Mark; he had balls chasing him through an active train tunnel.

Mark had just enough time to throw himself back towards the narrow path and against the wall; his back arched against the curved brick before the train rushed past him. He glanced in the direction the train was travelling in, his hair being blown over his face and the air rushing towards him, and saw Durrant, also pressed against the curved brick of the tunnel, his weapon in the wrong hand and too close to the train to swap hands. Mark realised HIS pistol was in his right hand and lifted it slightly to get the angle, knowing he couldn't miss, and let off two shots.

He winced as Durrant's body fell against the train and the momentum of the train carried Durrant onwards, throwing him against the wall and the speeding train. Mark inched back towards the engineer's room and out the way of the train as it rushed past him. He sat on the floor and steadied his nerves before reaching for his cigarettes. He tried to light one with trembling hands and struggled with holding his lighter steady. Eventually he got it lit and laid back on the broken door, exhaling and closing his eyes. From his back pocket, he took his list and his pencil and crossed Durrant's name off the list. There were three names left.

After he had finished his cigarette and burned the stub until any DNA evidence had been removed, he left the room and stood the broken wooden door back up in the doorway, before slowly making his way back up the tunnel in the direction he had originally come from. He was about to reach the platform when something caught his attention. Maybe Durrant has dropped something in the darkness which Mark hadn't spotted before. He flashed his Maglite on it and it looked like an invoice or receipt for something. Mark picked it up and examined it. It was torn and stained but Mark could make out a partial address, the same address as the freight yard Mark had researched previous. He put the paper in his pocket carefully and continued through the tunnel. Once at the platform, he hauled himself onto the platform edge and dusted himself off, straightened his hair and checked his pocket for his emergency ten pound note. He staggered over to the homeless man who was sleeping and gently shook him. The old man awoke with a start, holding tightly onto his dirty old blanket. Mark calmed him down and placed the money in his stained hand, closing his fingers around it gently. The homeless man's eyes widened as he stared at Mark's generosity and Mark had to move a little further away as the smell was unbearable.

He patted the man on the shoulder, got up, and made his way back out into the fresh, cool night and breathed a sigh of relief. There were moments where Mark didn't think he'd ever get out of that tunnel. He smiled and turned and walked towards the building he had left his rifle in. His tired legs dragged as he made his way up towards the rooftop to collect his rifle and sat himself down against his kit bag, reaching for his bottle of water in the bag. He tipped half of it over his dirty, sweat-ridden face and wiped it down with his sleeve, while drinking down the other half of the water in seconds, thankful to still be alive. He took a few moments to compose himself before dismantling his rifle and putting his equipment away in his kit bag, shouldering it and heading back down to the street and towards his stolen Audi A4.

Mark awoke suddenly from his nightmare, breathing heavily, sweat dripping down his brow and hair stuck to his head. His eyes shot around the room until he remembered where he was. He sat up in bed and grabbed his water bottle from the table next to the bed and took a long drink of the cold water. Marie had been walking towards him with her arms outstretched, a gun in her hand, and she was trying to hand it to Mark. Was it a message from Marie, encouraging him to continue on his vengeful quest, or was it his conscience catching up with him? He didn't know, but he was wide awake at this point and hopped out of bed and over towards the laptop on the steel table. The facial recognition software was running a check on pictures Mark had taken of his hit targets so far. He had to find out who they were working for and how many of them were not on his list. He glanced at the list pinned to the large notice board he had erected and looked down at the next name on the list: Jonathan 'Deadmoon' Winters, and it was his name Mark had put through all the search programs he had, to find out more about him. Mark lit up a cigarette and exhaled the smoke, taking a drink of his water to tackle the dry throat he had. He leant back in his large black leather recliner chair and smoked his cigarette as he watched the laptop screen flash through thousands of facial images. From prison mug shots to wanted posters to hacked government files, the screen flashed through them. On the other screen, the system was searching Winters' name for matching results revealing any link to this man Mark could use to discover who he was dealing with.

Ten minutes went by before Mark was considering going back to bed. He turned and stubbed out another cigarette and spun his chair round to leave when the laptop stopped searching and the screen switched to a black screen with a red rectangle, highlighting 'MATCH FOUND' as the alarm noise blurred out through the on-board speakers. Quickly, Mark turned to face the computer and clicked the screen as it brought up a restricted file pertaining to a Lieutenant Jonathan Winters, former SAS soldier, veteran of numerous campaigns across Europe. Like many soldiers returning home from war zones, he had found difficulty in adjusting to civilian life and, with the kinds of skills Winters possessed, he was soon working for freelance security firms providing security detail to VIPs and the wealthy before putting his combat skills to use as a 'gun for hire'. Mark read intently as he realised who he was up against. Winters had been awarded medals for bravery and his unsealed file revealed multiple performance reports from his superiors, including one commending Winters' endurance and courage in Mozambique when he and his squad were pinned down by enemy fire and Winters ran through a hail of gunfire, firing his own weapon as he did so, taking out five insurgents who were attacking a food convoy.

'Why didn't he just re-enlist with the army?' Mark said to himself as he scrolled down through Winters' service record. Mark smiled as he came across a picture of a young Winters. It was enough to go on, so he copied and pasted the picture into a photo program to age the picture, giving Mark an idea of what Winters would look like now. Mark's printer clicked into life behind him and the picture was ejected from the tray in full colour. Mark turned to take it and sat staring at it for ages. He turned back to Winters file and read further. He was proficient with explosives, most weapons, especially heavy weapons, but favoured a small Glock hand gun and the Browning small machine gun. Mark smiled knowingly, appreciating the same aspects of the weapons that Winters did. He couldn't envisage himself killing this man, but it was Winters' life or Mark's, and Mark knew this hit wouldn't be as easy as he hoped it would be. The obvious choice for Mark was a long-range shot with a sniper rifle and avoiding any hand to hand combat. This guy was tough and Mark didn't favour his chances toe to toe with him. Winters resembled Conan the Barbarian and Mark shivered at the thought of it, so decided he would head back to bed and revisit this in the morning.

He laid there, eyes open, thinking about the best method to take this target out. He refused to think of the person, with thoughts or feelings or a life. It was merely a target, a number that had to be taken out. Then something occurred to him and he sat bolt upright, staring straight ahead. In the chaos and trauma of the hits he had conducted so far, he had forgotten completely about the one thing which linked them all together.

'The bloody freight yard!!' he yelled out loud. 'Shit,' he said, slamming his fist down on the bed. Why didn't he see the connection sooner?

'All of them are connected to that damn freight yard!' he said. 'So perhaps this is their base?' Mark thought, as he lay back down smiling to himself at his, until now, lack of lateral thinking.

Now he had made the connection, soon he would have to find out WHY they were all connected to this freight company and Martin Underhill.

Chapter Fifteen

Later that morning, Mark was busy trying to get as much information as possible on the kinds of activities Lt. Winters was involved in during his various tours. He had been part of a special operations team which worked alongside US Navy Seals to provide security for UN food convoys delivering food to 'hard to reach' areas. From what Mark could research, there had been a revolt in a village where a large number of refugees were camped without food or emergency supplies and it was Lt. Winters' job to escort the UN convoy to administer vital equipment to ensure these refugees survived. A noble cause, Mark thought as he read down through newspaper articles and Lt. Winters' service record. So why would he end up on the wrong end of everything his vocation stood for, and what did it have to do with Marie? Was he just the 'hired gun', or did he know who was, if it wasn't him? Mark had so many questions and looking through screen after screen for information on Lt. Winters was giving him a headache. He decided he would take a break at the end of the page he was reading and go outside the bunker for some fresh air and a walk around to stretch his legs.

He scrolled down until he reached the section about Lt. Winters' discharge and last known address. It wasn't much, but it showed that, although there was no forwarding address for him, there was a previous address of where Winters was born: a remote home in Wales, on the Gower Coast. Mark stopped scrolling and quickly wrote the address before checking Google Earth for a satellite image of the property. It didn't take him long to pull up a few images, which he printed off and examined closely.

It showed a white stone building surrounded by a three foot wooden and wire fence and a large area of grassland surrounding it. Perfect, Mark thought, for someone who wanted to see someone coming from a long distance. There were hills and woods close by, which Mark was looking for to position himself safely so that Lt. Winters wouldn't see it coming. He didn't want to make contact with him, just one bullet, long range and he would be on his way. However, he didn't fancy driving all the way to Wales, waiting in his ghillie suit for two days, taking Lt Williams out, and driving all the way back home again, so decided he would have to base himself close to where Winters lived at a small bed and breakfast or hotel. He quickly searched online for places to stay and came upon a small, family-run B&B not far from where Lt. Winters' house was. He used his alias, Andrew Kemp, to reserve a room and would pay cash for it when he got there. He would use the back story that he was a rambler, to recon the local area. He would have to assume that Lt. Winters was heavily armed and would likely see him coming from some distance away, so he would need to be extremely careful not to arouse suspicion from the locals. He filed everything in a case file folder and placed it in his kit bag, gathering supplies and his rifle before heading to his car for the long drive to Wales.

Deep inside the Welsh countryside, in a farmer style kitchen, a mobile phone vibrated repeatedly but remained unanswered. It rang off before the vibrating began again until, eventually, a heavy hand dropped out of nowhere, onto the handset and picked it up, answering it with a grunt.

'Hmm,' the voice grunted, knowing the only time that phone rang was when there was a job for him.

The voice at the other end of the phone sounded agitated and nervous.

'Deadmoon, this is Vose,' the voice said from the other end of the phone. Winters' teeth ground together as he sat, slumped in the kitchen chair. 'You're not safe.'

Winters smiled and chuckled to himself as he sat up in his chair and felt for the whiskey glass in the centre of the table.

'Really, why's that?' Winters replied, unconvinced by Vose's warning.

'Someone's killing our men!' Vose replied, a more serious tone to him now. This made Winters sit up and listen.

'I thought this day would come. We make enemies in this line of work, Vose. You above all should know that. We get what we deserve,' he replied philosophically, sipping the whiskey and wincing as it burnt his throat as he drank. Vose was not philosophical; he wanted to stay alive, to survive, and he knew, if any more of his men were killed, it meant whoever it was doing the killing was getting closer to HIM and he didn't like that.

'Listen; just watch your back mate, yeah? Boss is trying to figure out who it is, in the meantime, keep your bloody head down, got me?'

'I think you should be more worried about whoever it is that's got YOU Roman, rather than worrying about me. I take care of myself,' Winters calmly explained, not threatened by Vose's warning.

He would do whatever it took to stay alive, but he knew this day would come, eventually. He had assassinated hundreds of people, so many he didn't even know their names or why they had been targets. He got paid to do a job, no questions. He pressed the hang-up button on the phone and walked towards the large kitchen window which looked out onto the rolling Welsh hills. He picked up his binoculars and scanned the landscape for movement. He wouldn't let Vose know it, but it concerned him that he was now being hunted. He grinned to himself; it would take someone very special to get a bullet into him and he was fully prepared for it. He walked into the well-lived-in living room and picked up his shotgun, rifle and a small black object with a button on it. He pressed the button and heard a high pitched humming from the outside of the property. He wasn't stupid, he had rigged the entire front and back garden with landmines so that anyone approaching would give him fair warning. The only thing that wasn't mined was the small stone path leading up to the front door. That was covered by a CCTV camera above the door. He relaxed into the green velvet-looking armchair and let his hand rest on his shining, perfectly kept Glock 22 pistol which was laid on the small coffee table next to his chair. He flicked the TV on with the remote and sipped more of his whiskey, and waited.

The M4 motorway was steadily flowing as Mark listened to the mid-afternoon weather forecast, doing a steady seventy miles per hour in the streamlined Audi A4. It was Mark's favourite jazz radio station he had been listening to but every half hour, the weather forecast kept Mark fully up to date with the weather in his region. He would take account of this later, and plan for all outcomes. He passed Pontyclun and continued onwards Bridgend, Birchgrove being his next stop-off. It would be here that he would put his car in storage and rent a more suitable vehicle for the rest of his journey. Mark had always favoured the Range Rover, but not the newer models, an older, tougher and more durable model which would provide him with decent four wheeled drive across the rugged terrain he expected to encounter. He glanced up at the sky as he lit another cigarette and took a swig from his Thermos flask of coffee. The sky was getting darker, and he knew a storm was moving in. The closer to his destination he got, the darker it became, and he glanced at his watch; it was just after three in the afternoon and he wanted at least to find somewhere to stay before nightfall and didn't fancy sleeping in the back of the car or Range Rover, especially if the weather was going to turn nasty. He listened intently to the weather forecast and screwed his face up at the announcement that a big storm was heading in his direction. He glanced up at the gathering clouds again and knew he couldn't outrun it for long. Potentially, he would need somewhere nearer for the night if the weather was bad enough to affect traffic. He spotted the sign for Bridgend and stopped for supplies; mainly cigarettes, coffee and food he could eat whilst driving, although he favoured a full English all day breakfast at a service station somewhere.

By the time he had reached Bridgend and filled up the petrol tank, Mark had decided that it wasn't a good idea to stop for a big meal, and instead bought sandwiches, crisps, chocolate bars and a few bottles of water and two or three coffees to fill up his Thermos with. He reached the checkout and paid in cash for his fuel and food so as not to be traced to his location. Instinct told him that, by now, the group he was hunting would have put the pieces together and realised he was taking them out one by one, especially if the owner of the Audi had pre-warned them. No one had reported the car stolen that he knew of. So far so good, he thought as he paid the young lad at the checkout and wandered back to his car, flicking on the radio as he turned the key in the ignition. He cursed silently as he tuned in the radio to the local stations and heard the traffic reports that there were roadworks in Llanmorlais on the B4295, just a short distance from his ultimate location. He would have to do what he always did, endure, and he sped out of the petrol station forecourt, heading towards Birchgrove.

After another half an hour of driving, Mark turned off when he saw the signs for Birchgrove and followed his satnav to the garage he had picked out before leaving and, after a short drive down an A road, he rolled up to the garage forecourt, parked up and went inside to find a salesman. He returned a short time later with the keys to his dark green Range Rover and got back into his car to park it up a short walk away, where it would stay until after this hit was complete. Enjoying a cigarette, Mark walked back to the garage and pulled the green Range Rover off the forecourt and drove back to where he had parked his car, in a private lock-up on a 'cash in hand, no questions asked' basis. After transferring his kit to the Range Rover, he was back on the road towards Gower, bypassing the B4295 to make up time. The B&B Mark planned to stay at knew he was coming and he had spoken to a lovely elderly lady who said she would prepare a hot meal for him for when he arrived. A good rest, a beer and a night's sleep was at the forefront of Mark's mind before heading out tomorrow to explore the surroundings and see if he couldn't locate his target; Lt Jonathan 'Deadmoon' Winters.

Forty minutes later and Mark was inside the quaint little Hillside B&B on the Gower Coast, so-called because it was built on a hillside and overlooked the vast expanse of Welsh countryside. It served as an ideal base from which to look around and potentially spot where the home of Winters was. He was provided with his room key and shown to his room by the same lovely old lady he had spoken to on the phone, who had told him he had a long trip and should rest. He smiled and agreed with her before being told that dinner would be served at six, which gave him time to wash and change. He picked up a handful of leaflets at the make-shift reception area on local attractions and there really wasn't much, except a good pub guide which Mark thought would make interesting reading, and a book about good rambling walks to take part in around the local area.

Mark smiled to himself; it would be perfect for what he had in mind. He needed to make himself a nice 'nest' where he would not be disturbed and where he could watch what Winters was up to.

After dinner, Mark felt much better, having showered and changed into more suitable weather attire. He stepped outside the B&B and glanced up at the sky. It was dark now and Mark figured he had a few hours to look around before they would be pelted by torrential hail and thunder. He took the pub leaflet out of his back pocket and lit up a cigarette as he wandered the narrow pavement, reading which pubs were good to visit. He decided he would try one nearest the B&B. The last thing he wanted was to be caught in the storm out here. Spotting The Old Bell pub a few hundred yards up the road, Mark marched along the road hastily, eager for that beer he promised himself when he got there, and reached the pub in no time. Walking inside tentatively, he adjusted to his surroundings. There was an old man in boots, a brown wax jacket and a labrador, sat at the table nearest the bar and a few tourist-looking customers dotted around the pub in various corners, and a roaring fireplace to Mark's right. He walked to the bar and ordered a pint of their Best bitter, paid and sat on the small round table in the bay window, facing the road outside the pub. He supped his beer and rejoiced in the taste after so long without one, savouring every mouthful as he relaxed into his armchair.

Mark couldn't have been sat there more than an hour before the place began to fill up. A small folk band had set up in the opposite corner and was joyously playing local folk tunes as people gravitated towards the tables that faced the band, singing and dancing along, and before Mark knew it, the pub was crowded. He took his leaflet out and realised this was the only pub for quite some miles so no wonder it was filling up. It was at that moment he noticed the tall, stocky and muscular figure leaning against the bar and an empty shotgun under his arm and a black collie at his feet. He looked the epitome of your average ex-British Army soldier, wearing the right clothes for the right weather, and the way he held that shotgun, Mark was convinced he was military and casually got out his camera phone and bought up the picture of Lt. Winters and examined it, looking back and forth at the stranger and the picture, before putting it away and breathing slowly. It was Lt. Winters, and more worryingly was that he was walking towards Mark's table.

Chapter Sixteen

Lt. Winters was even more imposing in person than his military record suggested, and he was used to the area and blended in well. Mark supposed that, with a history like his, the ability to blend into any crowd was an essential skill to have, especially if life depended on it. Winters motioned to Mark, towards the empty chair facing him, and Mark gulped and nodded, watching Winters sit down heavily. There was not much in the way of conversation to begin with, silent stares and nods, before, eventually, Winters spoke.

'You're not from round here?' he said in a deep, gruff voice. Mark shook his head and put down his pint.

'No, I'm only here for the night,' he said, hoping he was convincing. 'Just passing through.'

Winters laughed through a few missing teeth and nodded.

'Ahh, just passing through eh?' Winters replied. Mark worried he was unconvinced by his cover story. Then Winters did something unexpected. He put his hand out for Mark to shake.

Mark looked stunned but went along with it, feeling the vice-like grip of Winters' hand.

'Name's Jon,' he said, shaking Mark's hand vigorously. Mark could feel the circulation starting to wane so attempted to pull his hand away and smiled at him. 'If you wanna know anything, just ask, I know this place like the back of my hand,' he continued, winking at him.

'Kemp,' Mark said slowly. 'Andrew Kemp. Friends call me Andy.' Mark politely smiled and made his excuses to leave, deciding this was enough casual chat for one day. Once outside and down the road, Mark stopped to light a cigarette and breathed a huge sigh of relief. For a moment, he thought his cover had been blown.

It was getting all too close for comfort, Mark thought as he quickened up his pace, feeling a large raindrop hit his forehead and drip down his eye. He was going back to the B&B and straight to bed before he got himself killed. Winters could wait until tomorrow.

Mark slept soundly through the night, out of sheer exhaustion, and awoke the next morning to the smell of bacon and eggs wafting in under his bedroom door from downstairs. He quickly showered and changed, before heading down the heavily carpeted, sweeping staircase to the dining room where he was confronted by a room full of small tables and chairs as couples and a few families sat and enjoyed breakfast together. He found a vacant table and set himself down and, within a few minutes, the friendly old lady tottered in with a tray of the biggest breakfast Mark had ever seen, complete with teapot, coffee pot, milk, toast and fresh orange juice, and set it down on the table in front of him. She smiled sweetly and patted him on the hand as a mother would do for their child before school. He thanked her and tucked in eagerly, not realising how hungry he was until he had eaten. It wasn't long before the entire plate was empty and Mark was feeling full as he rose with the tray to take it into the kitchen area and convey his thanks to the landlady.

'Oh, don't you worry about that, my dear,' a voice came from behind him. Mark turned to see he was being followed, and smiled.

'I insist,' he said politely, receiving a warm smile and a nod from the old lady. He placed the tray down on the kitchen sideboard and turned to leave.

'Where are ye headed today then, presh?' she quizzed him as he held the door for her.

Mark shrugged and hesitantly answered.

'Not sure yet, I think I might explore that old white house a few miles across the moors,' he explained. She looked confused as she trotted towards the big bay window that faced the road.

'Old white house?' she said slowly. 'Oh, now I don't know, which one's that?' Mark stood alongside her and pointed toward the house.

'Ohh, that one!' she said, smiling before pulling Mark towards her to whisper in his ear. 'You don't want to go there, deary,' she warned in a hushed voice, 'he don't like visitors. He was in the army, you know?'

Mark laughed. 'I had heard,' he said, placing a reassuring arm around her before walking out of the dining room and into reception, then outside for a cigarette.

'Be careful my dear,' she shouted after him as he closed the door. Mark stopped for a second. Why would she warn him about it, he thought to himself as he sat on the wall and smoked, noticing the number of puddles littered all over the road. It must have rained hard last night but Mark hadn't heard a thing; he was asleep as soon as his head hit the pillow. That's what driving all day does, he thought, smiling again at the old lady's warning.

Back in Mark's room, he had prepared all of his kit in his bag and was ready to make his way out towards Winters' home. He carefully crept down the stairs and out via the front door before he could be accosted again by the old lady. She seemed to have developed a keen interest in who he was and what he was doing. He stepped down the three white stone steps that lead out onto the street and began his hike roughly toward Winters' house, having spent a few hours adjusting his ghillie net to blend into the surrounding countryside. With a determined look on his face, he crossed the road towards the miles of fields, moorlands and rolling hills, his target at the forefront of his mind. It was roughly a three-hour hike and initially, Mark planned to drive some of the way. After some calculations, he calculated that, from the position of Winters' house, he would see Mark coming long before Mark even knew he was there, and have time to prepare. The aim was surprise and for Winters to not see it coming. A clean kill was all Mark wanted, and that was exactly what he would get as he strode through knee high gorse, grass and rocks jutting out from the ground. Soon, the brown hue of the landscape gave way to lusher green pastures and Mark could make out the outline of ancient standing stones, long since abandoned. He stopped next to one and took out some of the food supplies he had brought with him, along with his bottle of water, and sat down to rest, estimating the wind speed and direction as he did so. It was very peaceful up here, although Mark worried his shot would be heard for quite some distance and could attract unwanted attention. He soon realised, after assessing the horizon, that there were no other houses around for miles, which made it easier to carry out his hit without being disturbed.

Reinvigorated by eating, he jumped up and picked up his kit bag, turning towards the sun and checking his compass against the satellite image of the house he had taken back in London. According to his calculations, he was another half-hour walk from his destination, and he set off due north, feeling refreshed. It wasn't long before he climbed a small rocky outcrop on top of a small hill which overlooked a steep decline into what Mark figured was a small valley. On the other side, to the left, was a small white house which sat in the middle of a flat field of gorse and heather, a wire perimeter fence surrounding it for three hundred and sixty degrees. Mark took his small infrared binoculars out and had a closer search of the area. It looked deserted, like no one had lived there in years. His eyes met with a wooden blue gate which led to a winding path and an old oak-looking front door. The windows were dirty, torn net curtains hanging from them. There was an old coal shed attached to the side of the building and the ruins of a stable or barn further out to the back of the garden. He was sure he had the right place, and checked the satellite image again to make sure. It looked like no one lived there, but Mark knew it was places like this where hitmen could hide away and not be bothered by anyone. He was sure there was more to this building that met the eye, and approached with caution.

He skirted round the hillside, ensuring he always kept a safe enough distance to be out of range of even the most powerful of sniper rifles, and kept to the higher ground so he could see anyone coming. A wind had sprung up, and this meant that he could be downwind so adjusted his course and edged closer to the white house. He found a suitable place to stop and, pulling up gorse and heather, camouflaged his kit bag and removed his rifle. He expertly assembled it and loaded it, positioning it so it was just in range of the front of the house, and laid the ghillie net over the top of it to hide it from anyone who may accidentally wander past, although way out here, Mark expected no one to be around. Carefully, he lifted a second ghillie suit over his entire body and lay down on his stomach, his eye to the telescopic sight, and waited, watching silently for any signs of movement. One sight of anyone moving around the property, and Mark would have to be quick to take the shot; one missed shot would give away his position and he would be vulnerable to a counter attack.

After an hour of no movement, and with the darkness closing in, Mark was getting the feeling that perhaps he had been tipped off by someone. Perhaps they had put the pieces together and figured out his plan, or perhaps the slimy toe-rag of a driver had squealed on him and talked about what he was up to. Whichever way it was, Mark had to think quickly. With no vehicle, Mark could safely assume his target was not home, unless he had removed his vehicle to give that impression and was also, like Mark, lying in wait under a ghillie net, waiting for the slightest movement, and it would be the end for Mark. As it grew ever darker by the minute, Mark decided he would make a move. He left his rifle set up where it was, took his silenced Glock pistol and several rounds of ammunition, and slowly backed out from under the ghillie net, all the way up the slope behind him, until the hill provided him with suitable cover. He then jogged stealthily around the hillside until he was facing the back of the property. Carefully, he climbed down the slope until he was in the trees surrounding what looked like the back garden. The back door to the property swung in the early evening breeze and Mark believed perhaps it could be empty, so carefully examined the earth inside the perimeter fence. He recognised the familiar humps in the grass, not as mole-hills as some would think, but mines. He thought fast and decided he would follow the path up to the door instead.

He reached the back door and, weapon drawn, used it to push the door open, stepping cautiously inside. Only silence greeted him while a breeze blew through the house, causing the door to creak behind him. He crept into the kitchen and spied the empty whiskey tumbler on the table. He felt the glass to see if there was any warmth which might give away someone's presence. There wasn't, so Mark progressed through to the living room. He passed an old TV set and ran the back of his hand against the screen to check for static. Mark checked for static build up on the screen to reveal if it had recently been turned off. There was no shock, so it hadn't been used in a while. He rounded a corner and faced some wooden slatted stairs. Slowly lifting one foot onto the first stair, praying there would be no creaks, Mark got within three stairs from the top before he had to pause as the wood beneath him flexed and groaned. He held his breath and waited; there was no sound, so he skipped that stair and reached the top, checking the landing as he did so, his weapon leading the way. He crept silently from room to room, without a single trace that Winters had been there for some time; either that or he lived this way all the time. However, what Mark found, tucked inside a drawer in the master bedroom, was the same freight company paperwork he had found on all the other hitmen he'd taken out. He tucked it back in the drawer and withdrew from the room. Just on the inside of the bedroom door, which he had missed before, was a little black box screwed to the wall with a red LED and a switch. Mark traced the wire along the landing, through a hole in the wall, down the exterior brickwork, and under the garden lawn. Curious about it, Mark flicked the switch and the red LED flashed. It must be the mines, Mark thought to himself as he reached for his multi-tool containing the wire clippers. He clipped the wires and the red LED faded. Satisfied the property was empty, he proceeded back downstairs again, careful not to make too much noise just in case someone was in the living room.

He was right to be cautious, as when Mark came into view half way down the stairs, he glanced into the living room and found himself face to face with two cold, hard, steel barrels of a twelve-bore farmer's shotgun, and Winters, dressed in military combat clothing, wearing a Kevlar vest, sat in the arm chair in front of the TV. He didn't look surprised to see Mark as the two men stared at each other for a few seconds, their guns pointed at each other, before Mark finally broke the silence.

'Well, it looks like we have come to a stalemate here!' he said with a half laugh. Winters stood up and Mark readied himself. Even if he was the best shot in the world, Mark knew he would end up with two massive holes in his chest if he moved too quickly.

'I don't like visitors,' Winters grunted angrily, 'especially those who come at me with a Glock 22 suppressed pistol pointed at my head!'

Mark scoffed and Winters relaxed a little, allowing Mark to take the remaining steps down the stairs so the two men stood facing each other.

'You here to kill me, I imagine?' said Winters, his eyes burning red. Mark glared back, equally able to bore into the man's soul.

'D'you kill my wife, Marie King?' he hissed at Winters. Winters shrugged and gritted his teeth.

'I kill a lot of people,' he replied, not taking his eyes off Mark the entire time. Mark's eyes darted around the room as his mind played through a scenario of disarming Winters, and he was looking for anything Winters could pick up and use as a weapon, like a secondary or hidden weapon.

'Who are you working for? Invictus Advoca?' Mark scorned at him, watching for any form of micro expression to tell Mark he was on the right track.

'Ahh, so you're that lawyer fella whose wife was shot!' teased Winters. 'Sorry to disappoint you my friend, but that wasn't MY handiwork.' Mark glared at him.

'Lt. Winters. Pleasure,' Mark replied, watching the smile grow on Winters' face. 'Why should I believe you?'

'Mr King, you are in way over your head. You are out to sea with no sign of the shore, like a boat, drifting on a wave,' he whispered hoarsely. 'I wouldn't have left a single trace for you to use to come seeking revenge.'

'But you know who killed her?' Mark spat at Winters, who seemed quite amused by the whole scenario.

'Perhaps,' Winters chuckled. 'Number one rule, Mr King, do not underestimate your enemy.

Mark hissed at him scornfully, raising his pistol a little higher.

'They can't be underestimated if they're dead!'

'Seeing as I'm in a good mood today, I am going to give you to the count of five to get your sorry arse off my property before I blow you into two pieces. One...'

Mark heeded the warning but would not let Winters see his fear. He lowered his weapon and took careful steps towards the front door, his eyes not leaving Winters as he counted down. Mark reached for the handle and pulled open the door, casually striding down the path and back towards the tree line he had come from. Winters stood at the door with the gun still pointed at Mark.

'Come back 'ere again and I'll not be so forgiving!' he shouted. Mark made a mock salute to him, which caused Winters to shout 'five' at him before firing a shot into the air, sending birds from the trees in all directions. The sound of the shot echoed around the hills as Mark disappeared over the small hill.

'OK,' Mark said defiantly, 'you don't want me to come back there, that's fine. I can kill you from here!'

Chapter Seventeen

The night was cold and damp as Mark lay motionless under his camouflaged ghillie net. He was safe from the wet and cold as the net was insulated to prevent the user from being spotted by heat seeking equipment from the air or the ground, and he hadn't moved a muscle for hours, so much so that his joints were stiffening up. He longed for a five-minute walk around but he knew Winters would be watching. He looked through his powerful telescopic sight and saw slight movement of shadows under the front door. He was probably checking out the security, Mark thought to himself as he focussed intently on the front door. Within a few minutes, the front door opened and Winters appeared in the doorway with a small black box with a switch. He was frantically flicking the switch on and off, then back on and off again and getting angrier by the second that whatever it was he was trying to make happen, wouldn't happen. Mark lined up his crosshairs, almost chuckling to himself as he'd disabled the landmines while in the house, and had Winters' face in the dead centre. Winters must have been angry that, on his way to bed, he had checked the mines and realised the wire had been cut and so had come out to inspect them himself. Mark caressed the trigger and took a long, slow deep breath, exhaled and took another breath as he heard the scream from his hiding place.

'KING!!!' screamed Winters, the long, gurgling howl held in his throat as loud as he could go.

Mark felt sure Winters looked him straight in the eyes as Mark pulled the trigger. His powerful long-range rifle let off a 'pop' as the bullet found its target, right in the centre of Winters' forehead, sending him quickly to the floor, killed instantly. Mark exhaled a long, hard sigh of relief before rolling over and out of his ghillie net. He quickly disassembled his rifle and packed it, together with the ghillie net, into his kit bag and quickly made his way down to the house, pistol drawn, inspecting Winters' dead body. He was impressed, considering he had actually gotten the clean shot he had waited patiently for hours to get. The scattered birds that had their sleep interrupted by the sound of gunfire, returned to their roost, satisfied that they were not being shot at. Mark stepped into the house and straight upstairs to the bedroom to retrieve the paper from the freight company he had found earlier. He then made his way down to Winters' storage shed, where he retrieved two large jerry cans of petrol, and soaked the house completely, from top to bottom. He rewired the switch for the landmines using some electrical tape he found and exited the house, moving Winters' body into the open doorway. He walked to the end of the path and pushed the switch. With lightning speed he threw the switch towards where Winters' body was lying, and it bounced off his chest and fell near to his hand and Mark turned and ran as fast as he could back towards the hill he had been hiding on. He reached the top just as the first line of mines exploded. With an almighty crash like thunder throughout the small valley, the entire house exploded into a massive ball of flames. Mark lit a cigarette as he walked away, silhouetted by the fireball behind him, with a smile on his face, and headed back to the B&B.

Mark slipped in quietly to avoid detection by the old lady, and took off his boots, putting them in his kit bag, and tip toed upstairs to his room, where he had filled the bath up with water before he left. He turned on the hot tap and within a few moments, the bath was hot, and filled with bubble bath. He bundled all his kit, including his clothing, into his bag and folded his jeans, jumper and black hiking jacket neatly on the bed before getting in the bath. Moments later he heard footsteps outside of his bedroom door and a light knock on the door.

'Mr Kemp. Is everything all right?' the old lady whined. 'I thought I heard a noise?'

Mark smiled and got out of the bath, wrapped himself in a towel and opened the door.

'Why, Mrs Grey, whatever is the matter?' he said, smiling innocently at her from around the door.

She looked Mark up and down, seeing him covered in soap bubbles.

'I thought I heard you come in, but I can see you're already here. It must have been another guest.'

Mark smiled as, confused, she turned to walk away. Mark shut the door and breathed a sigh of relief as he dried himself off and sat on the edge of the bed, thumbing through all the paperwork he had taken from each of the hitmen. The only thing they had in common apart from their chosen vocation, Mark thought, was this freight company. Emptying the bath and leaving it to drain, he finished drying himself off before packing up his equipment, dressing, and walking down to his old Range Rover and locking it in the boot space. He returned to his room a short while later and tidied everything up, removed any forensic trace of him ever having been there, and settled down to sleep. He had a long drive tomorrow.

Mark approached the freight yard office, a plain and simple building Mark assumed used to be quite a hub of activity at one stage, to be greeted by a young receptionist who took his fake details to pass onto the manager who would come to collect Mark to talk about his 'shipment' in more detail. Mark was grateful to be above ground as time below ground was getting to him somewhat. He was led to an office where a man in a suit was waiting for him. Overweight and strangely oily, Martin Underhill, the manager, greeted Mark with a damp handshake and it became obvious to Mark, judging by the brand new Jaguar parked outside with the personalised number plate, that this Mr Underhill was into some underhand dodgy shipping dealings to afford a tailored suit and car such as that. Mark seated himself opposite Mr Underhill and studied him carefully to see if there were any signs that might have given away any clues that Mark had been discovered. Satisfied he was in the clear, Mark smiled at Mr Underhill.

'So, Mr Kemp,' he said eerily, 'I gather you are looking for a logistics company who can transport some, shall we say "delicate artefacts"!'

Mark crossed one leg over the other and leant forward slightly.

'Yes, I have some rather unorthodox items to be shipped and, as I am sure you can understand Mr Uphill, the utmost discretion is required.'

Mark winked and Mr Underhill laughed nervously.

'Er, it's Underhill?'

'Yes, of course,' Mark replied, brushing off the deliberate error.

'Discretion is something we comprehensively understand. Might I enquire as to the nature of these items?' Underhill smiled a greasy, slimy little smile that Mark just wanted to wipe off his toady-looking face.

'Let's just say, I don't want ANYONE to find out,' Mark replied, smiling.

Mr Underhill looked more serious, nodded and smiled, shuffling papers on the desk.

'I completely understand. Rest assured Mr Kemp, we can cater for this. Although, the price does, I am afraid, increase if these items are not legitimate?'

Mark nodded again. 'I wouldn't have it any other way.' Mr Underhill was confident Mark was not an undercover police or customs officer.

'No one has any interest in what we ship here. No one has caught us yet. Would you like a tour?' Mark nodded at him and Underhill got up from his desk and waved his arm towards the door.

'Please,' he said, arm outstretched.

Mark didn't trust the guy, but led the way into the corridor. He smiled as Mr Underhill led the way around the yard. During this tour, Mark noticed that some of the workers loading and unloading items in crates seemed to be armed.

'Armed workers?' inquired Mark, trying to look impressed.

'Ah yes,' Underhill said uneasily. 'We can never be too careful who may "stray" into our territory. These guys double up as security overnight.'

'Ah see. Excellent,' Mark replied, slapping Underhill on the back so hard it made him cough and stumble. Underhill laughed nervously, straightening out his ill-fitting suit out and clearing his throat.

'We keep security tight. As you may have noticed, the area is fully covered by a state-of-the-art CCTV system included movement sensors, laser alarms, armed guards and security codes on every door, to which I have the only access, apart from the workers.'

Mark's eyes widened as he attempted a smile; he glanced down at the hidden camera in his briefcase handle, and made sure it captured all the details with it.

'I think I have all the details I need,' said Mark with a smile, 'I will be in touch within twenty-four hours to arrange collection of my shipments.'

'There is, of course,' Underhill whined, 'although I hate to mention it, the case of payment?'

Mark smiled and made his excuses. 'Ah yes, it slipped my mind!'

Mark set the briefcase down and opened it, pulling out papers and a folded set of bank notes. He handed it to Mr Underhill who quickly concealed it in his inside jacket pocket and checked to see if anyone saw. Mark and Mr Underhill shook hands and Mr Underhill escorted Mark back to his car. Mark now had everything he needed and thanked Mr Underhill again as he waved him off. Mark smiled wryly to himself as he drove.

Once back at the bunker, Mark gathered a large amount of ammunition, two M24 sniper rifles which Mark preferred, as this model was the military and police's version of the Remington 700 rifle Mark trained with at Sandhurst which had been the standard US Army sniper rifle since 1988; a Glock 22 handgun with silencer; home-made smoke bombs in small glass canisters which he planned on using to mask his escape; and the usual combat gear. He printed out the pictures and saved copies to his hard drive. Grabbing his homemade latte, he reached for his map, plotting the best way in and out without being seen. He also consulted a list he had located of known associates of Hix and Vose. During his research, he tied them to the shipping company as they seemed to be on the books regularly, probably as cover employment. Mark had his targets, plan, weapons and equipment. This time, he WOULD NOT slip up.

Chapter Eighteen

Night fell as the freight yard's automatic lights flickered into action, making a faint pinging sound as the bulbs warmed up. A thick fog was crawling in while the sound of distant foghorns echoed, muffled by the fog. Mark arrived at the shipping company, this time ready for business. He parked in an old disused warehouse next to the freight yard after reviewing the footage his hidden camera had taken and making a note of all the places not covered by CCTV. He eyed up the cranes and forklifts as they sat silently and driverless. As per his earlier visit, Mark had allocated a crane to use as a vantage point but had brought along some specialist equipment he found at the bunker: small remote control camera tripods which were movement-sensitive. He had attached small rapid fire rifles to these and wired the trigger up to the flash so that whenever they sense movement, they would turn and fire. He crept silently and stealthily through the corridors of containers and warehouses, clutching his kit bag and placing these tripods and hidden locations, all the time mapping his route. Finally he climbed the crane where he mounted one of his two sniper rifles. He took out his small notebook laptop and set it up next to him. The display showed an interactive map with eight flashing red dots. These were the tripods. He clicked the option marked 'activate' and watched as they all swung round to locate any movement before resting still. He didn't want to arm them yet as he wanted to wait for hell to break loose. Mark sat silent and still, waiting.

It wasn't long before armed guards and thugs wandered about on their patrols. Mark had learned since his last 'hit' and has removed the telescopic sight cover so nothing reflective could be seen. He swung his M24 sniper rifle around and calculated which guard to hit first so the others didn't see. Mark took aim at the first guard, waiting until he was out of sight of the others, slowed his breathing down, controlled his heart rate and felt his finger lightly on the trigger. He took one last breath in, eased it out carefully and squeezed the trigger. The only sound was the much muffled thud of the silencer as the guard dropped to the ground, thanks to Mark's clean headshot. The M24 rifle was quieter now as he had muffled the silencer. Swinging round to the next guard who was on a part run, part jog to where his comrade had fallen, Mark tracked him, waiting until he stood over the body of the other guard. Again breathing deeply and slowly, Mark caressed the trigger, calming himself down from the rush of adrenaline, lined the crosshairs up and braced for the muffled thud. The second guard dropped to the ground, over the first. Mark moved away from his scope and smiled. He had taken him out with another clean headshot.

Mark hit three more guards in quick succession, just as he had done the previous two, before reloading and moving to another location on the roof of the nearest warehouse.

He reached for the drainpipe which ascended to the roof of the warehouse, and pulled himself up, nestling in a spot just out of sight from the ground. He left his rifle there and, spotting a skylight, lowered himself down into the warehouse. Once inside, he made his way to towards the offices he had passed with Mr Underhill and tried the locks on each, careful to only move when the small black CCTV mini cameras were revolving in the opposite direction. He found an office with a filing cabinet and searched through the files, taking what may be useful and placing them in a bag hung from his shoulder. He stopped and ducked, hearing the sound of voices. He replaced the cabinet drawers and grabbed his second rifle, crawling towards the door. Opening it slightly, just enough to get the muzzle of his second M24 rifle through, Mark shot three guards, one after another from the doorway. He also shot out the cameras with precision aim.

All had gone quiet and Mark seized this opportunity to move to the other side of the freight yard to see what he could uncover. Light on his feet and stealthy, Mark moved between the rows of containers, slinging his rifle over his shoulder and pulling out a silenced pistol. A few guards spotted him close up. He took aim and fired three rounds at them with the pistol before moving on. The gurgle and lack of screaming confirmed to Mark they were dead. He found a black Mercedes with blacked-out windows parked up outside a container and skilfully, with no damage, gained access. He quickly jumped in and shut the door. Leaning over and opening the glove box, he pulled out a cell phone and charger and a leather-bound diary and some papers. He put this into his bag and waited until he was confident the coast was clear before moving on. He moved around like a ghost, and no one at the yard he encountered lived to say they saw him as he quickly shot two more guards running behind him. Finally he reached the wire fence and the office he was taken to earlier that day.

Climbing the steel fire escape staircase, he easily snapped off the small lock and opened the door. The lock on the inside fell to the ground with a 'ping'. Mark picked it up and put it inside the nearest drawer before looking around for what he was after earlier: a safe. Packing small explosives onto the safe door he stood back and ducked behind a desk with his weapon drawn, detonating the explosives. The door fell away revealing more paperwork inside. He noticed a strange logo on the paperwork but he didn't have time to look into that now; he could hear voices and what he thought was a large minivan approaching. Tilting the blinds down, he saw between eight and ten guards with semi-automatic machine guns jump out and run between the containers.

'Part two,' he whispered and pulled a device from his pocket, no bigger than a memory stick.

He pushed the button on it which activated the sensor controlled machine guns he hid earlier. Suddenly there was a tumult of gunfire and deathly screaming as a few of the guards ran back towards the minivan, ducking for cover left, right and centre. Mark smiled as he heard one guard shout to another, 'It's an army of intruders, fully armed!'

Mark crept out of the office, back to the cover of the Mercedes. Rolling underneath it silently, he placed a magnetised tracking device on the undercarriage of the car and made his way back to the shadows but not before he caught sight of a familiar face: Roman Vose, who by now was leading the guards back towards the office. He rolled one canister of explosives he made earlier towards them; it wouldn't do any damage and was purely a dry ice smoke mixture designed to sit in the air for a minute or two, just enough to mask his escape.

After dispatching another guard who seemed to have run at him from an open container, Mark took a quick look inside. It was filled with green and black storage boxes Mark recognised from his military days. Quickly stepping inside the darkness of the container, Mark allowed his eyes to adjust and used his pocket Maglite to see what was there. He saw rows upon rows of the same military boxes. He prised one open, being careful not to make too much noise to uncover his location. Straw, then underneath that, cold hard steel and instantly Mark knew what was going on: weapons hauling. Not wanting to burn this opportunity too much, Mark took his mini camera out and took a several snapshots including details of their destination. Germany. He realised that if he was to uncover what Marie was murdered for, he needed to follow this lead. He left the container and sealed it back up using the outside bolts. These people needed *something* salvageable.

Doubling back to the first crane where he stashed his first sniper rifle, Mark climbed back up into the cab, waiting for Vose to appear in his crosshairs. He did but only for a second.

A second was all Mark needed to fire his shot and his reactions were quick. Vose hit the deck onto his knees, clutching his thigh, and crawled into what seemed to be HIS Mercedes before speeding off round past some containers. With that, floodlights seemed to light up every section of the yard and Mark, thinking it was best to take this opportunity to leave, planted an explosive device under the crane and ran back to where he parked his van. Driving a few feet, he turned out of the driver's window, retrieving the detonator out of his pocket with two buttons on it. He pushed the first one and all the remote machine guns he positioned at various points around the yard exploded, causing total mayhem and confusion. Mark flashed his laser sight into the windows of the office, attracting the attention of the guards.

'He's over there,' shouted one guard, waving his hands over his head towards the entrance. A second guard responded.

'He's hiding in the office, surround him!'

The sound of foreign voices echoed around as gunfire rattled the corrugated metal roof of the office. Mark pushed the second button, which activated the explosive under the crane. There was a thunderous explosion and sudden silence before Mark heard creaking metal and steel and high pitched grinding. Looking up, he saw the crane about to buckle, swinging precariously, creaking and groaning. Before anyone below could move, it came crashing down on top of the office building with an incredible smashing of glass and an almighty explosion. Mark smiled again and, lighting up a cigarette, drove off leaving a scene of complete and total devastation with bodies, fires and broken containers and a smashed crane lying all over the place. Anything he left behind would not be traceable at all. Just the way he liked it, total mystery.

Pulling into a remote area, Mark's intrigue got the better of him. He flicked through some of the papers he removed from the safe and searched down through a list of employee and contractor names.

'Useful,' he said to himself, but then he noticed something a little more serious: photographs of himself and Marie leaving and returning home at different times of the day.

'None of the children, thank God,' he sighed, relieved. But the list of names of employees and contractors rang a bell. 'Time to scout them.'

Mark was relaxing at his desk with a glass of twelve-year-old Scottish malt and a cigarette looking through the paperwork when he found the address of Martin Underhill. He sipped the Scottish malt and leant back in his chair. The taste and scent of the whisky reminded Mark of his father and the holidays they used to have in the Highlands of Scotland. He smiled as he remembered with fondness the times they used to spend walking around the Highlands, his father with his shotgun and teaching Mark how to shoot. When this was all over, he vowed to himself he would spend time there again. He would still have his old home to sell before he moved to New York as he couldn't stay there, especially after all this. If he survived, he was going to Scotland for a long, restful holiday.

Images flashed through his mind of him walking through the rugged landscape of the Highlands, to the sound of distant haunting bagpipes. The thought of spending time at the prestigious Carnegie Club, with its pool, sauna, spa, golf course and bar was an inviting one. He pictured himself sat in one of their tall armchairs, looking out of the window across the glen and the lochs but his beautifully crafted image turned to grief and anger as he remembered a trip he and Marie took there just before they got married. This image bought him back to reality, and he sat up in his chair and stubbed out his cigarette.

Mark's conversation with Underhill revealed that he was involved in something sinister, but he didn't have enough answers to connect to weapons dealing to Germany. Obviously he couldn't go back to the freight yard as there wasn't much left of it so the next logical choice was to go to see Mr Underhill at his home. Mark grabbed his gear and made his way to his van to pay the fat man a visit.

The sound of something moving in the kitchen, as Martin Underhill crept into his large luxury rural home during the middle of what had been a horrific night, got his attention and set his nerves on edge. Perhaps it was one of the children or his wife waiting up for him. He moved into the large study and put his bag down on the nearest chair. He chose not to put the light on and the pale moon shining through the net curtain onto the patio was the only illumination the room had. No matter, he thought, I'll only be a minute before going up to bed, but perhaps a small brandy to calm the nerves is in order. He moved towards his decanter in the cabinet and as he was about to put his hand on it to pull the oak cabinet door open, he noticed a figure clad in military combat gear and saw the shine of the moonlight on a Glock 22 silenced pistol. He had seen many of those bandied around the yard during his time running the establishment for his ever absent boss. He dropped his hand down and froze, as a voice came out of the darkness.

'Move and I'll shoot you in the head.'

He slowly turned around to face the figure at the door, legs shaking and arms up in surrender.

'Are you going to kill me?'

He breathed a small sigh of relief when the answer from the mystery figure echoed around the room.

'That depends on what you tell me.'

Prepared to say virtually anything to save his own skin, Martin Underhill suddenly believed he MIGHT get out of this alive. Remembering his wife and children were asleep upstairs, his voice quivered. 'Are my wife and children OK?' he asked. The reply was short.

'They are, for now.'

Underhill relaxed a little.

'They are tied up and gagged and one word from me and my accomplice will cut their throats.'

Underhill froze once again and, terrified, agreed to talk.

'SIT down!' the figure ordered as Underhill fumbled in the dark for the chair opposite, facing Mark. Underhill did so without question and kept his arms up. 'Put your arms down,' the figure tutted at him.

He obeyed and stared in horror as the figure stepped into the moonlight.

'YOU!' he said in hushed shock and disbelief. But no answer came, for the mystery figure was Mark and he was holding a silenced pistol to Underhill's forehead at this point. Mark sat in the chair facing Underhill.

Mark's questioning of Martin Underhill was extensive.

'Illegal arms smuggling Mr Underhill, now that is a dangerous vocation.'

Underhill looked embarrassed as he answered, 'I just manage the yard. My boss is a dangerous man to know.'

'I see, and your "boss", what does he want with these weapons?'

Underhill confessed to the whole operation and seemed only too willing to talk about it in great detail.

'We received them via a logistics company a few days ago. They are to be sent to Germany for a private buyer. I don't know his name.'

Mark raised his eyes in disbelief.

'But I know the shipping address and delivery schedule. I can call him if you like?'

Mark smiled as Underhill moved from his chair and lifted his gun a little higher, forcing Underhill back on track.

Mark felt in his pocket for the recording device he had been keeping on all the time to get Underhill's confession and was pleased with the fact he had questioned him the way he would cross examine a witness in court. It felt good for Mark to be doing this after everything that had happened, as it made him feel almost normal again.

Mark made his way to the door. Underhill's voice quivered again.

'What about…?'

'Your wife and children?' Mark interrupted, anticipating his question and replying nonchalantly. 'No idea, last time I checked they were fast asleep. But if I were you, I'd get myself a good lawyer!'

Martin Underhill couldn't tell, but Mark was smirking as he silently disappeared from Underhill's sight and out through the ornate kitchen patio doors from where he had entered an hour beforehand. Lying in wait for someone like that wasn't ideal but as Underhill wasn't even home when he arrived, Mark had limited options. But it gave him a laugh as he really didn't like the slimy, oily little bastard.

The following day, Martin Underhill scurried across the grass clutching his briefcase as he nervously prepared to provide all the details on how Mark King had taken him and his family hostage at gunpoint and how he had killed two or three neighbours to gain entry to his house to kill him. He also planned to describe how his daring escape had worked and he had foiled Mark King's plans and that he had men after him, and that he expected them to call imminently to confirm they killed him and would be bringing his body as proof. The truth of the matter was that Martin Underhill had made the call to his superiors the second Mark King had left his property, but had to use his mobile as King had cut the main telephone line before breaking into his house. The mobile was destroyed so there was no chain of evidence. The black executive Lincoln stretched limo was parked on the tarmac opposite a gleaming white Gulfstream G550 private jet with its ladder down awaiting its passenger. Underhill knew he would likely be disciplined as both back doors and the front door of the limo opened simultaneously. Three men clutching Uzi nine millimetre sub-machine guns, locked and loaded and ready to go at the first hint of trouble, stood motionless and menacing, glaring at him. Someone from inside the car had told them to stand down, as they relaxed a little when Underhill's fat and flushed frame cast an embarrassing figure in a tight fitting suit and red face, white hair all over the place and a clear look on his face which gave away that he hadn't slept in at least a few days. He reached the car and Roman Vose's six foot six figure against Martin Underhill made Underhill shudder as Vose chewed his gum and stared intently at him.

Vose didn't like him and made no secret of it, and prayed his boss would give him an order to put bullet holes in his horrible fat frame. He fumbled his way into the back of the limo and stared in horror at the person sat looking at him with eyes that seemed to bore into his soul and stare judgementally at every single thing he'd ever done. A person whom he had only ever heard on the phone, and who he instantly knew was his boss. This man, who owned an empire, was staring at him with disappointment and disgust and a mild look of curiosity about what he was about to say, and could easily have him killed just by clicking his fingers. There had never been a time he had feared more for his life, not even when Mark King was holding a silenced pistol to his forehead. He tried, in a trembling voice, to explain what had happened and he stammered and stuttered as he did so, all the while being stared at coldly by his boss. His boss just kept staring, and at one point it looked as though he would pull a gun out from his jacket and put two slugs into his chest and throw him out of the car and not blink. Underhill was terrified, and rightly so because his boss didn't yet know King was still alive and would surely want to know why Underhill didn't raise the alarm and have him arrested, which would have saved them all the trip now and the worry and stress of trying to work out a way to eliminate a man who NO ONE could find. Underhill gulped as his boss raised one eyebrow. This is it, he thought, the end.

Thomas Lundon got out of the limo, cane in his left hand, looking at his pocket watch intently. Roman Vose looked expectantly at him, waiting for the order to execute Underhill and was disappointed when it didn't come. Lundon instructed one of the other two men to 'get rid of the rubbish in the back of the car to somewhere where he can no longer get into any trouble'. Vose smiled at the thought of Underhill dead but was still disappointed he wasn't the executioner this time around. The two men got into the car and it sped off the runway towards the small hangar behind them. Thomas Lundon beckoned to Vose to follow him whilst an aide helped Lundon onto the steps leading up to the plane. Vose followed, and the shutter door was raised. Inside

Lundon sat opposite Vose in a luxurious leather recliner, with a laptop on a small table on one side and a decanter with brandy on the other and an ashtray with a box of cigars in it next to the decanter. Lundon sighed, irritated by what Underhill had told him. He explained to Vose that it was KING who had destroyed the weapon's shipment bound for Germany and that now, he would have to find new goods to send to his buyer. Also it was King who had put a bullet in Vose's leg. Vose rubbed it at just the mention of the event, which had left it healing but sore. The two men devised a plan to hunt down and kill Mark King wherever they could and asked Vose about Mark King's remaining family.

'Boss, there was no trace of them, no bank transactions and not a single shred of evidence to track down either the mother-in-law, or the two brats. It's like they've vanished.'

'They are probably all together, holed up somewhere like frightened rabbits,' Lundon replied. Vose smiled. 'Unfortunately.'

'Now there is no way to use King's family to lure him out into the light.' Vose rubbed his wound and gripped the side of his seat in anger.

'I promise you Vose, you will get your revenge soon enough.'

Vose hoped Lundon was right; he had a bruised ego, bruised bones and was eager for payback.

'Boss, what does King want with you, anyway?'

Lundon paused for a moment before turning to Vose.

'I upset him because he "wouldn't play ball" and he is a threat to the businesses.'

Vose shook his head despairingly and Lundon raised one eyebrow to this response. Vose ignored it but knew what it meant as he looked out of the plane window to watch the ground slowly fall away as the plane took off.

'I expect it was Mark King who took out Hix as well,' Lundon smiled, taunting Vose. Lundon never liked Hix anyway. This just made Vose even angrier; even though he didn't like Hix, he also didn't like being shot at and hit twice in the space of a week!

Chapter Nineteen

The lonely, battered Ford Mondeo which was parked outside the house for days it seemed was looking like a stolen car, dumped in a prestigious neighbourhood by kids of the wealthy who had rebelled against their rich, well-bred parents. There were old takeaway boxes and drinks cans covering the back seats and the smell was unbelievable.

The neighbours had reported it there earlier that day. At first they had thought it was an undercover police car judging by what happened at the house not so long ago. The police tape remained attached to certain parts of the door, garden and gate posts outside, and in an X shape across the front door where Mark had used the door to leave that night.

In the front seat with his head tilted back was a very decrepit, sleep deprived, coffee-overloaded journalist who had not gone back to work since he heard of Marie King's death. He camped outside the Kings' residence because he couldn't bring himself to leave. He was suddenly awoken in the dark by the sound of tyres on gravel. He looked up to see a black Mercedes Vito van pulling into the drive. He picked up his camera and realised he had not connected the battery, so fumbled in the glovebox for a spare. It was only seconds, he literally had seconds off his target but when he looked back up, there was no one. Not a single soul around. It was definitely King, no doubt about it.

He grabbed the spare battery and took pictures of the foreign plate Vito van. Suddenly, a figure appeared at the van again.

'It IS you, King!' he said as the clicking of his camera made him focus on what he was doing. He took around a hundred pictures before King got back into his van and reversed off the drive and drove off into the night. Ian Hawking put down his camera and smacked the steering wheel in celebration.

'I got you, you bastard!' he shouted before he started the ignition and drove away from the house, satisfied he had got what he came for: evidence!

What Ian Hawking hadn't seen during his fumbling in the glovebox for his spare battery was Mark King taking pictures of his own of Hawking's car before he disappeared around the back to the kitchen door.

Meetings were the order of the day, including a briefing on the Al Azidi situation. The wife of the lawyer prosecuting him during the trial, had been murdered, the lawyer himself had gone underground and there was no useful intelligence from the office shooting other than the mumblings of a security guard who said nothing 'untoward' had occurred prior to the shooting and the new cleaner seemed nice and not really anything to pay attention to.

'New cleaner?' said Agent Nathanial Williams thoughtfully to himself as he perched on the corner of Rachael, his superior's desk.

He flicked through the evidence file while he waited for the briefing to start. He was a seasoned agent, having been attached to this unit for several months since Al Azidi had resurfaced. He was even more interested in this lawyer Mark King who had seemed to have everything going for him before his wife was murdered.

'Strange,' he said aloud, 'that his wife dies, the case is dismissed then King vanishes?'

As far as his supervisor was concerned, that was what MI6 wanted in the first place, however, in his line of work, there was no such thing as a coincidence. His superior came rushing in.

'Talking to yourself again, Nate?'

'Hey Rachael,' Williams responded without looking up. He was too busy mulling over Mark King.

'Do you want to get your arse off my desk, AGENT Williams?'

He obeyed, moving himself to the chair and smiling but not taking her warning seriously. They had worked together years before on an undercover operation when she was NOT his boss and occasionally he lorded this over her whenever they didn't agree on something. Agent Williams followed her into the briefing room and there were seven others all stood waiting to be seated around a pale pine boardroom table. There were several large screens around them, hung from the walls and on arms which could be pushed back against the walls when not in use. There was a copy of the same file in front of everyone and Williams' boss called the meeting to order.

'Thank you everyone! Several hours ago, we received intelligence as to an alleged witness, the security guard at the office shooting, who said there was a new member of the cleaning crew that night that he had never seen before.'

'King,' Williams mentioned. Rachel nodded at him and continued.

'A cleaner had reported being struck over the head by a masked stranger while having a cigarette prior to his shift starting.'

Williams got up and addressed the attendees.

'We have discovered some "anomalies" as you will see on screen and in your files. Why is this connected to the shooting, and is this stranger Mark King?'

The big screen TV switched on and he dismissed the meeting.

'Everyone use your contacts to find out anything else that may have not been right that night.'

Agent Williams and his boss headed down to the ops room.

There was an extreme sense of tension in the ops room as Agent Williams had come into an operation in the Middle East, mid-swing. He was silenced and told to wait while a desk of military operatives made frantic phone calls on headsets and watched a huge cinema-type screen in the centre of the ops room. Everyone was talking with people rushing about. On the screen was a desert war zone with a building in the centre which seemed about to be blown up. The room went quiet as a female operative looked around at Rachael.

'Ma'am. Request authorisation for strike?'

Before pausing, she bit her thumb nail whilst crossing her arms, a nervous habit she had gained as a child. She paused again and gave the order in a serious, quiet but authoritative voice.

'Strike authorised, target acquired, weapons free.'

The strike was launched, and the room fell silent after the drone had decimated its target.

'Sit-rep. Strike confirmed?' she demanded.

A voice came over a radio from the Operations desk.

'Target destroyed. Repeat. Target destroyed.'

There was a moment or two's silence before she turned to everyone, congratulated them on another al-Qaeda target destroyed and asked them to resume normal duties. Agent Williams looked on at her, knowing what kind of responsibility she held and how seriously she took it. He felt sorry for her having to shoulder such a burden but knew she was specifically requested for military intelligence because of her impressive success record in the field. She reveled in the excitement but the responsibility of the death of others took its toll on her daily.

Rachel looked over at Agent Williams and she knew he was right. She wasn't about to give him the satisfaction of knowing it, but inside she *knew*.

'OK, everyone, listen please. Dig up EVERYTHING you can about the office shooting: CCTV, witness statements, forensics, reports, and cross reference them with any other incidents which match the same details, specifically the fact that the operative used a guise to gain entry to the building.'

Williams intervened. 'Also include anything where the primary weapon was a sniper rifle, but no reports filed and where a body was absent.'

Within seconds, results came in and people shouted results at both Agent Williams and Rachel.

'Right,' he replied in his familiar Scottish accent to the numerous responses from the team, 'Now we're getting somewhere!'

Rachael pulled Williams to one side and handed him a file. He looked at her, confused.

'Rachael, what's this?' he asked, looking surprised that, after their history, she would want to share *anything* with him he didn't have to fight for.

'It's something that may be of interest to you,' she said, smiling, 'it seems it could be connected to this shooting, I want you to look into it.'

Williams opened the file and read the description. His eyes widened.

'A female assassin?' He smiled, impressed by what he saw. Also he noted privately that, in the photograph that had been taken of her, she was very attractive.

'Yes,' Rachel replied, noting the look on Williams' face, a look he used to give *her*, 'her name is Nadia, that's all our boys have been able to come up with so far. Ruthless killer, merciless and she uses her charm to get close to her victims. I'm waiting for the Psyche team to do a full eval but for now, she's your responsibility.'

'Right away!' he replied, astonished at her request.

Mark King was polishing his rifle after deconstructing it and cleaning every single inch, just the way he had been taught at Sandhurst Military Academy. He put his rifle cleaning kit down and went over to his equipment table, where he had laid out the pictures of the car he saw at his house when he decided to divert there on the way back to his bunker. It was becoming a habit, and he knew he had to stop but he wasn't ready to just yet, even though it could draw attention from anyone. He looked at the pictures and noticed something he hadn't noticed before, a familiar face in the car window with a camera! He looked again but couldn't make it out so reached for a box under the table.

In it he found a round magnifying glass. He put it against the picture of the car window and was both amazed and shocked at what he saw. Ian Hawking camped outside his house trying to take pictures of him. He slammed the magnifying glass down on the newspaper he had next to him and immediately reached for a cigarette. Lighting it up and feeling the slight burn against the back of his throat took the edge off his anger, whilst a sip of single malt helped ease the racing heart rate. What on earth was Ian Hawking doing carrying out surveillance on HIS home? His EMPTY home?

He wandered over to his corner sofa and pondered this thought as he sat back and relaxed, retrieving the remote control for the CCTV around the bunker, a routine he had stuck to since the day he erected the CCTV system around him. He pressed a button which armed the electric fencing and the landmines in the grass areas surrounding the bunker. He was ready for bed but couldn't seem to get the image of Ian Hawking out of his mind. Perhaps he needed to pay him a little visit? But that wouldn't be good, he would be tempted to shoot him and make it look like suicide so decided against this. Mark desperately wanted to talk to him but there was no need right now as he was being diverted from his mission. Although Mark had no idea where he should go; if it was Germany, he didn't know which location to look at. Without a shipping detail or log, he wasn't even sure if he knew where those weapons were destined for. He researched the ship's name and latest route on the web to see if that yielded any clues. According to the publicised ships log, Holtenau was the vessel's next stop off before returning to the UK. Maybe Holtenau was the best place to start.

Mark grabbed his 'go bag' and filtered through some of the piles of fake passports he had made for him and chose an alias. The yacht broker identity looked promising as he knew a great deal about luxury yachts. After getting cash, he grabbed his keys to the Vito and prepared to make his way to the airport. He glanced at his watch; it was just gone ten PM. If he could get a flight in the next hour, he would be in Kiel, Germany for first thing tomorrow morning. He yawned and grabbed his cigarettes to light another, always a sure-fire way to keep himself awake. He realised he didn't have many so would have to stop off and buy more. He also needed food and a coffee too. Remembering a good Costa near to the airport where an attractive barista called Laura worked, Mark decided he would stop there. He stopped himself short at that point as he realised he found someone other than Marie attractive, and hadn't looked at anyone like that since the first time he met Marie. As he set the intruder alarm system to 'armed', meaning anyone who gained entry into the facility would be blown to pieces by the strategically placed mines hidden all around the place, he looked up decent but discreet hotels near to the airport so he could crash when he got there and found one he liked the look of, the understated Inter City Hotel Kiel, which was conveniently located next to the train station: perfect for quick movements around Germany. He reserved a room under the same alias as his passport, to be paid on arrival for several nights. He had no idea how long he would need to stay or what he would uncover when he arrived. At least he could relax knowing that under this alias, no one would look for him. All he could think of now was supping a steaming hot toffee latte and he half hoped Laura worked the graveyard shift.

It was a cloudy descent as Mark gathered his small carry on possessions together and put on his safety belt ready for the landing. He was irritable and desperate for a cigarette and coffee as the announcement came over the Tannoy advising that they would shortly arrive at Hamburg Airport and that the weather was cloudy, at four degrees with a feeling of two degrees. Mark already felt the chill. He had taken minimal clothing with him as most of what he needed would be obtained when he got there. A stewardess came past asking everyone to fasten their safety belts. He got her attention, and she addressed him in his alias name, Russell Green.

'Yes Mr Green, what can I get you?'

'Where are the best places to buy clothes when we land? I didn't expect this weather!' he said with a smile which caught her eye.

She wrote on a piece of paper a list of shops which were high quality and reasonable prices and he thanked her, putting the piece of paper in his pocket. She was sweet and attentive, he thought to himself as the plane touched down on the runway. It taxied to its terminal and the usual instructions came over the Tannoy before people stood ready to retrieve their hand luggage from the overhead storage areas. Mark waited and picked up a copy of World News Media's latest magazine about luxury property developments for sale in Germany.

He also noted there was an article about yacht brokerage which he thought would be of use, considering his cover was a yacht broker. He read it and, as he had done many times, memorised every word to be used at a later date. After most of the passengers had disembarked, he retrieved his bag and made towards the exit, thanking the stewardess on his way out. He made his way out via Terminal 2 and quickly eyed up all the exits and potential escape routes, along with anyone who looked suspicious or that may follow him. He may have been relaxed about travelling to Germany but he hadn't lost the notion that, a few months ago, his face was all over at least the national news due to the Azidi case. That seemed like a lifetime ago, he thought as he felt for the piece of paper the stewardess had given him. He located a coffee shop just inside the airport, Café Treff and ordered croissants and a large black coffee, paid and chose a seat at the back so that anyone wandering by wouldn't notice him. He re-read the note and found, in German, more than merely a list of shops and some directions. He translated in his head and was shocked by what he read.

'Sir, it is not my place but, I felt I should warn you. There is a man a few seats behind yours who has been making notes about you since we left London. Please do not be alarmed but I think he could be a reporter. Good luck with the shopping.'

Nina X

Instantly, Mark was on the defensive and hadn't really noticed anyone sat behind him on the plane.

'More to the point,' Mark thought to himself, 'who the hell would make notes about ME and follow me to Germany?'

He was so careful using aliases and untraceable phones and money, he couldn't possibly think of a way in which anyone could have got a link to him. He was uncomfortable as he looked around at all the people filing past him. It could be any of them. As he got up to leave, he noticed the stewardess in blue, walking her small wheeled suitcase across the airport. She clocked him and smiled as she walked towards the public phone booths to the left of Café Treff. She nodded for him to follow and he did so, taking up the phone next to the booth she was in. She dialled the internal number of the phone next to hers and Mark picked up. She seemed concerned for his wellbeing.

'Oh sir, thank goodness. You got my note?' she panted, her eyes darting around her constantly.

'Yes Nina, thank you,' replied Mark in a hushed voice, 'now, tell me everything you know.'

Nina settled down and explained what she had seen.

'That passenger I warned you about is behind us, across the airport, just within sight.'

Mark casually turned around, acting out actions with his hands which were not relevant to their conversation so as not to arouse suspicion. He spotted a man in a brown suede jacket and grey chinos leaning up against the wall reading a paper.

'Thank you sweetheart,' he said, putting his hand on her shoulder. 'Why did you notice it was me he was taking notes about?' he asked.

She leaned in closer so as not to be overheard.

'The notes mentioned your seat number, description and your name.'

'Great!' Mark said encouragingly. 'What else did he write and what makes you think I am in danger?'

'I would not speak to you but, Sir, I saw the word, how you say in English, a hit? Forgive me sir but I thought you may be the target of a mugging or kidnap?'

Mark reached for the piece of paper she gave him earlier and a pen and wrote a quick thank you.

'Thank you Nina, you have been a darling,' he said, holding her hand tightly in his.

She smiled tenderly at him. In any other circumstances, Mark would have made more of it as he had a feeling she liked him.

'Stay on the phone and pretend a conversation is ongoing with your boyfriend. Keep it going until I'm out of sight!' Mark explained.

She nodded and Mark thanked her over and over and then hung the phone up. Shouldering his bag and with the piece of paper in his hand, he walked 'accidentally' straight into her, sliding the paper into her jacket pocket, made his apologies and caught sight of the man in the brown jacket lifting his phone to his ear.

He was spotted so made a quick retreat as the man motioned quickly after him. Mark spied a door marked 'Private' and, purely out of curiosity, checked the handle. It opened, and he passed through quickly to cover himself. He was in a long white and grey corridor with a sign on the wall in German: 'Gepäckabfertigung' (Baggage Handling). Mark made his way towards the sign and turned a corner. He heard the door turn after him and suddenly came up on a door marked: 'Flughafensicherheit' (Airport Security).

Again he tried the handle, and the door swung open. He located the arms cabinet and picked the lock quickly before grabbing a handgun, silencer and a magazine of ammunition. He locked and loaded with lightning fast speed, just time to hear the door go. He rushed behind it and a hand came around the corner holding a silenced pistol. Mark allowed the man to walk into the room before putting the gun to his head and ordering him in German, 'Drop the weapon.' The man did so and Mark aimed a foot to the back of the man's knee, causing him to drop to the ground. Mark went round him to face him. 'Why are you following me?'

The man refused to answer so Mark hit him on the chin with the handle of the gun he obtained from the cabinet. Blood dripped to the ground, and the man pushed himself back upright again. Mark held the gun to his forehead and pulled back the hammer ready to fire. This changed the man's mind.

'I was hired by someone, I don't know his name.'

Mark's face turned serious; he was furious and close to kicking the man half to death.

'Why?' he shouted, his voice deepening, pushing the gun tighter to the man's forehead. The man glared at Mark and through gritted teeth, explained.

'To follow you because I know you are. You are Mark Lucas King, disgraced lawyer.'

Mark felt the anger build, but wanted to know exactly who was following him and why. The man loosened up and explained.

'We had located you because of the alias you used, Russell Green, which was one of your old client's names who was deceased.'

Mark was struggling to keep control of his temper. He held tightly on, thinking he needed this man alive, at least for now.

'Go on,' Mark demanded. The stranger continued.

'You represented his estate during a fierce battle of inheritance.'

Mark cursed himself for being sloppy and said it was no surprise they had found him.

'Who are you people, the people who murdered Marie?'

'I know nothing about that,' replied the stranger looking confused, 'I was supposed to follow you and update my "client" on where you were going and what you were doing.'

The truth dawned on Mark at that point and he realised they knew he was there.

'You take a message back to your "client": if they continue to hunt me or my family, I will locate them and kill them all!'

The man hissed at Mark and nodded, before he knocked the man unconscious and wiped the gun clean. He put the gun in the man's hand so that his fingerprints would be on it and located the security alarm. He punched it and waited until people were running down the corridor outside the security office. He had about one minute before the guards came to fetch their weapons and he timed it perfectly, slipping out of the door and into the crowd, unnoticed, and out of the airport and into the street.

Chapter Twenty

Mark figured the best way to get to Holtenau from here was by car. He knew he could check into the hotel after midday but was still reeling from his encounter with the man in the brown jacket. He made his way towards the Europa Passage Shopping Mall in the centre of Hamburg. It had everything he needed there for clothing to 'fit in' around Germany. He found a small newsagent and stocked up on cigarettes; he bought sixty and a bottle of water. He took a packet and put the rest and the water in his bag as he lit up, feeling more at ease and satisfied. A thought had occurred to him that if they tracked his alias and alias passport, they probably knew he had a hotel reservation, so diverted hotels. After calling around a few in Holtenau and offering to pay cash, he used a name he made up on the spot so as not to make the same mistake again. He relaxed. OK, so they knew he was in Germany but they didn't know why and they couldn't trace him now. Mark entered the Europa Passage shopping centre and made straight for 'Wormland Men's Fashion', purchasing a few pairs of trousers and jeans, some shirts and a few jackets. He worried that he wouldn't take these with him when he returned to London, but money really wasn't that much of a problem now. Next he needed a hire car and a rifle so looked up a military surplus supplies store between Hamburg and Holtenau and the nearest car hire firm.

He found one quickly and paid cash for a week's hire, knowing he probably wouldn't need it. The dark grey Audi Quattro Q7 3.0 TDI four-by-four came with a full tank of diesel and it was only a one hour ten minute drive to Holtenau. He decided not to cancel his booking for the first hotel he booked and played along with the game, checking in and paying for his room. He left his bags in the car and walked to the room, made a coffee and headed out again to the hotel down the road where he checked in, paid in cash and headed up to the room. Now if they came looking for him, they would start in the wrong hotel, at least buying him time by creating a distraction.

Mark ran a bath in his new hotel room at the Maritim Hotel Bellevue and made a coffee; staring out of the window, he lit up a cigarette and researched the port of Kiel-Holtenau so he could get an idea of what he was up against. Opening his rented laptop, he typed in the search box the name of the port and got a satellite image of the place so he could pick out the best vantage points. He wasn't sure what he was looking for other than the same container he encountered in London but there could be no guarantee it was still en route or whether it had been picked up, only that the ship would arrive in three days and he needed to use that time to find out who it belonged to and why it was being shipped. More to the point, HOW it was being shipped. During his bath he wondered if all of this was somehow connected to the Azidi trial. He went right back to the start and realised that it all started with Azidi and that THAT was the root cause of Mark's involvement in this whole situation.

Mohammed Al Azidi stood on top of a container overlooking the vast Kiel-Holtenau Port whilst he surveyed the rows of storage units and felt the comfort of his AK-47 and his knife in its holster. He smiled, knowing soon he would be head of the most deadly and well-armed unit in Europe. His men were heavily vetted and all 'brothers' from the Middle East who were supportive of the cause. It wasn't a jihad, far from it, but it was the start of something he totally believed in: the unconditional destruction of the western world. He didn't like who he was working for as he was a westerner himself, but if the person he was working for should turn on his country of origin and go against his government, who was he to stop him? After all, as soon as he took power, he would have him killed anyway, so it really didn't matter. Azidi waited for a call from his German contact to confirm whether it was Mark King, that bastard lawyer from Britain who tried to have him put away, who was coming to Germany but, as yet, no word had come. He was getting concerned but reminded himself that this contact had never let him down before so he was sure there was a perfectly good explanation for his delay in contacting him. He would leave it a few more hours before doing any investigations.

In the moonlight which cast eerie shadows over the surrounding buildings, Azidi finished his cigarette before calling it a night.

The thought of Mohammed Al Azidi being involved in this was a chilling prospect as Mark sat outside the café not far from his hotel and smoked a cigarette. He shouldn't be surprised because it made so much sense now, but what he could do about it? There was no doubt in Mark's mind; Mohammed Al Azidi HAD to be eliminated. But he was sure Azidi wasn't the man at the top, he HAD to be getting his orders from someone else. It frustrated Mark that just when he thought he was in sight of the ultimate target, something else came along and shifted the balance. He was getting impatient, but he knew he couldn't afford to make too many quick moves or it could all go horribly wrong and that would be the end of it. Mark took the last sip of his coffee but just as he did so, he glanced at the reflection in the café window and noticed a man sitting in a car opposite, intrigued by Mark, or at least, that's the way it looked. Mark glanced left and right along the road until he spotted a coach, full of what looked like tourists, about to pass between the café and the car opposite. He saw his chance and, as the coach masked his movements, he vanished up the road, across the road and back down the other side, using an oncoming bus as cover.

The man in the car was worried; the coach had blocked his view, and he now had no clear line of sight to the café. When the coach moved, he couldn't tell where his man had gone. He had to move and, as he fumbled around for his keys he felt cold, hard steel on the back of his neck and froze, rooted to the spot in fear. A voice came from behind him.

'Turn around, slowly.'

Frans Luca froze and watched as the muzzle of the silenced pistol moved from his neck to his stomach to mask it from passers-by. He was staring at the face of the man he'd followed. The man who looked like a spy stood out somehow, but he smiled begrudgingly and resigned himself to defeat.

'My name is Frans Luca,' he said nervously, 'I am a private detective. I have been following you.'

Frans Luca was definitely an eccentric and a local, however, one thing that Frans Luca wasn't was brave when staring down the barrel of a silenced pistol. With his back against the wall, Frans Luca explained further.

'There is a meeting of a powerful criminal gang in Germany tonight.'

Mark's face drew in as he felt his blood boil and his heartbeat increase.

'And why would I need YOU?' Mark growled as he pulled the hammer back on the revolver. Frans burst out into a sweat and began to shake.

'I know the location and the time?' he answered quickly and in a panic. Mark raised his eyebrows at him.

'How did you come across this information?'

Frans Luca trembled.

'I cannot say. I will accompany you there.'

Mark put the hammer back up on the gun and lowered it, concealing it in his jacket. He wanted the major players.

'I believe the head of this organisation is terrorist Mohammed Al Azidi.'

The name chilled Mark's blood, and he agreed to gather intelligence on the meeting, thinking he may find out where this shipment of weapons was going. Mark trusted Frans Luca, as no man will lie with a gun pointed at his head

'OK,' Mark relinquished, 'I am following a shipment of illegal weapons from London to Germany and I think Al Azidi is behind it.'

Frans nodded, and they discussed a plan together to get access to the meeting and gather information on who was who.

Mark's Quattro pulled up outside the alleyway adjoining the location Frans Luca had described during his interrogation, clad in his usual steel combat gear and carrying a two-piece custom AMP DSR-One sniper rifle in a leather carry case and his favourite A CZ Kadet suppressed hand gun with silencer. He also carried various throwing knives and a US Army Special Forces Combat Knife which he 'acquired' through Frans' various sources. He was ready and pulled a two way radio out of his side leg pocket and radioed for Frans.

'Hey buddy, you read me?'

There was no reply.

'Hey, where are you?'

The radio crackled but still no response. Mark was getting concerned and irritated.

'Hey! Where the hell are you!?'

After the third attempt, Frans replied which got Mark concerned but then, he was overweight and was probably rushing.

'Here, sorry.'

Mark gave a sigh of relief.

'Don't go silent on me like that again!' he scolded.

'Cover the vehicle!'

Mark got out and manually locked the car to prevent the 'bleep' from drawing attention to them. He found a drainpipe and silently climbed to the third-storey window. Once there, he tied a length of military issue rope to a retractable harness around his waist and then to a spike he shot into the wall with his grappling hook. He tied the rope onto his retractable harness and leaned himself into the window, releasing the safety off his silenced Kadet pistol in case he should encounter any problems. They were just in time as there seemed to be a large crowd of people on the ground floor. They were gathered as if waiting for someone.

The voices quickly died down as a solemn hush came over them. A figure appeared from behind a lorry and stood up on its bonnet to address the crowd.

'Azidi!' Mark thought and thought it so hard he suspected for a second that everyone down there would have heard him.

Mark steadied his rope and lowered himself down further so he could hear what Azidi would say. Azidi addressed the crowd.

'My brothers in arms, my loyal friends.'

Mark felt the grip on his 'Kadet' pistol tighten as he heard the evil monstrosity spout pure and unadulterated hatred but continued to listen.

'When our "delivery" arrives, we will take the streets of Berlin and seize control of the city and use it as a base to launch our jihad against the western infidels.'

If only Mark had a better grip, he could unhook his rifle and put a bullet between the eyes of that smarmy, slimy evil terrorist scumbag and put an end to his little party. But he had no quick escape and no sooner would he have let off the first bullet than the entire entourage would have turned their fully automatic weapons on him and turned him to sawdust. That would NOT serve well to honour Marie's memory, nor would it suitably delay any terrorist uprising. They would carry out their plan without their 'leader'. Mark listened intently to what Azidi was saying and took in every last word. As soon as could, he would put a bullet in Azidi for each wrong word he said against the free world, and more for the way he spoke to him in court.

At that moment, something strange happened; Azidi seemed to raise his hands in the air as if he was praying to Allah to the triumphant roar of the crowd.

'Kafir infidel! Qatalah, waqal 'annah sawf naerif ma abadiat al'alm!' (Bastard infidel! Kill him; he will know what an eternity of pain is!), he shouted, looking Mark right between the eyes.

The entire room turned to him. Their weapons quickly pointed at Mark as he heard what sounded like a thousand safety catches all being turned off at once. Mark's eyes quickly assessed the situation as he targeted who to shoot first; perhaps he could get two or three shots off at Azidi before being shot. Amid the confusion which ensued, Azidi had vanished. Mark popped off two shots into the crowd as suppressing fire to enable him to buy himself enough time to escape.

Bad guys flew everywhere and Mark winced as the sound of bullets ricocheting off the metal ceiling girders around him rang in his ears as he thought it was time to go. He grabbed his retractable harness buckle and kicked off from the wall he had his feet on. Within a second, he half leapt out of window and down the drainpipe to the car, a hail of gunfire ripped past him. Frans was nowhere to be seen and his car was unlocked. Suddenly police sirens filled the air and the flash of blue lights almost blinded him. Mark looked ahead and saw two police cars blocking his entrance. Mark turned to run, but yet more police blocked his path. He was cornered with NO way out. Looking desperately at his gun and the amount of armed Bundespolizei forcing him back, further and further back, he was out-gunned and out of ammunition. Glancing up, he realised, during the rush to get away, he had left his grappling hook and rifle up above the girder he had hold of, and only had his pistol as his defence. Mark King was completely surrounded. As a sea of Bundespolizei parted, a man walked through calmly and collectedly, wearing a long trench Crombie and black leather gloves. Mark put him as being in his late sixties to early seventies but still as commanding as he had been in his younger days. He spoke English well but with a heavy German accent Mark could only associate with a World War Two German Commandant of Colditz.

'Vell, I hate to break up zis little party but you really shouldn't run around spying on people viz such…' He looked at Mark's loaded and gripped pistol. '… Toys.'

This was Detlev Kastner, nicknamed 'The Wolf' by those who know him and fear him, the head of the German

Intelligence Service. His piercing blue eyes seemed to stare into Mark's mind and read every single thought he was thinking right now.

'Zere is...' Kastner said with a certain satisfaction and almost a laugh in his voice, 'no escape.'

Mark closed his eyes in defeat and frustration as the Bundespolizei relieved him of his weapon and cuffed him. One officer walked him past Kastner and the two men stared intently into each other's eyes before Kastner motioned for him to be taken away. Kastner paused and took in the sight in the alley way. Kastner spotted a face, peering from the shadows from behind a large industrial wheeled bin before it vanished. Kastner narrowed his eyes and did nothing to prevent the escape. Azidi was gone.

Chapter Twenty-One

Mark was tired and had sat in the interrogation room for hours without a cigarette. The injuries he sustained firstly from getting out barely alive from the third-floor window of the warehouse and secondly from the rough treatment of the Bundespolizei using cable-tie cuffs on him and then roughing him up before finally sitting him down in this interrogation room. He didn't feel fear, not with his legal experience, he was angry and his head hurt. The lights from above Mark made his eyes hurt, and he was sick of waiting to be seen. He was interrogated for hours by idiot Bundespolizei officers who knew little English and really didn't appreciate his sense of humour and continuous references to the Second World War. However, they did at least partially listen to his protests about a terrorist plot in Berlin.

Behind the two-way mirror stood Kastner, listening intently to the entire interview before taking a file and entering the interrogation room to sit in front of Mark. Kastner threw the file down on the steel table; Mark averted his eyes, sighed and looked directly at Kastner. Again those cold piercing blue eyes seemed to stare right through him.

'I find it difficult to believe your story vizout any evidence!' Kastner taunted.

The only evidence he had was that he caught Mark with a gun outside a warehouse which had been emptied by the time his men searched it and there were no weapons found.

'Ve checked out zis "ship". Ve found zere vas NO vecord of any shipment of any container ship due into Kiel-Holtenau zis veek at all.'

Mark couldn't believe what he was hearing. He had SEEN it, the paperwork in London, the shipment itself in the container, there was no way they could have diverted the ship at that late notice, was there? Mark's mind was going a million miles an hour, scarcely able to take in what he was hearing. He was furious now. Not only that he had been careless enough to get caught, but it seemed he had come all this way for nothing. Now under the authority of the German Intelligence Service and looking at a prison sentence in a German prison, he thought about the only real outcome.

'Game over,' he thought.

That was it. He would serve his time and come out with no way of getting home and nothing really achieved. Kastner was still starting at him and didn't flinch at Mark's angry outburst.

'It's true! Let me take you there!'

Kastner smiled, knowing the more this man got angry, the more it would prove his point, that he was dangerous. Kastner explained.

'It vas strange zat ve found none of your fingerprints or any information at all on you, Mr Gveen.'

Mark's throat was dry and hoarse and he was REALLY hoping for a cigarette. Kastner got up and left the room, leaving Mark alone. It was a good hour before he came back.

'It zeems, Mr Gveen,' Kastner announced as he closed the interrogation room door and sat down in front of Mark, crossed legged and flicked through the police report.

'...Zat due to ze lack of evidence of anything suspicious going on in Germany, (and I vould know in my position), zat I can only serve a caution on you for firearms offences.'

Mark felt a rush of relief, and it showed.

'BUT, if you vould be prepared to be escorted to ze airport and put on ze next flight back to London, ve vill drop all ze charges against you.'

Mark thought although this decision was a little odd, he had no choice but to accept. He nodded reluctantly and Kastner stared at him intently. He knew something wasn't right, but he couldn't prove it and had to let his suspect go, at least to put him under surveillance until he left the country.

It was another hour before Mark was released. He exited the headquarters between two security service guards. Kastner pointed at the guards.

'Zey vill escort you to your hotel vhere you are to vash up and collect your belongings before being escorted to ze nearest airport and flown directly back to London.'

Before Kastner turned to return inside, an adjutant hurried up to him and passed him a file.

'Sir, you are letting him go? You know who he is?'

Kastner didn't want to release a prisoner, but Simms frustrated him by challenging his authority.

'Yes zank you Simms, I am very avare of Mr Mark King.'

Outside it was mid-afternoon and Mark had been there for the best part of twenty-four hours. He looked at his watch and realised that the container ship was due in to Kiel-Holtenau port later today. Mark cursed aloud in English, prompting one guard to usher him forwards with a sharp dig to the shoulder. He remembered what Kastner had said about being no record of that ship, or any other vessel, arriving this week into Holtenau. Mark spotted the security service four-by-four parked opposite with two suited German security officials seated in the front. He made it obvious he had seen them but they didn't respond.

'What a joke!' he remarked and whistled the 'Great Escape' theme as he got into the waiting police car.

Throughout the journey back to his hotel, his mind was sharp and going a hundred miles an hour. Could he use an escape route at the hotel? Was it possible he could roll out of the car and get up and run? He slyly tried the handle on the car, but it had been locked. One guard noticed and smiled, shaking his head in wry disgust that their prisoner really thought they were THAT stupid. He had purposefully chosen a room with a window in the bathroom and the first night he was there, he had tied thirty feet of black military grade rope to the outside drainpipe and down to the ground below. If required, he would have to use that.

Mark received confused looks from the concierge as he was led into the hotel lobby, flanked by two armed Bundespolizei, who just stared at him. He walked over to the desk and advised he would check out immediately. He paid, and they handed him his passport and he advised them he would return the key to them on the way out. The concierge looked nervously at him while bobbing his head in agreement.

'Mr Green, is everything OK?'

'Oh yes!' Mark joked, 'just my private security detail. I'm actually a celebrity in the UK!'

Joke though it was, Mark left there firmly under the impression that the poor concierge believed his story. Mark thought to himself, smiling, 'This will be useful!'

Up at the room, Mark slid his passkey into his room door lock and turned the handle the second he heard the click. He glanced at his watch again and wondered where the container ship could be headed if not here. He gathered his things and took his bag into the bathroom after changing into a fresh pair of black combat-style trousers. Luckily he had spares of most things so had slipped his harness belt on unnoticed by the guards. He advised them, in German, he was taking his bag into the bathroom to load up his toiletries. One guard nodded and Mark made the excuse he needed the toilet due to bad food the night before. Not wanting to follow him and be subjected to this, the guards sat down outside the bathroom door. Mark locked the door and opened the window. He felt for the end of the rope and clipped the buckle to his harness belt. He slung his bag over both shoulders and stepped out of the window onto the ledge. Sliding the window shut quietly, he looked down to see if anyone was below. It was clear, so he began his quick but careful descent down to the ground below. Once his feet were on the ground, he knew he would have roughly five minutes before the guards noticed he was not responding to the shouts he could already hear and from above. He unclipped the rope, tightened the handles on his bag and jogged away through the café/restaurant section and through the lobby. On his way past, he slid the room card onto the finely polished reception desk, and winked at the young female receptionist sat next to the concierge he had spoken to on the way in. Mark noticed the concierge, who he had immediately thought was gay and fancied him, winked back thinking it was he who had been winked at as Mark was already out of the door and along the street to a taxi rank he spotted on the way in. His taxi took him past the main reception doors just in time to see the police questioning reception. His cover had been blown, and he turned his head away so he wouldn't be noticed.

Mark was relieved to find his hire car still parked up where he had left it. Although covered in police tape and notices in German which read 'Police aware, awaiting collection', he was glad it was still there. As he ripped it off, he felt along the underside of the chrome running board for the spare key he had duct taped. He breathed a sigh of relief as his hand rested against the key. He jumped in and started the engine. He noticed that something was rolling around the passenger foot-well and, upon inspection, noticed it was a receipt and Frans' mobile phone. He opened the phone, and it clicked into life; he also picked up the receipt and read it. It was for a hotel between here and Bremerhaven, 269 km west of Kiel-Holtenau. He grabbed the bag from behind the driver's seat and got out his map.

'Why Bremerhaven?' he said to himself. 'What significance does that have for Frans?'

He didn't know but when he looked at the map and information he collected on all major ports in Germany, he read:

'Bremerhaven is located at the mouth of the River Weser on its eastern bank, opposite the town of Nordenham. Though a relatively new city, it has a long history as a trade port and today is one of the most important German ports, playing a crucial role in Germany's trade.'

'Bingo!' Mark said aloud.

If the ship wasn't due in Holtenau, it MUST be en route to Bremerhaven. He did a quick calculation; it would take just under four hours by sea but just under three by road. He would still have time to stop at the hotel listed on the receipt. That MUST be where Frans was holed up. The problem was, whoever was now after Mark was intelligent enough to figure it out sooner or later; if Frans was clumsy enough to leave his receipt in the car, what other mistakes had he made? Mark prayed he had been more discreet and put his foot to the floor as he sped off towards the autobahn, determined to smack Frans in the face for leaving him and keeping something from him. Mark checked the driver door panel for his cigarettes and ignored the no smoking signs in the car as he felt that satisfying feeling of nicotine at the back of his throat. He hadn't realised how much he missed it when he was living with Marie who, despite being as much of a cigarette lover as he was at university, got all health conscious after Hope had been born. Hope: he felt bad he had thought little about his children these last few days.

Mark stared at the road ahead, heavy thoughts running through his mind. He stuck to the back roads as news of his escape from the hotel would, by now, have reached Kastner, whose revenge would be swift and ruthless. He was now a fugitive on the run and they would try to stop him at all costs. He wasn't worried about Kastner right now; his mind was on getting the truth out of Frans before it was too late and finding out what else he knew. He stopped for food and fuel, being careful not to use a card or visit any location where his presence would be on CCTV. He thought a skirt around Hamburg would cause him to be recognised or stopped, so he stuck to the smaller, single-manned fuel stations and garages as he found them. Mark also stocked up on cigarettes and plenty of food so he would require fewer provisions later on and would be less traceable. His mind wandered back through the past few weeks. It amazed him how quickly life as he knew it had changed. He worried about the children and their safety. As far as anyone knew, he didn't have ties to New York so they would not think to look for them there to use them as leverage or harm them as punishment against him.

He dismissed this thought as it caused him too much pain, instead, focussing on what that shipment of arms meant for Germany. He knew Azidi seemed to run a sleeper cell out of Germany and would inevitably need this shipment to carry out his plan. Mark's choice as he saw it was simple; take out the shipment, or wait until he was has present and eliminate both Azidi and the weapons together. He didn't know which one was the best idea, only that the first one risked the shipment being used by a substitute cell if he didn't take the cell out himself. He couldn't allow anyone to leave alive or they would start up again somewhere else. Also Mark didn't want to risk starting a war with a terrorist group that would bring death to him and his family. No, this had to be done quietly. Kastner now knew of the plot; whether he believed what Mark had said or not, Mark would not take any chances so opted for taking out Azidi AND the shipment in one.

This plan, however, involved the biggest risk and was logistically problematic. He still had weapons and Azidi didn't know who he was. There must also be a bigger plan here, it cannot just be a small independent terror cell at work, and they always work from a higher authority. So who was it, al-Qaeda, ISIS, an independent terror cell or something even more sinister, an organisation? It had to be. These people were equipped with heavy fire and intelligence, resources small terror cells wouldn't have or be able to fund. So, a new mission faced Mark; uncover who is at the top and do everything to stop them. It was becoming clear to Mark now that the pieces could fit together: the Azidi case, Marie's death, Hix and Roman Vose, the weapon's shipment and the attempts on his life. But where did Frans fit into all this? Was he an informant sent to keep Mark from getting to the truth by distracting him from the REAL issue?

Mark's car rolled into the parking space outside the entrance to the seedy looking 'Happy Hotel' half an hour's drive from Bremerhaven. He looked again at the receipt he had found in his car prior to leaving Holtenau and his eyes felt heavy. He hadn't slept in nearly two days and was feeling it now. He locked up the car and walked towards what appeared to be a reception. He could hear loud music and screams from the various open windows adjacent to the carpark. It was a two-storey motel, and it looked every inch like something out of a *Criminal Minds* episode. Exactly the spot Frans would hide out in. He wasn't very bright but on this occasion, Mark would have chosen similar. Somewhere that accepted cash didn't ask questions and definitely didn't report its guests to local law enforcement. He glared at the spotty looking teenager reading his *2000AD* comic and watched as he shouted at guests down the hallway from reception. Mark took his notes out of his pocket, ready, and asked which room Frans Luca was staying in.

'I'm looking for my friend; I think he may be staying here. A short, fat guy, looking nervous?'

The kid behind reception shook his head.

'No, not heard of him,' he said, glancing around the room nervously.

Mark had realised he wouldn't use his real name to check in so described him, making sure the kid saw the wad of notes Mark had hold of. Suddenly the boy seemed to regain his memory.

'Room two-zero-one, down the hall,' the kid said, pointing down the hallway. Mark smacked the notes into the boy's hand and flashed him his gun from inside his jacket.

'Hey kid,' he said as the kid went back to his comic. He looked up again quickly at Mark. 'RUN if you want to live!'

The boy's face went white, and he looked in horror at Mark before he obliged and took off back down the hall, back to his comic. Mark smiled wryly and gently turned the door handle of room 201. It was locked, just has he had expected. He pulled a pick lock device from his left knee-level pocket and easily and quietly picked the lock. He moved inside, weapon drawn, and stealthily moved around the darkened room. The bed was unmade and there was a cup of coffee on the bedside table. Mark waved his hand over it; it was still hot so Frans seemed to have been expecting company. He moved back towards the door and noticed a shoe behind the floor length curtain of the window in the small reflection of the mirror hung on the wall. Mark turned and inched over towards the window. He gauged where the head of this person hiding behind the curtain would be, held the muzzle of the gun against what he presumed to be the head, cocked it loudly and shouted for Frans Luca. The curtain moved and Frans reluctantly stepped out from behind his rather obvious hiding place. Relieved to see it was Mark, he put his hand on his shoulder and breathed a sigh of relief. Mark grabbed him by the scruff of his collar and threw him onto the bed. He walked round the bed and turned on the bedside lamp. Frans lay there, a look of sheer terror on his face. Mark aimed the gun down at Frans' crotch.

'Start from the beginning and tell me everything you know about Mohammed Al Azidi and the weapons cache.'

Frans Luca gulped, smiled helplessly and nodded.

Chapter Twenty-Two

Frans Luca checked into the City Hotel, Bremerhaven as Alfred Monet, a stockbroker from Berlin, and made sure the concierge knew his cover story, just like Mark had suggested. He requested a room at the centre of the hotel and paid cash. The concierge smiled and passed him a pass key. Shaking slightly, Frans took it and made his way towards the lift and up into the room. Once there, he checked for the inside window Mark had told him to find, and tied the trusty black military grade rope to the outside of the window, onto a rather old-fashioned looking satellite dish bracket, and left the window open. Moments later he heard the sound of boots against the window sill and realised that would be Mark. He stood there looking sheepish and ashamed at having lied to Mark and running the way he did without warning and being responsible for Mark's capture and subsequent run in with 'The Wolf'. Frans looked at Mark, hoping to be forgiven but, to his dismay, Mark was NOT in a forgiving mood. Mark walked past Frans and threw his equipment onto the bed.

If anyone tried to look for Frans here, they would be met with stiff resistance and the element of surprise once again belonged to Mark King. Just the way Mark liked it. Mark took out of his bag the various pieces he salvaged which made up his two-piece custom AMP DSR-One sniper rifle he retrieved before reacquiring his hire car, plus copious amounts of hollow point and armour piercing ammunition. He wasn't taking any chances here, especially if 'The Wolf' caught up with him which was virtually inevitable. He also, from his sock holster, took out his Kadet US issue army knife, at which Frans' eyes widened. On the way to locate Frans, Mark had made an unofficial stop off and a closed military surplus supplies store and 'borrowed' some equipment which he had the genuine intention of returning once used. He left no trace of a break-in. From under his jacket, he produced his silenced pistol with separate suppressor and again, copious amounts of ammunition. Frans looked horrified at Mark and made a comment in German.

'I don't want to know where you got all this from and the less I know the better.'

Mark turned on him in a second, whipping the knife from the bed and under Frans' throat. Frans got the hint and backed off, muttering to himself, forgetting that Mark spoke German and understood it.

Setting the map out on the bed, Mark pulled a red marker from his pocket and circled Bremerhaven container port. It was just a short drive from where they were staying and Mark had no intention of leaving ANY trace this time or missing a target, especially one like Azidi. He sat down and beckoned for Frans to make coffee. Frans did as he was asked and soon the two of them were sitting, drinking coffee and discussing the best assault pattern for the container port. It was much the same as the one in London, only on a much grander scale, so Mark had to REALLY cover all his angles to gain entry, hit his target and get out again with minimal effort, maximum effect. Also he didn't want to decimate the place like London either. He wanted a silent, effective kill that would send a message that Mark, now involved, was a force to be reckoned with and not to be underestimated. Frans was to provide Mark access, in and out again without too much of a problem. They both sat back and sipped at their third round of coffee and Mark noticed that Frans was shaking.

Frans had told Mark everything, about Kastner's suspected involvement, that Frans was employed as a distraction for Mark and that, because he had led him to the warehouse in Holtenau, his card had been marked. Mark could see the poor man was terrified and softened up on him, letting his anger go. Seeing a man so shaken and desperate made Mark feel sorry for him rather than angry. Mark got up to find his cigarettes and patted Frans on the shoulder to comfort him. Frans put his hand on Mark's which, although it made Mark a tad uncomfortable, also reinforced how scared Frans was.

'I don't want to die. I only wanted this whole awful sorry affair over with so I could go on living my life in peace and quiet.'

Mark related to that and told Frans about his history. Mark checked his watch and realised the ship would have docked by now but, according to the arrivals and departures conveniently published on the web, no ships were due to leave until the morning. They had time to kill and Mark needed to relax and unwind before the hell storm erupted all over this man, this Thomas Lundon, Frans had told him so much about. Mark had done his homework on him already and Frans Luca had filled in the blanks. According to Frans, it was HE who may have orchestrated Marie's death and Mark's professional and personal demise. It had to end and Mark would end it; here, in Germany. Mark handed Frans a tumbler of the strongest whiskey he could find on the market on his way to the Happy Motel.

'Here, drink this. It will calm your nerves.'

Frans gulped it back and seemed to relax a little. Mark poured him another one and explained all that had gone on from the beginning.

By the time Mark had finished, Frans was blubbering like a baby and blew his nose on the corner of the bedsheet. Mark winced in disgust so he got up to polish his rifle and load it. Before he knew where he was, Frans had got up from his chair and was hugging him, squeezing him until Mark coughed. Mark didn't quite know how to handle this so nervously patted him on the back while Frans cried into his flak jacket. This man was no spy! He was a normal person with emotions that had been in the wrong place at the wrong time and he didn't deserve this.

'I promise you I will help you.'

It only made Frans cry more and thank him repeatedly.

'You are a good man, Mark.'

Mark looked uncomfortable with this and almost forcibly put Frans back in his chair. Mark looked at his watch again.

'We'll attack at three, during security details shift change when they are at their most vulnerable. We'd better get some sleep.'

Mark opted for the sofa whilst Frans got the bed. It wasn't the most ideal setup but there was little choice.

Mark moved to the window for a cigarette. He stared out and the Germany skyline as little lights came on in each building. He thought back to his honeymoon when he had done the same thing as he quickly smoked his cigarette. He missed Marie more than he had realised at that moment, but then he hadn't stopped to think about it before, so much else had gone on. He heard a noise behind him and thought he saw a woman in white walking towards him with outstretched arms. It couldn't be Marie? She was getting closer and all he could do was hold his arms out to her. Mark surveyed her body and saw she was bleeding. Within a second she was bleeding from multiple bullet wounds all over her body and her face conveyed signs of pain and desperation. Just as she came within arm's reach, she vanished and he awoke with a start, loading his gun and pointing it round the room. The room was black, and he had fallen asleep after finishing his cigarette. He quickly surveyed the room and realised he was dreaming and let out a long breath as if he had been holding it for ages. He checked his watch: two-twenty AM. He strode over to the bed and shook Frans, who was snoring and had an eye mask on. He jumped him and rolled off the bed, creating a loud bang on the floor. He jumped up confused and scared, shouting something about being blind. Mark laughed to himself; at least it was a sign they were both alert. It was time to prepare for the onslaught.

The lights of the tall cranes nestled against the quayside flashed in the darkness as muffled noises of containers moving and workers shouting to each other echoed to where Mark and Frans were perched. Due to his rather portly figure, it took a while to get Frans up and onto the vantage point overlooking the quayside. A large container ship was moored and its huge ropes pulled tightly as the slight movement of the water rocked the ship gently. It was piled high in places and not in others as a yellow dock crane busily removed the containers. Mark thought to himself that, as they were lead-lined, it wouldn't be advisable to get stuck in one of those. He peered through his night vision binoculars down to a group of people stood at the bottom of a set of steel stairs which led to the port authority offices.

'What can you see?' he asked nervously.

Mark could see Roman Vose in his leather jacket, sub-machine gun slung over his shoulder like a sentry at a prison camp. Next to him stood Azidi and what looked like bodyguards, followed by a Japanese man in a suit and long hair. He looked like the buyer and Mark relayed this back to Frans.

'A "business deal" no doubt. These people are into all sorts.'

Mark nodded and surveyed the rest of the dockside for security personnel. He saw eight or ten security guards all wandering about. This was a high profile meeting and carried high profile security measures.

'Contractors,' whispered Mark in a hushed voice. 'Ten, max.'

He could feel Frans' breath quicken and his hands shaking as he passed Mark his rifle. Something about this didn't feel right but Mark couldn't quite put his finger on it. He was on edge and he didn't feel like this in London. Used to trusting his gut, particularly in court, Mark didn't entirely dismiss this emotion, but he pushed it to the back of his mind, as he needed clear focus to get the job done. He COULD take them out from here, but he wouldn't be able to vouch for the weapons cache. THAT was as important as his target. He had to get closer to find out which container it was in. He spotted the crane operator and realised that he would have an itinerary in that cab and Mark needed to see it.

'Stay here where you can't be seen,' he said to Frans, who nodded nervously.

Mark hopped down, moving his way expertly through the shadows. He passed within feet of several guards and his first thought was to take them out with his knife, but nobody would die that didn't need to die, that was his promise to himself. If his life was threatened, he would defend himself, but he could get to the crane without killing anyone. He made his move across the dockside and into the shadow of the ship. He hoisted himself up the mooring rope and onto the deck, where he moved along unnoticed until he got to the mooring rope at the other end of the ship. He slid down the rope to the foot of the crane and shimmied up the ladder to the cab. Just as the crane moved, swinging a container against another, he made his move.

Mark quickly jumped the crane operator from behind, hand over his mouth so he couldn't scream, and hit him over the back of the head with the butt of his pistol. The guard fell limply into Mark's arms and he laid him down checking his pulse. He was still alive and would wake up tomorrow morning with an almighty headache. So far, all was going according to plan. Just as Mark had predicted and prayed for, there was an A4 paper printed and stapled itinerary with all the containers listed in their number order. Mark took out his night vision binoculars again and scanned the ship and the dockside. He read aloud in a hushed voice,

'Containers are numbered throughout fore to aft with odd numbers, i.e. in this case 01, 03, 05 and so on up to 75. The bay spaces for 40' containers are numbered throughout with even numbers: 02, 04, and 06, up to 74.'

Mark scanned the pages and found another set of instructions.

'The purple 20' container in the first bay has the bay number 01. The light-brown 20' container in the second bay has the bay number 03 and the light-blue 40' container, which occupies a space in the first and second bays, has the bay number 02. The magenta-coloured container has the bay number 25, the dark-green number 27 and the light-green number 26.'

Mark thought for a moment. If there were seventy-five containers in the itinerary, and they were numbered one, three, and five, up to seventy-five, why was the one to Mark's left in his line of sight marked seventy-six? It was an inconspicuous container which didn't really stand out from the others apart from the fact it had the wrong number on it. Mark realised he had found it, and upon closer inspection with his binoculars, recognised it as the same one he had encountered in London. He smiled to himself, had a quick check of what was going on below and spotted Roman Vose below waving incessantly at the crane cab. He could make out something about being quicker before the radio the crane driver was carrying in his belt crackled into life.

'Be quick, we have a deadline!'

Mark picked up the radio.

'Roger, ten-four,' he replied in his best low, deep voice.

After getting familiar with the mechanism, he loaded a few more containers onto the dockside before he came to the one he wanted. He set the control console in the cab to automatic and climbed out of the cab and down the ladder, pausing periodically to check for Roman Vose and any guards. They had gone.

'Shift change,' whispered Mark, 'at last!'

On the way down, the crane had lowered the container just enough to reach. He jumped, placing plastic explosives in the tubing which bolted containers to one another when stacked, and quickly hurried away.

Once on the ground, Mark made his way back to his original position where a very nervous Frans was waiting eagerly for his return. Mark got behind his rifle and did a sweep of the dockside. The new guards were now on duty and making their way towards patrolling the dockside to take over from their colleagues. He had his sights firmly trained on the metal staircase which led to the port authority offices which were two cabins stacked on top of one another. He held the detonator in his hand ready and informed Frans about what it was and how to use it. Then he waited, picking his moment carefully.

He looked for Roman Vose but lost sight of him; presumably he was away at his car calling his boss to provide an update, all the more reason to get on with it. He found the tranquillisers in his hip holster and loaded his pistol with them, with that he jumped a passing guard who was blissfully unaware of their presence eight feet below them, and shot him in the neck. He quickly dropped to the ground and Mark dragged him away. Mark then grabbed his cap, so that silhouetted against the night and the ship, he looked like he belonged. Each guard he came up against nodded to him without realising he was not one of theirs, and Mark quickly dispatched them with the tranquilisers one after another, dragging their unconscious bodies to a convenient hiding place: four down, six to go. He would have to use his hands as he was low on tranquilisers. This would involve a more cunning plan. He tiptoed up behind a guard and, arm around his neck, knocked him unconscious with a whack of his pistol butt. He had to move quick before the remaining guards realised some of their number were missing. He jogged silently towards the port authority cabin and hid underneath the window and listened in. From what he could see, they were discussing target designation.

'Great,' he whispered to himself, 'now I have multiple targets to take out!'

He counted six Arabic voices in total and pieced together that these were Azidi's men. He wouldn't lose sleep over taking them out, but at a distance, it was much safer. He repeated the mantra he had been taught at Sandhurst.

'Never put yourself at unnecessary risk in a combat situation.'

Those words echoed at him from a visiting SAS major after whom he named his two children. He ran back to his rifle where Frans was, by this time, white with nerves.

Frans looked concernedly at Mark.

'You seem never to be bothered by who you kill,' he said coldly.

Mark looked puzzled.

'Who have I killed so far tonight?'

In Frans Luca's lack of combat experience, he really wasn't sure who was dead and who wasn't until Mark reassured him.

'No one's dead so far, just unconscious.'

Frans relaxed more. Suddenly, noises came from the port authority office. Something was wrong so Mark lined up his sights. He caught two of Azidi's soldiers with one shot, clean through before the pandemonium set in. People were running about all over the place and Roman Vose's voice rang out before vanishing between the rows of stacked containers. Mark fired off another few shots which took out another of Azidi's associates and narrowly missed Azidi himself. Mark slapped the floor in frustration and his hand stung. He would deal with the pain later. Sweeping the dockside with his rifle, he lined up another Azidi associate in his sights, this time on the run. The rifle recoiled, and the target fell, blood spatter still flying. Mark was already on his next target and he too dropped to the floor dead. That was it, there was one more: Azidi himself. But he couldn't find him so took his rifle on the run. Mark ran through the maze of containers until he spied a shadow. He looked up and realised he could get the drop on this target from above so scaled the containers, inching along the edge of the overhang, unhooking his rifle. He took aim, steadied himself for the recoil and fired. Mark's hollow point grazed Azidi's shoulder, and he hit the side of the container he was hiding behind from the impact of the bullet. He shouted insults at Mark in Arabic and Mark gritted his teeth and managed a wry smile.

'A piece at a time, scumbag,' he shouted to Azidi, before moving quickly to the ground.

He flew against a container as a hail of semi-automatic weapon fire ricocheted all around the containers surrounding him. He was panting at the shock of such fire and held his ground flat against a container until he heard the click of a reload. He was round the corner in a flash, sending off two, then three shots before running towards the shooter. As he rounded the corner, he caught sight of his target trying to reload his sub-machine gun. It wasn't Azidi this time but a surviving shooter. It all seemed to happen in slow motion as both men lifted their weapons at once. Mark slowed his breathing right down and felt his heart slow. He breathed out narrowly through his lips and his finger pulled back on the trigger.

As he did so, bullets flew towards Mark, but to no avail; Mark was already on the fly and forward-rolled out of the way as the shooter flew backwards, taking a bullet to the chest and hitting the ground with a thud. Mark found his feet and ran towards his target, who was still alive.

'For Marie,' he said as he pointed his pistol towards the forehead of the shooter.

He replied something in Arabic and spat blood at Mark. Mark smiled and pulled the trigger, killing the shooter instantly. Voices behind Mark made him regain his bearings, and he moved quickly toward the voices, grabbing the shooter's sub-machine gun as he did so. Now he was fully armed, and the gun had a full magazine, ready to go. Mark ran, firing the sub-machine gun toward the voices, and heard the screams as the bullets bounced off the lead-lined containers and hit their targets somewhere.

'Fluke, sorry about that!' Mark shouted, laughing as he ran.

He was almost enjoying this. In fact, he was enjoying it so much that he didn't see the back of Azidi as he ran straight into him. Both men fell to the ground, but Azidi was first to his feet. Mark heard his rifle drop behind him and stared coldly into the eyes of Azidi who was now stood over him laughing.

'Stupid infidel!' Azidi taunted, but Mark was already working on plan B.

As Azidi dropped his gun and pulled an equally terrifying knife from his belt, the blade glinting in the floodlights of the container yard, Mark felt his hand on his silenced pistol, whipping it out in front of him before Azidi could bring down the knife into Mark's chest. He fired four or five shots into the chest, neck and head of Azidi and rolled out the way just in time for Azidi to crash face down onto where Mark lay seconds before.

'Stupid terrorist!' he remarked angrily.

Surveying his surroundings, Mark realised the noise had subsided, and it seemed everyone was dead, or unconscious. He staggered back to his look out point where Frans Luca was lying flat on his fat belly to avoid stray bullets. Mark patted him on the back as he sat, rested his weapons and examined his injured leg. It wasn't a bullet, but it was a bad cut, from the sharp edge of the side of a container he fell against. He didn't notice the pain while he was running, but when it all calmed down, he felt the sharp sting as he tried to put weight on it. Frans, upon noticing Mark had been injured, ripped off a sleeve from his shirt and tied it tight around Mark's wound. Mark looked appreciatively at Frans whilst trying to get his breath back. Mark smiled as he reached for his detonator to blow the container. He clicked it but nothing happened. He clicked it again and again but still no explosion came. Mark examined it and realised he had damaged it during the fire fight. Frans put his hand reassuringly on Mark's shoulder and picked up a spare explosive and detonator.

Mark went to get up but Frans prevented him from doing so because of his injury. Instead, Frans climbed down the ladder, and made his way over to the container to place the explosives on it. He got there and threw it in where the first one had been placed. He turned to Mark who was, by now on his feet on top of his vantage point smiling at Frans. Just as Frans was making his way back to Mark, smiling and rubbing his hands together, a single shot rang out from the darkness and Frans fell to the floor, his face confused and contorted. Mark's face dropped as he dashed down to where he could see Frans lying dead on the dockside, bleeding from a head wound from a sniper rifle. Mark pulled up his weapon and fired it at every point he could assume a shot would have come from. The ping of bullets against metal rang out along with a single, familiar voice.

'See now, Mr King, you have messed in the affairs of our organisation for too long now and my boss wants me to kill you!' Vose's voice echoed up at him.

Mark turned his rifle towards the voice and fired off three shots in that direction.

'VOSE!!!!!!!' he yelled. He heard the voice curse in pain and all fell silent.

Mark fell on the lifeless and bloodied body of Frans Luca and cradled him in his arms, heartbroken at the fact he couldn't protect him like he promised he would. Angrily and reluctantly, Mark realised he had to go, so shouldered Frans' body as much as his already depleting strength would allow him, and placed him between two containers. He staggered up and pressed the detonator. The hanging container exploded with a burst that went skywards, and the explosion repeated as the ammunition inside the container ignited. Mark staggered off back to where he and Frans had parked the car and looked back mournfully at the container yard. Vose just made it to the top of Mark's hit list, and he would not stop until Frans Luca's death was avenged.

Chapter Twenty-Three

Back in the UK, Mark pored over the maps he had laid out on his table whilst sipping gently at his twelve-year-old malt. As he drew in the satisfying nicotine, his eyes levelled on something he had not spotted before. If Roman Vose made it to Bremerhaven before he got there, surely he would have needed transport and a route to and from Bremerhaven container port. Perhaps the CCTV may hold clues. He sat down and spun his leather wheeled office recliner over to where his many computer terminal monitors were, and typed furiously to get up the CCTV for that area. Before he was killed, Frans Luca had provided Mark with vital information concerning the terrorist's movements and, now they were all dead, he had virtually no way of tracking them. He paused as he thought about his friend Frans Luca and how he needlessly died trying to help him. He had been cruel to him initially but, from his position, it looked like he had been betrayed before he found out the truth.

Mark deeply regretted Frans' death and everything that had led up to it but now was not the time to mourn for those who had fallen. Mark shouldered this grief privately and had spent the last week berating and chastising himself for letting Frans die. At least his family were safe. He had buried this grief deep inside because that was the only way to survive and it had kept him alive this far.

His thoughts inevitably turned to Marie and what she would have made of running around killing people. She would have been mad at him for taking revenge but, as time went on, he remembered less and less about what life felt like before all this started. And he wasn't finished yet. He had more to do, a lot more. Someone had ordered Azidi to carry out this attack and used Roman Vose, authorised Frans Luca's death and Marie's death, although it occurred to Mark that everyone he seemed to get close to in this, ended up dead. His thoughts drew back to tracing Roman Vose and the screens in front of him which were now loaded with information. He knew he had hacked the FBI and CIA files, assuming that Roman Vose's accent was transatlantic. Thinking he may find something from the FBI, he decided that was a good starting point. He wasn't a hacker and had only used what Frans had told him about on the way from Holtenau to Bremerhaven.

Mark knew he only had a matter of minutes before the FBI and CIA hackers shut down his connection and was relieved it couldn't be traced to his location even with their superior devices as it belonged to the military and, even though the UK and the US were allies, they were still abiding by an agreement NOT to hack each other's systems. Screenshotting everything he found, his large printer clicked into life behind him, automatically printing out everything he had screenshot. He slid over to the printer in his chair and grabbed the freshly printed files. Mark couldn't believe his luck when Roman Vose's face was on the top page.

Roman Vose was an ex-CIA assassin, which explained his skills and technical talent with a sniper rifle. Mark closed his eyes in horror as he remembered that fatal shot which killed Frans Luca. Vose's profile read like a hitman 101 instruction manual, showing he had taken part in operations in Afghanistan, Bosnia, Ireland, Istanbul, and, more recently, Syria, although Mark wondered, knowing the current situation in Syria with ISIS or Daesh or whatever they wanted to call themselves, which side Roman Vose was on, or even if he HAD a side. Vose had also been on many bodyguard details but then Mark noticed there was a blank in the dates with sketchy information about Vose being headed to Russia, then back to the US where he seemed to resume his duties under the CIA. Secondment perhaps, Mark couldn't tell, but he had a feeling Vose had defected to Russia and was working with the Russians AND the US, playing one off against the other. This was a long time ago, and he soon found correspondence which showed that Vose had either left the CIA or had been 'burned'.

Mark thought for a few minutes before concluding that he was 'burned' but, with his skills, had evaded burning and had killed those sent to kill him. He sat back in his chair and stared at his 'most wanted' wall. He got up and removed Azidi from the wall, moving him to the bottom of the list and, using a red permanent marker, drew a red cross all the way through Azidi's face. In his place, he moved Roman Vose's image, which had been third on the list until today. He stood there for a while, finishing his cigarette, just staring at the faces of those who remained and those who he had taken out. What bothered him the most, he thought as he turned to his giant white board and drew a brainstorming spider diagram, was if these were all the 'little guys', who was the guy at the top and why did he feel it necessary to authorise Marie's murder. Frans Luca he could almost understand, as it was Frans who turned against them to help Mark locate the shipment of weapons, so in their eyes, that was a betrayal, but Marie was never involved in anything like this and was merely an innocent victim. He HAD to find out who was responsible and figured that Roman Vose was the ticket to this. To get to the guy at the top, he needed to locate Vose and make him talk, if he could. Mark grabbed the TV remote and nonchalantly pressed 'standby' to turn it back on. Sky News came up with Jeremy Thompson reading the headlines. Mark's eyes widened. News was breaking of a terrorist plot in Germany where the arms deal had gone wrong and there was a shootout between the 'seller' and the 'buyer'. Mark turned up the volume and leant forward, reaching for another cigarette. He relaxed in his chair and smiled.

Thomas Lundon threw the remote across the room after watching the Sky News report about the alleged terrorist arms deal gone wrong. He shouted and gestured at a sorry-looking Roman Vose sat in a leather chair opposite him in the study. Vose had a black eye and several bandages and scars. He was also limping again and seemed to have bruised ribs.

'Please boss, let me kill this guy! It wasn't my fault; he turned up out of nowhere, like a ghost!' he pleaded, realising it was now about self-preservation.

Much as Vose respected Mark King, he knew deep down, when it came down to it, it was kill or be killed. Thomas Lundon was red in the face and making his way angrily over to where Vose was sitting.

'He must have had an army with him to cause that much damage,' pleaded Vose, trying to make excuses as to his obvious failure.

'You came with recommendations, Vose. Idiot! You had to KILL Luca!' Vose looked at the ground shamefully. 'He was a very important source of information! And you let King get away!'

Lundon's blood pressure was rising and Vose was scared. Now King had gone to ground again, it was, again, impossible to locate him.

'It's NOT good enough!'

Vose was terrified. He held his head, nursing his relenting headache which had not gone away since he arrived at the villa later on in the day in which Mark King blew up their arms shipment.

Thomas Lundon strode around his study and out into the highly decorated hallway which led to his private spa. Roman Vose nervously followed as Lundon touched each of the huge oil paintings which lined the hallway which led to the marble reception area of his private villa. A maid approached Lundon with warm towels and a dressing gown which he took and dismissed her instantly, showing his irritation at everything around him.

'My "brothers" in my youth formed this organisation, along with those who had been members and are members still, with one sole purpose: the organisation of control. Since before you were born.' Lundon stopped when he reached a gap in the paintings. 'This is where MY painting will hang one day.'

Vose gulped, feeling sure he would be shot or killed in some psychopathic and torturous way for having failed his boss so miserably. There was no end to Lundon's anger and frustration as he screamed again at Vose and anyone else who would listen.

'We will NOT be INTIMIDATED BY MARK KING!' Vose limped behind Lundon again as Lundon spun on him. 'What are we supposed to do now, Vose? WHAT?!'

Vose just stared helplessly at Lundon, who was getting more and redder in the face. He calmed for a second, getting his breath before he pressed a buzzer on the wall and his private doctor came running, taking him by the arm and warning him about his blood pressure and heart rate. Lundon pushed the doctor away from trying to steady him and cursed him too. He turned on Roman Vose again.

'You have ONE last chance to locate and eliminate Mark King or this time, YOU will be the one eliminated!'

Vose's face went white as he knew his boss would carry out his threat. Lundon was escorted away by his doctor as Roman Vose was left in the hallway with his thoughts. He was ashamed. He was deeply ashamed because he had never failed on a hit until he met Mark King.

Roman Vose wandered up and down the halls of the gigantic villa, wondering what the hell he was going to do. He would have to get himself a new team to go after Mark King again, but he was wrestling with his morals. COULD he kill him? Each time they had met, King had almost fatally injured him and, one day soon, would eventually get the best of him and send a bullet with his name on it, buzzing through his skull. But Vose respected Mark King for being so tough and resilient and difficult to kill and he appreciated WHY King was coming after him, but what Mark King didn't know was that it was

NOT Vose who had killed his wife, and it wasn't Hix either. In a fit of rage, Roman Vose punched anything he could see, doorways, doors, walls, tables and chairs and grabbed random people, mostly maids and servants and asked them hopelessly, what he should do. Vose's mental capacity was starting to wane.

They stared terrified at him and ran off, after which he then looked round in a rage for the next poor unfortunate soul to vent his anger on. Vose was more angry at himself than at Mark King, and he knew sooner or later the two would meet again and, considering Vose thought Mark King was a soft target to begin with, his realisation had dramatically changed in the past week and he was now scared. Roman Vose, the big assassin and henchman was *scared*, and he didn't like that. He didn't like it one bit.

Detlev 'The Wolf' Kastner sat poring over the CCTV images of Mark King's interview. He knew the offender's REAL name, and it bugged him that this man dare contravene and blatantly defy HIS orders and go off on this mad killing spree, tearing up Bremerhaven's largest container port like that. He compared the grainy CCTV images of the shoot-out at the container port to that of the interview a few days before that and he knew it was the same person. He had inspected the scene in the most extreme detail, looking for ANY kind of clue as to the whereabouts of this man, this... killing machine on a mission to ruin his country. Suddenly, something clicked for Kastner. In all his years of interrogation, in all his dealings with some of the worst scum he could imagine, with his level of experience, something resonated with him.

That word he had just said out loud; that word somehow held the clue to what this insurgent's next move would be and where he had vanished to. Was he still in Germany? His hotel had said he checked out, but no one under the name of Russel Green or Mark King had boarded any flights or trains or rented any cars, anywhere in Germany. He was totally bemused.

Kastner sat and thought for a while. He was getting too old for all this but he had ultimate power here. He knew he couldn't go on in this job forever, two wives divorced and one buried had taught him that, and his children who didn't even call or write anymore. Was he really the monster everyone thought he was? He felt like it sometimes, but the world is an evil place and he was good at his job; he faced, fought and caught the evil which ravaged this world and it was up to HIM to clean up the mess. His pay-cheque was handsome, as were all the benefits which went with such a position, plus he had a nice little nest egg he could fall back on if things went south. His mobile rang, and he looked at the number. He answered in his usual serious tone, concerned about the caller and the nature of the call. It was a short call but one he had been dreading. It wasn't his superior, it was much worse than that.

'I am doing all I can to locate this intruder to my country and I am calling in every available resource and asset to capture and eliminate this loner, this sniper, this Russel Green.'

However, the person on the other end of the phone seemed to have more intelligence at their disposal than Kastner did and he hung up the phone, gripping it tightly.

Kastner checked all the records of flights and trains again before reaching for his phone and calling the airports, one at a time, requesting all their CCTV in the last 7 days. He realised this would be a mammoth task so called in some of his most experienced agents. He got up from his desk and went downstairs into the central operations room where agents were busy tracking all kinds of threats to Germany's security. As always, because it was rare he came to the ops room, everyone turned to stare in fear at Kastner when he entered the room. He held his hands up to get everyone's attention. He needed no words to do this, and surveyed the room, carefully, as if he was looking for a rat in a pipe network.

'No one is going home until we have a fix on Mark King. I want him, alive if possible, but I want him and I want him TODAY!' growled Kastner, his face flushed.

Everyone stared, motionless, at his request. His eyes grew narrow, and he straightened his back, angry at this apparent insubordination, and clapped his hands before breathing in and out a few times to calm himself down.

'NOW,' he said in a much calmer voice, 'you want to go home? Find him!!!'

He screamed, and the room erupted into a tirade of phone calls, CCTV images, panicked, frantic and chaotic before eventually a rhythm formed as they pulled up countless images they had gathered from all across Germany of Mark King as Russell Green. Now the 'Wolf' was a little closer to his 'prey' and was going on the hunt!

Something had occurred to Mark as he was walking the corridors of his secure bunker. It was well stocked, all of it with modern equipment. He wondered how Nial Atkinson had acquired such a site, even considering he was ex-military. He decided he would dig deeper into the history of the place and look through the boxes of old papers stored in a secure storage cupboard on the second level of the bunker. Atkinson had told Mark they were his old financial records he stored there as it was about as secure as he could get, and he didn't want them falling into the wrong hands.

'The wrong hands?' Mark said aloud to himself as he made his way up to the storage area.

There he found boxes upon boxes of paperwork, looking like old military files. He decided he needed a break from chasing Roman Vose for a while and picked a few of the files to look into.

Within a few hours, he was sat on the floor, surrounded by hundreds of partially open files. There was information here about missions Atkinson had been on and old photographs of him as a young soldier. One in particular stood out: Nial Atkinson with what looked like a company of other soldiers, posing with their arms around each other and guns over their shoulders. Mark took it, attempted to clean it up and put it in a frame. He thought back to his time at Sandhurst and wondered what life would have been like if he had pursued that career instead of the legal career he had chosen. He knew he couldn't bear to leave Marie, which is why he allowed her to persuade him to go into the legal profession rather than the military. He was grateful really as he had enjoyed his career, but perhaps he wouldn't be in this position if she hadn't persuaded him to leave the dream of the military behind. Perhaps she would still be alive, although she would not have stayed with him if he had stayed in the army. He needed answers and decided to re-visit the nursing home where Nial Atkinson now lived, almost at the end of his life. Mark wondered where Nial Atkinson had the money he had, considering he was in the military although he was a senior ranking SAS officer. Something here just didn't add up.

A nurse came with a tea trolley as Mark and Nial Atkinson faced each other across a chess board. Mark, as usual, was losing. Atkinson looked up and smiled at the nurse who placed two cups of coffee on the table next to the two men. Atkinson wasn't supposed to have coffee but considering how popular he was amongst the nursing staff, they gave him virtually anything he wanted. The truth of the matter was that he wasn't half as gaga as he allowed the nurses to think he was. He had spent years infiltrating the enemy and lying low for weeks before a strike was ordered and he was good at it. He learned how to acquire things in the home he shouldn't have. One such acquisition was a small cache of small arms hidden in his room. Mark looked at Atkinson as if trying to read his thoughts. Atkinson smiled without even looking at Mark and told Mark exactly what he was thinking.

'You want to know what I know,' said Atkinson, smiling.

Mark shouldn't have been surprised at this. However, Atkinson always had a way of surprising people. He cared deeply for this man but there was something he always seemed to hide from the world. Perhaps it was the horrors of war and conflict, or the suppression of the stress of killing in the name of queen and country; no one really knew, but Mark knew something wasn't right.

Atkinson looked up, his face turned serious.

'I know what you want to ask me.'

Mark looked embarrassed at being found out, and rightly so, for Atkinson gave Mark a dressing down for snooping into affairs which were not his.

'You shouldn't go snooping around in affairs that don't concern you. You may find out things you didn't want to know.'

Mark apologised and Atkinson took it well.

'The contents of that bunker are MY life. I haven't been there in thirty years and with very good reason,' Atkinson explained cagily, looking at Mark before turning away.

'I'm sorry Nial, but if it concerns Marie and these goons trying to kill me, it concerns me too.'

Atkinson smiled and nodded.

'How are things going?' Mark shrugged and made a move on the chess board. 'Do you like gardening? I like gardening. I think you ought to go on a holiday Mark, get away from it for a while.'

Mark shook his head in despair and was thinking Atkinson really was as gaga as he made out to be. Atkinson's tone turned deadly serious, and he scolded Mark.

'Mark, please don't think me stupid enough not to know what you've been doing. I do still follow the news.'

He had easily put two and two together to figure out it was Mark who was doing all this killing.

'Besides, your injuries give you away. Would you pass a gunshot residue test?'

Mark looked back at Atkinson. For some reason he feared this old man even though he was brittle and elderly. But there was something about Atkinson which still told Mark he still had it in him to break him in half and snap his neck if the situation called for it. Atkinson frowned as Mark showed him the picture he found of him and his battalion as youngsters. He realised it was time to tell Mark the truth, and he would not like it.

'After my comrades and I left the military, we worked as guns for hire, working for the highest bidder. Some of the members formed a secret organisation which amassed them great wealth, hence my income.'

Mark listened intently, watching, as the old man's eyes wandered back to a time when he was younger and happier.

'They eventually grew so powerful and had so much influence; they began to get control of large companies, corporations and eventually turned to politics.' Atkinson looked sorrowful and distant, his eyes slightly glazed over. 'Many of the group turned against their respective governments and grew too power hungry, even for me. I argued with the group and eventually had to escape underground and never spoke to any of them again. I purchased the bunker off record with some of the money I had and spent the best part of five years living in hiding so I could not be traced. Eventually, when I got too old for the bunker, I made my will, sorted all my financial affairs and retired to this place where I could live the rest of my life in peace and safety.'

Mark was amazed. He sat there staring at the old war dog in total disbelief. Atkinson smiled and gave Mark a wink.

'Hence the secrets I hide in his room. One day, Mark, they WILL come for me. They always do. They leave no one alive.' Atkinson's smile turned to intensity and fear. 'There are forces in this world, Mark. They will kill without hesitation and they will not mourn loss.'

Mark felt sick, especially when, before he left, he turned to Atkinson with one more question.

'What is the name of this organisation?'

Atkinson looked up grimly and replied distantly as if remembering a long forgotten fear or sadness. He could barely even say their name and his voice trembled, 'Invictus Advoca,' he said absently.

Chapter Twenty-Four

The crowds filtered through check-in desks at Madrid-Barajas Airport in Spain as Mark shouldered his carry-on luggage and calmly glanced around the airport, scanning the crowd for anyone who might pose a threat to him. Satisfied he was not in any danger, he checked in through security and headed towards the taxi rank outside the airport, not wanting a repeat of Germany. He adjusted his Aviator sunglasses and tucked his passport back into his back pocket. He took out his tourist map and checked out the rates, times and costs of boat charters to his destination, the Island of Cabrera and the fourteenth-century castle which was where Nial Atkinson advised he would find someone who could provide information on Invictus Advoca's current movements and arrangements. He was to meet someone Nial Atkinson only described as 'El Toro' or 'The Bull' and he didn't know who this person was or even if they would be any help to him.

Mark located the car hire company based at the airport and confidently but politely advised them that there was a car, paid for and reserved in the name of Nial Atkinson. The young lady at the desk took a note of Mark and his details and handed him the keys and directed him to the carpark. When he got there, he wandered the bay numbers until he found the bay number listed on the paperwork. He was shocked to find it was a red

2015 Porsche 911 GT3 RS. Mark shook his head and smiled at the silly old fool for providing him with a car HE would drive rather than what was practical for Mark. However, he was amazed and wasted no time getting in and getting her started. On the passenger seat was a note written in black ink, it read,

> *'I thought you could travel to Valencia in style.*
> *Check the boot.*
> *Nial'*

Mark looked puzzled but smiled at Atkinson's gift. He got out and opened the boot to reveal a massive silver case. He flicked up the locks and opened it. Inside, nestled in cut foam, were an Israeli-made DAN .338 Sniper rifle, a Kadet standard issue US army knife and a Glock 23 .40 S&W suppressed with an Osprey silencer. Mark couldn't believe it. Also tucked into the foam, was a prepaid phone with a single number programmed into it. Mark took it and turned it on; it was fully charged. He dialled the pre-programmed number and Nial Atkinson answered it, advising Mark he assumed he got the car and 'gifts' with no problem. Mark laughed.

'Silly old fool, but generous!'

Atkinson scolded Mark for this and advised him he thought Mark 'might need a few supplies'. Mark was grateful to Atkinson for the help. He silenced Mark as if he was on a Black-Ops mission and gave him a set of instructions. He was to meet a 'friend' of his, El Toro, and would find him at Cabrera Castle on Cabrera Island and to follow co-ordinates thirty-nine degrees north, two degrees fifty-seven east.

Mark looked down in the case and found the military compass Atkinson had also supplied. Underneath the foam was a massive supply of ammunition, some boots, black combat trousers and a Kevlar flak vest, hat and night vision binoculars. He really had thought this through, Mark thought to himself as he thanked Atkinson who hung up. Mark grabbed the Porsche keys and checked his tourist guide. How the hell was he going to explain this lot if he was stopped by the Spanish Policia Local or Guardia Urbana if he was pulled over? A voicemail clicked up on his phone; it was from Atkinson advising him that, before he worried what he would do if the Guardia pulled him over in his car, Atkinson had taken care of that.

'Who the hell IS this guy?' Mark said aloud.

Mark wondered if he really knew Atkinson at all. But then he realised, Atkinson had been in combat in so many theatres of war over his career, he probably made useful contacts. Still, Mark couldn't wait to get behind the wheel of the Porsche. Zero to sixty in three seconds, a three point eight litre flat-six engine kicking out four hundred and seventy-five horse-power and hits nine thousand revs per minute, Mark loved it. He also loved the satnav with Valencia programmed as a destination so all Mark had to do was to drive. After an hour into the two and half hour drive to Valencia, Mark pulled over for fresh water, cigarettes and something to eat. He bought a visitor's handbook and read about his destination out loud.

'The Cabrera Archipelago Maritime-Terrestrial National Park (Catalan: Parc Nacional Maritimoterrestre de l'Arxipèlag de Cabrera, Spanish: Parque Nacional Marítimo-Terrestre del Archipiélago de Cabrera) is a national park that includes the whole of the Cabrera Archipelago in the Balearic Islands (Catalan: Illes Balears, Spanish: Islas Baleares), an autonomous community that is part of the Spanish State. The park covers one hundred square kilometres though eighty seven square kilometres are covered by water. The park attracts relatively few visitors due to its remoteness. There is no permanent population, but there might be at any given time just under one hundred National Park staff members and other personnel on the islands.'

He considered stopping off at Ibiza before he headed to Cabrera to visit the clubs he heard so much about. But he decided he was too old and didn't really need the distraction. He would charter a boat and go around the Island, direct to Cabrera. After a short break and a refuel, Mark was on his way.

The roaring Porsche 911 GT3 RS pulled into the carpark opposite the Land Ahoy Boat Charter company and was met by a young man in overalls, in the process of jet steaming the *Mallorca 4*, a Sessa C44, forty-five foot Sunseeker motorboat. Mark approached the young man, who seemed to know what he was doing with boats. It was Pablo Valentin, the owner of Land Ahoy Boat Charters and he took people on guided tours to Cabrera Island where Mark was to meet this 'El Toro' contact of Atkinson's. Mark offered him five hundred euros for passage to the Island and be in constant radio contact, to collect him and possibly one other passenger.

Pablo agreed because he knew Atkinson and, after a fashion, beckoned Mark on board to set out first to Palma, Mallorca, then onto the Island of Cabrera. Pablo advised Mark it would be a five to six hour trip and if he wanted to pass the time, he could help load food and supplies on board.

After an hour of loading the boat with all the supplies they thought they would need, Mark sat back and lit a cigarette while Pablo passed him a cold beer. He was grateful of the rest and refreshment and they toasted the boat before gulping down the refreshing Spanish beer. Mark lay back against a box and enjoyed the warmth of the Spanish sun, a much different weather system than the UK and Germany. He was tired of globetrotting chasing killers but he felt it necessary to pursue these people wherever they went. Pablo motioned him on board so Mark grabbed his case, his beer and left his cigarette in his mouth as he walked towards the Sessa.

With a top speed of thirty-four knots or thirty-nine miles per hour, it would take roughly five hours to get to Palma Mallorca so Mark took this opportunity to sleep for a while. He left Pablo explicit instructions to report anything suspicious, and, as Pablo knew what kind of business Atkinson had been in, he knew what Mark meant. As Mark made his way below deck to the larger of the two bedrooms, Pablo loosened the safety harness of the M16 machine gun he kept hidden in a removable panel under the controls, switched the radar on and kept his eye on the horizon. He anticipated trouble and had to be ready for it.

The jerking of the Sessa's engines slowing down awoke Mark from what had been a deep sleep. He freshened up and came up to see they were pulling into the beautiful Nazaret Harbour. Mark had elected a blue cardigan, short sleeve white shirt and grey chinos. He came above deck wearing his Aviators and remembered that since he bought them, he was just looking for an excuse to wear them. Pablo, as usual, wore his deck shorts, flip-flops and Musto jacket with sunglasses. They made their way ashore and Mark followed Pablo as he led him to a small marina café. A short while later, both Pablo and Mark were sitting at the Garito Café drinking coffee and eating. The pair sat and discussed their route to Cabrera and Mark called Atkinson to provide an update.

'We're resting. The Garito Cafe,' he said smiling.

'I trust you met Pablo?' Atkinson laughed.

'Yeah. Not much of a conversationalist.'

'Never was! I could tell you a story about the last time I was at the Garito Café and a waitress who used to work there?'

'Too much information,' Mark laughed, smiling to himself, 'speak soon.'

He hung up the phone and sat back and relaxed to finish his cake and croissant. Mark decided he would have a scout around the local area before they head off to Cabrera and stretch his legs. He visited a few novelty shops and noted it was very touristy here in some parts, but the parts he preferred were the local, backstreet cafes, and shops and out of the way places. He stood on the corner and lit a cigarette. He glanced up to notice someone across the street; they seemed to be watching him and they looked out of place. Mark didn't know what it was about it, but he knew something didn't feel right and he was always taught at Sandhurst to go with your gut. Luckily, as he was wearing Aviators, it didn't show when his eyes moved so the stranger opposite wasn't sure if he had been spotted or not so he moved a little down the dusty street. The stranger moved too.

'Once more,' Mark said quietly to himself as he walked, 'and I'll have you!'

Mark walked a little further and turned a corner, and the stranger moved again. Slightly panicked but remaining calm, Mark looked around to see how to get behind his target. He found a stairway into what appeared to be an empty home. Waiting until something distracted the stranger, Mark sped through the open wrought-iron gates and up the stone steps to the rooftop. Peering over the edge, he noticed the man was wandering aimlessly up and down trying to work out where Mark had gone. Mark looked at the rooftop opposite, only a six foot jump, so took a run up and leapt silently over the roof to the building on the other side. Mark found a doorway and slipped through, apologising to people in their rooms as he made his way downstairs and out onto the street. He followed the stranger down an alley and relaxed when he realised he hadn't been spotted. Turning a corner, Mark felt for his Glock from under his shirt in its back holster and flicked off the safety catch. He held it out before him and whipped round the corner, face to face with the stranger. It took both of them a few seconds to register they faced each other before Mark fired questions at him.

'Who are you? Why are you following me?'

No reply came, and the stranger tried to get past Mark. With a lightning quick move, Mark blocked his path, grabbed his shirt collar and hit him hard over the back of the head with the butt of his Glock. Mark rifled through his pockets but was disturbed by a car pulling up, doors opening and people shouting in Spanish. It was time for Mark to leave as he holstered the Glock and calmly walked in the opposite direction. He hurried back to Pablo, who was anxiously waiting for him.

'Trouble?' he asked with a thick Spanish accent. Mark nodded and replied sharply.

'We best be going.'

But before he could blink, Pablo was on board the Sessa and starting the two powerful Volvo Penta IPS 600 engines. He shouted to Mark, who was still stood on the Marina watching for the stranger and his 'friends'.

'Come on!' Pablo called and Mark leapt onto the boat and Pablo hit the throttle, roaring out of the harbour and towards Cabrera Island.

Mark was relaxing on the deck of the Sessa C44 with a cigarette and a laptop loaned to him by Pablo and he noted to himself that the only thing missing was the twelve-year-old single malt. He was desperate to dig into the history of the Invictus Advoca organisation and find out as much as possible. Mark logged into his secure email and noticed Nial Atkinson had sent him an email with many large files attached. For an old guy, he really kept up to date with new technologies. Mark downloaded the attachments, showing senior members of the organisation who were long dead, and some who were not.

There was a history of the organisation, of which Atkinson was a crucial part at one stage. There were connections to the Vatican, German High Command, which explained why Kastner caught Mark in Holtenau, London and the head of the current organisation was a man by the name of Thomas Theodore Lundon. A picture was attached, which was a CCTV image or something a covert photographer had taken, but it was difficult to gauge where Lundon was. He was slim and elderly, with grey hair and a very expensive suit. He was flanked by two people Mark instantly recognised, Roman Vose and Hix Lomas. Mark scowled when he saw Vose there and gradually things seemed to fit together.

Azidi was subcontracted by Thomas Lundon to take delivery of a shipment of weapons while Kastner turned a blind eye, however, Azidi was planning to conduct a little scheme of his own and carry out terrorist attacks in Berlin right under Kastner's nose.

'So it was possible,' Mark thought to himself, 'that Kastner was part of Invictus Advoca but didn't know what Azidi was up to on the sly and was about to bust it open!'

Mark was doing the same thing that night in Holtenau. It all made sense to Mark now, especially that it was Thomas Lundon who ordered the hit on Marie. NOW Mark had a name and a face. The face looked strangely familiar but he couldn't place it. Perhaps he had come across him in his past and only subconsciously remembered it.

Mark had exactly what he was after now, except one thing: details of Lundon's whereabouts and personality. Perhaps this El Toro could help provide information on exactly what type of person Mark was dealing with.

Soon, they past S'Estanyol De Migjorn Point and turned south and headed directly towards Cabrera Island. Soon, Mark could see the ominous castle loom up on the horizon. Pablo explained there are many ghost stories about this island and that few people came here. It was also a national park so there were wild animals roaming and he warned Mark to be careful. Mark, by now, had sheathed his new rifle in its leather carry case, pocketed the ammo in his various combat pockets in his trousers and flak jacket, holstered his knife and Glock and was carrying water.

'Thanks for your help Pablo.' Pablo smiled and nodded. 'Anchor close by, I have a feeling you may be needed.'

Mark began the hill climb, which led up to the castle.

Chapter Twenty-Five

Within an hour of Mark and Pablo parting company, Mark had reached a rocky outcrop under the castle. Light was fading, and the temperature was falling. Mark used his binoculars to scope the castle walls to look for a way in when something glinted in the fading sun. Mark's first instinct was to focus on it but then he saw the quick muzzle flash of a sniper rifle and ducked as the bullet chipped the rocks to the side of him. Hitting the deck hard, his first thought was that Lundon's henchmen had followed him here and that they guy following him in Nazaret Harbour had found out their location. Mark crawled to a better vantage point and within two moves, had fixed up his rifle and was scoping the rocks where the muzzle flash came from.

Something caught the corner of his eye and he rolled, mid-air, behind a rock just in time for another bullet, then another to ping off the surrounding rocks. Mark's blood was pumping now, and he realised he was pinned down.

'What a bugger I didn't bring any grenades with me!' he thought.

He waited for a moment, correctly assuming the shooter was reloading, and made a run for it. His way was pounded by automatic gunfire and he realised either the shooter had NOT reloaded but merely changed weapon, or there was more than one shooter.

Just as he approached the wall of the castle, he heard laughter and saw the shooter stood on the wall high above him.

'If I wanted to, you would be floating home right now!'

Mark did not take kindly to this.

'I'll shoot you off that wall if you don't shut up,' he threatened, trying to get a fix on the man, not wanting to be outdone by some deranged Spanish mercenary.

'Ha ha!' squealed El Toro, 'no one has ever got the better of El Toro. You want I shoot you now?' He continued to mock Mark.

'So this is the contact Atkinson told me to come and see!'

Mark peeked out from his cover position and shouted that Atkinson had sent him and used his real name.

'Reynaldo Clemente! A friend sent me!'

There was silence.

The nurse eased the frail old man into his electric bed in his room and dimmed the light down. His breathing was laboured and his lungs crackly. Nial Atkinson gave a sigh as if, in silent resignation, he contemplated his end of days. The nurse looked soulfully at him. She remembered the first time he came to this place, vigorous, full of life but hiding dark secrets and the scars on his body were testament to the life he sometimes described to her. If he didn't have more medication soon, it would be too late for him to recover from this infection. Nial, being the man he was, sensed something was wrong with the nurse and took her by the hand, patted it and winked at her. She couldn't help but smile at this sad gesture and realised he was probably a serious catch in his younger days.

'Goodnight Major.'

Nial smiled.

'Goodnight, my dear.'

She turned to leave, but not before she cleverly picked up the cell phone under the pile of hospital notes she had left on his table. She shut the door and made her way to the nurse's station. Once there, she made her excuses to go on her break and grabbed her coat and cigarettes and disposable lighter and went outside. She walked around the back of the nursing home to the smoking area, out of sight of residents and other staff and drew the cell phone from her apron pocket. She picked it up, opened it and checked the last dialled number. She hesitated for a moment and braced herself before pressing 'dial' and putting the phone to her ear.

'Mr King. Mr Mark King?' she whispered with a tremble in her voice, 'this is Susan, a nurse from Sunningdale where your friend Mr Atkinson is a resident.' She paused again. 'It's about your friend.'

It was nightfall when El Toro and Mark sat in two armchairs front of a roaring log fire which crackled in its huge ornate fireplace. They raised their whiskey glasses, toasting each other, and Mark gazed up at the stag's head above the fireplace as he ended the call from the cell phone Atkinson had provided for him. El Toro spotted Mark's interest.

'There was a priest hole behind the fireplace which led to tunnels deep beneath the castle and out to a small hidden harbour at the north end of the island. I have a boat there.'

El Toro also noticed a deep sadness in Mark that was not there before. He asked about the worry written all over Mark's face. Mark took a deep breath and began his story, right the way through from his court case battle with Mohammed Al Azidi, to Marie's murder, and everything that had happened since. El Toro sat back in his chair and crossed one leg over the other whilst Mark lit a cigarette as he explained.

'My life has changed so much in the past three months.'

It was quite a story and Mark wasn't even sure if El Toro would believe him but something he saw in El Toro's eyes, something which looked like familiarity, glimmered and gave Mark a good indication he believed his story.

Mark spent an hour explaining his life story as El Toro got up to put more wood on the fire and refill their whiskey glasses. Mark was very warm in front of the fire and it sounded like it was a rough night out tonight.

'It is rough. When you live on an island, Mark, it's what you have to put up with.'

Mark smiled, thinking this was somewhere he could get used to.

'Sounds like paradise,' he said distantly. El Toro looked at him, knowing he had seen sights he would rather forget. El Toro, being an expert interrogator in his former life, questioned Mark.

'Bad news from home?'

'A friend of mine is elderly and isn't well but was refusing drugs and I don't know why.'

El Toro's eyes narrowed. 'Señor Nial?' he asked.

Mark looked puzzled.

'How did you…?'

It was El Toro's turn to tell a fireside story, so he unravelled the mystery surrounding how El Toro and Atkinson knew each other.

'Nial and I go way back. We were captured together in Bosnia. Special Forces. They fed him many kind of drug to make him tell them what he knew. He did not crack.' Mark was horrified. 'That is why he no take a drugs now.'

'He'd rather have the pain than the memories?' Mark asked.

'Wouldn't you?' replied El Toro, looking seriously at Mark.

As Mark listened, El Toro threw a lot of names into the conversation, some of which Mark had recognised from his research, and some were new to him. It was at that point that Mark reached into his bag and bought out the photograph of Nial Atkinson and others during their military days. El Toro chuckled.

'I remember the day and night after that picture was taken. That is me,' he said leaning over and pointing himself out in the picture and going left to right, naming all those he could remember.

His finger stopped on the man stood next to Atkinson and he trembled. He sat back in his chair as if he had seen a ghost and stared at it. He stared at it so hard Mark half expected it to burst into flames at any moment.

'What's the problem? Who is that?' Mark asked, pointing at the man in the photograph, the man El Toro had not named.

El Toro looked shocked at Mark, as if he was dumbfounded that he didn't know who that was. Mark turned the picture over and examined it in more detail. El Toro got up and leant against the fireplace. From behind the stag's head, he pulled a picture in a cardboard frame and brought it over to the small polished oak carved table they were sharing. He pulled his double-barrelled shot gun closer to use to prop himself up. He placed the picture on the table purposefully, the way a secret service agent would place evidence or an offender file in front of someone in interrogation. Mark stared at the picture, identical to the one he had found. A few, if not all, of the people in the photograph, could hold a copy of the same picture. Mark stubbed his cigarette in the waist high stand-up three-legged ashtray and exhaled as he looked around the room, as if for some flash of inspiration. El Toro stood over him.

'Why you want so much information?'

Mark was slightly intimidated by this but wasn't about to let it show, not even to El Toro. He jumped up to face El Toro, who looked equally surprised at this as Mark was at having had El Toro stood over him. The two faced each other before sitting back down. El Toro stared at Mark for a long time before drawing in his breath.

'Many of the people in that picture had formed part of the Invictus Advoca, initially as a justice group to defend those who felt they couldn't turn to their governments or authorities for help, people who required strength outside the law.'

Mark scoffed at this.

'Like the A-Team?' he laughed.

El Toro didn't share Mark's humour and stared at him angrily. Mark realised he wasn't joking and looked sheepish at having made a bad joke at a bad time. El Toro continued.

'Many of them assisted because they believed in justice. Real justice, not the rubbish people try to be palmed off with through the courts!'

This comment hurt Mark, as he had always tried to be just when trying a case. El Toro neither cared nor stopped talking.

'Soon, a few of them banded together privately to discuss how disgusted they were because Invictus Advoca was branching out to undertaking professional "hits" and murdering innocent people, taking over countries and supporting terrorist regimes. This angered us and we tried to leave.'

'And went into hiding,' Mark said, nodding.

'Most were hunted down and killed by the then-head of Invictus Advoca, a man who had forced his way to the top to create corruption, murder, deceit and bribery.'

El Toro stopped, almost afraid to mention his name. Mark was getting impatient.

'Who?'

El Toro stared Mark in the eye as his finger pointed to the man with his arm around a young Nial Atkinson.

'OK, so they were friends,' thought Mark as he looked just as puzzled. Puzzled, that was, until El Toro spoke his name.

'Thomas Theodore Lundon.'

Mark's eyes widened in horror as he went dizzy at the gravity of what El Toro had just told him.

He stomped around the hall in front of the fire with a whiskey in one hand and a cigarette in the other, shouting insult after insult while he comprehended the enormity of the situation. The man he was hunting, the man who ordered the murder of his wife, was the best friend of Nial Atkinson. Now he REALLY didn't know what to do. No wonder Nial was so helpful towards Mark when he explained what he was doing. El Toro walked over to Mark and put both his hands on Mark's shoulders to calm him down and stop him wearing a hole in the fire place rug. He spoke carefully and quietly to him, giving Mark no choice but to listen carefully to what he was saying.

'Listen to me Mark, this man needs to be killed dead. The world is not safe while he lives.'

Mark was breathless and panicked. How could he have missed that? It made little sense. El Toro picked up the picture and stared at it again, not being able to place three or four other people in the picture.

'Another picture exists of the ENTIRE Invictus Advoca organisation heads around the world.'

Mark looked up at him.

'They meet once a year in secret to discuss their "empire" and if you want to take the organisation out, you will have to hit the entire organisation in one.'

Mark nodded. He agreed but El Toro, although he had suggested the idea, really didn't think Mark would take up the idea!

'Taking out the entire organisation is suicidal and impossible.' Mark wasn't for turning. 'It would create a vacuum for other members to be promoted within the organisation and carry on its work in place of those you might kill.'

Mark looked lost and hopeless.

'What am I supposed to do? What was the point in Marie's death, what did SHE do to deserve to die?'

El Toro sat Mark down, passed him a cigarette and a brandy from a decanter on the table and explained exactly how the Invictus Advoca worked.

When he had finished, Mark was stunned. He was loaded with useful information about how to infiltrate them, but he was still stunned. El Toro added that there were four members of the organisation, heads of it, who were unaccounted for and probably had assumed names. Mark had no idea how to trace them if El Toro and Nial Atkinson didn't know their names. Decades to change names, places, and hide; Mark felt lost. The only thing on his mind was the question of how he would pull the trigger on Thomas Lundon, being a friend of Nial Atkinson. Mark reached for his cell phone.

The nurse had returned to Nial Atkinson's room whilst he was sleeping and returned his phone. It was lucky that she did as, shortly after the nurse closed the door, it rang. Atkinson reached with a trembling arm and answered the phone. His voice seemed no different to the caller than it did days earlier when they had sat and played chess face to face, discussing Invictus Advoca.

'Nial? Mark. Tell me about the photograph.'

Atkinson's face dropped, and he realised he would have to be, for the first time in his life, one hundred percent honest with Mark. He sighed, propped himself up on his pillow, and explained his relationship with Thomas Lundon, why Nial Atkinson wasn't his real name, why he owned a nuclear ex-government bunker at an undisclosed location and why he was now in hiding under this assumed name, at Sunning Dale Nursing Home. None of this was easy to do for Atkinson, but seeing as he concealed himself from his family for their protection and had set up trust funds in their names, he couldn't be traced and had little use in life left. This was his last confession.

Thomas Lundon stood on the exterior balcony at the old abandoned UN military base he had secured, and watched next to the control tower, as a fleet of black Range Rovers rolled out onto the dust track the other side of the large metal fencing. He smiled to himself as he made his way down the steps to his car flanked by Roman Vose and another two men, all heavily armed with Uzi 9mms and M16s. The sound of the standard military issue, steel toe-capped boots echoed around the entire base to the fading sound of the Range Rover engines. Lundon could see the last of the Range Rovers was towing a trailer with a large black inflatable, and thought back to his briefing to his men. He also watched the two private Black Hawk helicopters take off from the helipad and had taken great delight in imagining what kind of impact this would have on anyone who he was chasing. He had fifteen men taking part in this operation, more than enough to bring in one man.

But what Thomas Lundon didn't expect was that Mark King was no longer one man, he was five men and three of them were heavily armed.

However, Thomas Lundon had Mark King and was advised he was last spotted in Valencia in Spain associating with some boat owner. He knew he wouldn't be far from there and had sent his 'staff' out to scour the coast of Spain for any place Mark King could hide. Lundon's most trusted intelligence operatives worked through the night to work out what kind of locations would Mark King be going to around this area. They had identified several areas of interest, including an island off the East coast, of significant interest, seeing as it held a fourteenth-century fortified castle. But there was no way to infiltrate a building like that without attracting serious attention. Any attempt would advertise his location to his enemy. He had learned many things from his military life and giving up the element of surprise was the quickest route to defeat. He pulled out his two-way radio.

'Get into position. We will wait until the storm has passed and send in a few agents to see if they can recon the building. Let's test their mettle.'

The radio crackled into life as a passenger in one vehicle had just pulled out. He replied and Lundon gave a further order.

'Before I authorise a helicopter drop into the main courtyard, I'll need three teams of three. Alpha and Bravo teams will insert west of the objective by air whilst Charlie team will mount an amphibious assault, all under the cover of darkness.'

However, he had to wait until the current storm had blown over before being able to mount this kind of assault. He looked up at the watchtowers and his guards nodded to him as his driver drove his car into a fortified carport with blast doors. Lundon was no military leader or tactician, but he was desperate and he had performed this role many times before. He would wait here for his glory to be reported to him. And he would enjoy every moment.

The nurse returned on hearing the sound of Nial Atkinson talking and paused at the door, watching the old man talking like he was twenty years old again. She smiled at him as he beckoned her in and she helped prop him up on another pillow. He placed his hand in hers as she sat in the chair next to him while he held the cell phone in the other hand. He went into detail about what happened, nearly forty years previously, to his friendship with Thomas Lundon.

'I first met Lundon in the army and we had saved each other's lives several times, becoming firm friends. When we were recruited by a black ops unit to conduct counter terrorism around the world, specifically working for the US Special Forces unit Delta Force, we were recruited together because of our closeness and ability to work fantastically together.'

Nial Atkinson put the history so eloquently and slowed now and then to catch his breath. The nurse squeezed his hand in encouragement periodically, while smiling at him warmly and sympathetically.

Mark King remained silent on the other end of the phone, patiently waiting for Nial Atkinson to catch his breath. The nurse looked concerned and so administered a further dose of morphine after Atkinson agreed to take the drug again now he had explained to Mark exactly what he had been doing. He set it out in plain words for Mark exactly why he was involved.

'Tom wanted to recruit you to his organisation, Mark. But upon following your developing career years before, he decided you would never agree to be part of such an unjust organisation and risked exposing it if you decided not to join. That was when your death warrant was signed.'

'It was no good having someone who had been invited to join the Invictus Advoca wandering around after refusing, so he would have to be killed to tie up loose ends,' Mark pointed out.

Atkinson paused again to get his breath and his nurse lifted a glass of water with a straw in for him to drink from and gently dried his mouth with a neatly folded, pristine white face towel. Atkinson always loved the luxuries, once stealing a solid silver cutlery set from an African dictator he helped eliminate and giving it to a friend as a wedding present, but not before removing two of each of the set he stole for his personal use.

Atkinson regained his composure and strained back the tears as he continued to tell Mark about how crazy the military life had made Thomas Lundon, even though it made him a billionaire.

'Tom would have people brought to his villa in the Mediterranean to torture and kill them for fun, relinquishing all control over reality and moral standing. He's a madman Mark, and madmen are dangerous.'

Atkinson was growing angry and hurt as the tone in his voice changed. The nurse got up to mop his fevered brow and hold his shoulders in a loving gesture as if to say 'calm down'. Atkinson continued.

'Tom had grown power-thirsty and lost sight of the original mission of the Invictus Advoca, using it instead to blackmail, murder, pillage and control people, towns, societies and governments all over the world. Wherever Invictus Advoca went, devastation and suffering followed.'

'Then it's time someone took him down,' Mark growled determinedly, angered at how upset his old friend was getting.

Mark listened as Atkinson urged him to fail in his mission.

'If you attempt to destroy this evil organisation, you will need to use every skill and every resource you have and be prepared that it won't be an overnight solution. It may take months, even years to fully work your way up the chain of command. That is why I have sent you to El Toro.'

Chapter Twenty-Six

Mark sat, aghast at what Atkinson was telling him, unable to comprehend how his life was being mapped out for him without him even knowing. Mark had always considered himself intelligent, yet here he was, up to this point, oblivious to the life going on behind the scenes. What made him angry were decisions about his life being made on his behalf. No one had the right to do that. He felt stupid and paced up and down again; until El Toro came over, once again, to calm his nerves and sit him down to listen.

'How do you know it could take years to destroy Invictus Advoca?'

Atkinson made a stark admission. 'I worked so closely with Thomas Lundon before he turned into a power hungry monster. I was considered "High Command" and I know how they operate, their reach and the lengths they would go to, to keep their organisation a secret so it remained operational.'

Mark's head swam with all this information. How could a secret organisation be running governments behind the scenes? This was what he saw in films, not reality!

'It is the organisation that is the enemy here, King,' Atkinson reminded Mark gravely, 'not just the men who run it.'

Mark felt a cold shiver run through him. 'I just want my wife's killer, her REAL killer brought to justice.'

'These men know nothing of justice,' Atkinson said sharply, upset at what he was being forced to remember.

'My kind of justice. And it doesn't involve a courtroom,' Mark reminded Atkinson.

The two friends ended the phone call with the usual pleasantries.

'Take care of yourself, you silly old fool.'

Atkinson gave away a look towards his bed where his 'attaché' was stashed and smiled.

'Don't mock a senior rank and, if I was twenty years younger, I would have beaten you senseless for that comment.'

Mark was grateful Atkinson WASN'T twenty years younger because he knew his word was true, but he also wished he was twenty years younger because he would be here with Mark as an ally and his skills were formidable, hence why he had to hide from Invictus Advoca. They knew what skills Atkinson possessed and what kind of influence he held over old contacts and in countries he still did business with. He was not just some old 'codger' in a nursing home breathing his last and reminiscing about old times. Mark smiled at the thought of the justice Atkinson would have visited on his old 'comrades' had he been younger and more physically fit. He, even in his old age, was as hard as steel and there was no denying it. El Toro patted Mark's shoulder.

'I recommend we get some sleep.'

Mark was still unsure of his next move to trace Thomas Lundon. He couldn't possibly sleep while all this was running through his head. He needed a plan, he always needed a plan, and he didn't have one and this hurt and worried him. How would he hit his target, with NO knowledge of his location or whether Mark would be met with an army when he went walking in, knocking on the door? So many things were buzzing through his mind and he opened the oak door to his room. It was made up and his gear was already out and ready. He checked each of his weapons and put his Kadet knife on the floor under his bed, loaded and cocked his Glock pistol and placed it under the pillow, and loaded and locked his rifle.

He was ready for anything but had nothing to do. Mark hoped the next morning would bring fresh insight and more ideas about the whereabouts of Thomas Lundon. Mark lay down and closed his eyes, trying desperately to put it all out of his mind. As he eventually drifted into some form of sleep, his mind inevitably turned to memories of Marie and his children and, after a while, Mark King was unconscious.

It was just after ten AM when El Toro rudely awoke Mark.

'The storm had passed and breakfast is waiting for you.'

Mark washed and changed back into his black combats and headed down to the main dining hall of the castle's private residence, where he wasn't disappointed. There was a cooked breakfast and a continental waiting for him and he eagerly tucked in, suffering from a headache from the whiskey the night before, plus all the questions still buzzing through his mind. He located El Toro in a room with a huge banqueting table and a map laid out on it. He smiled at Mark and bid him good morning. Mark looked interestedly at the map laid out on the table.

'If we are to locate Thomas Lundon, we need at least to look for areas he might be based. From what Atkinson had told me about Lundon, he never stayed in one location for long?'

El Toro nodded and agreed.

'We needed to look at areas with road, sea and air access.' Mark smiled and finished a mouthful of breakfast. 'Shouldn't be too hard.'

El Toro led Mark to a row of computer monitors and a laptop on the tables adjacent to the map table.

Within half an hour, the coffee was pumping and so was the blood pressure of El Toro and Mark as they busily searched the internet for areas of interest and marked them with flags on the map. They switched between the screens and the map, occasionally stopping to have coffee and for Mark to smoke. On one such break, Mark looked out of the small window that overlooked the vast expanse of sea which surrounded them. This was a beautiful island. The fact no one ever came here made it so much easier to be at peace here. He would come here again once all this was over and done with.

El Toro joked with Mark as he put another marker on the map and, after a little more searching, 'Eh Mark, looks like we've run out of locations that a billionaire bad guy could hide!'

Thomas Lundon wasn't hiding, far from it; he was busy mounting his offensive against Mark King which would see this thorn in his side put to rest forever and it couldn't come soon enough as far as he was concerned. He had cost him a fortune in revenue thanks to his little escapade at the container terminal in London AND in Bremerhaven and taken out some of his best, most skilled, experienced and trusted men and that wasn't good for Thomas Lundon. He had been so used to having everything his own way, he took a while to come to his senses and mount a meaningful reaction to this one-man army. Lundon wondered where Mark had received such extensive training to hone these skills, why he suddenly wanted to hit Lundon where it hurt and what his motivation was. Lundon was militarily trained but knew nothing about the psychology of a man on a mission. Lundon almost envied Mark at being so young and fit to do this, as those days were over for Lundon. He preferred the controlling aspect of running such an empire as was at his disposal. He wandered back to his car and lit a cigar, and stood, staring at the sun rising over the trees. Today would be the day he would catch this man, this missionary. He had decided years ago that Mark King was a valuable potential asset but his commitment to justice and 'doing the right thing' posed too great a risk to his organisation and there could be no allowing people like that to go about knowing such an organisation existed. People who were recruited to the organisation only ever had one invitation; there was never a second chance. Once he had explained the organisation to them, if they didn't join, they died; it was as simple as that. It was this mentality which had ensured that Invictus Advoca had survived for as long as it had and why it only had the best assets at its disposal.

When he was younger, and still in the military, he had envisaged heading up an organisation that operated above the law, one that would grow powerful and direct armies, supplies and missions of its own, answerable to no one, not government, not dictators, not sovereigns, no one. It would choose where and how it got involved in the world. Its power would come from those who had no use for or right to use it. He had obtained that and, aside from a few rebels which every successful unit had which needed to be weeded out and dealt with, he had succeeded in all he had set out to accomplish and revelled in its covert nature and success. Under its umbrella, he had terrorist organisations, religious movements, military and para-military forces, world leaders, politicians, judges, entire police forces and even royalty. It had taken over the Mafia, parts of the Catholic Church and even several countries' governments, infiltrating nearly every part of society. No single organisation had ever done that since the Roman Empire and Thomas Lundon was very proud of that. It couldn't be that ONE MAN, one bitter, angry and vengeful man, could put any of this in jeopardy. He wouldn't allow it. Mark King, it seemed to Thomas Lundon, had no chance.

Mark and El Toro stared at the map full of flags which they had created, realising they really had their work cut out for them as they tried to piece together where Lundon could be based as of now. The problem, as El Toro has put it to Mark earlier, was that even as they narrowed down their search results, by the time they even got close to the correct location, it was almost certain that Lundon would have moved from that location or not even been there yet. It was like trying to find a needle in a hundred haystacks blindfolded when the needle kept moving itself around. Mark thought back to his Psychology experience.

'It may be like that,' he expressed with a glimmer of hope in his voice, 'but if you hide a needle in one hundred haystacks and keep moving it around, eventually you have to leave the hay disturbed.'

El Toro patted Mark on the back and told him, 'You have finally cracked, my friend.' El Toro laughed as he went to replenish the coffee and snack supplies. Mark sat down, not feeling any nearer to locating this man whom he had come all this way to kill. He felt hopeless and cursed himself for allowing his mind to wander to thoughts of giving up and going home, to live the quiet life and forgetting this whole damn saga. But his resolve won through and he smacked his legs in encouragement as he stood up and surveyed the map full of flags. Process of elimination, he thought to himself, putting himself in the shoes of someone like Lundon and piecing together what he knew about him already.

'He loves power so it would need to be a location which commanded power and control.'

Mark removed five or six flags to eliminate places which did not fit these criteria, all the while explaining his feelings to El Toro.

'He had a great deal of money and influence.'

Mark removed any flags of locations which were not influential locations or that would be low cost to Lundon.

'He would need somewhere with access to air, land and sea escapes and entrances.'

He was about to remove the flags relating to any locations which did not have at least two of these, however El Toro had beaten him to it. Mark looked at El Toro, confused how he would know this. El Toro patted his machine gun and raised his eyes at Mark. Mark smiled and realised El Toro knew Nial Atkinson, so anything was possible.

'Lastly, he needs total secrecy and security.'

Mark removed any locations which didn't match these two needs. Suddenly, they had removed all but a few of the locations they had flagged on the map.

Back at the computer monitors, El Toro and Mark studied satellite images obtained via the internet of the four areas they had shortlisted which met what they thought was the criteria Thomas Lundon would require to conduct such operations as Invictus Advoca had been conducting for God knows how long.

'Most are fortified facilities belonging to various government and private agencies around the world but these two stick out.'

Mark flew over to El Toro and gazed at his screen. El Toro was right, two stuck out. He rubbed his sore eyes and glugged down the rest of his coffee. El Toro sucked loudly on a large Spanish cigar and blew a smoke ring before putting his hands on Mark's shoulders.

'We need a break! You should have a wander around the castle to see its many historical sights.'

Mark agreed and, putting out his cigarette, stretched before getting out of the chair and walking towards the door. El Toro, whose arm was still around Mark's shoulder, escorted him to the door, describing the best way around the castle. Mark was grateful for the break from all the stress and was actually looking forward to a wander around an empty castle to see all it offered. El Toro walked back to the window and stood there, waiting and watching. He said aloud to an invisible enemy, 'Come on then señor. You make-a your a move. I wait a for a you!'

He knew something was coming, a lifetime of military exercises with Special Forces had provided him with instinct and reasoning. He knew the storm prevented anyone who would attack them from doing so. Now that the storm was over, they would attack before another storm front moved in.

Chapter Twenty-Seven

Agent Williams sat staring at the vast array of computer monitors while blowing hard on his coffee as he pondered the patterns he was seeing. Someone kills a bunch of terrorists in a London container terminal and then the same thing happens, days apart, in Bremerhaven in Germany, with the same precision kills, the same motive and the same untraceable weapons used. His forensics department had spent weeks trying to trace the weapons used but what frustrated him most was that they were no clearer to identifying either the weapons or the killer. CCTV had a partial image but nothing that would amount to reasonable to use and wouldn't stand up in court.

It was true; he admitted to himself as he got up to grab another coffee and head out for a cigarette which previous to this case, he had given up, it was virtually a cold case. Then a call came in requesting his presence in the office upstairs. He huffed at the thought of having to wait for his cigarette break. He made his way upstairs and used the laser eye scanner to enter the room. There he found a file and a young female investigator waiting for him. He read through the paperwork hoping it was worth cancelling his cigarette break for, or this girl would be reprimanded. His eyes shone as two plane tickets and hotel reservation paperwork fell out. He picked up the tickets and read out the destination whilst looking up at the young girl who would accompany him and with whom he would meet their CIA counterparts:

'Bremerhaven, Germany?' he questioned thoughtfully.

El Toro 'The Bull' stood rigid, rooted to the spot with his fully automatic machine gun, pump action shot gun, Uzi 9mm and knife as he watched the disturbance in the water out of the window. He had been trained well enough to know when he could spot something that wasn't right and he was convinced he had spotted two or more divers in the water and, after checking the island schedule, had realised there was no dives booked today so it could only mean one other thing: whilst they were blissfully planning to locate Thomas Lundon, HE was planning to attack THEM. Big mistake in a fortress like this, it was impenetrable, and he had made a few 'unofficial' modifications to its defences. El Toro reached under the window frame and found the black panic button. He pressed it and listened for the sound of crunching gears as the steel blast proof window protectors slid down over every single window in the house. The room went dark and then a red light lit up the room, the computers instantly switched to every single CCTV camera on the island and another bought up a radar screen. From the concealed speakers, El Toro heard the female voice he had programmed.

'Attention all personnel. The castle is now in lock down.'

Another monitor advised 'intruder alert in sector seventy-nine', bringing up a 3-D map of the island divided by a grid overlay. El Toro ran to the fireplace and flicked the concealed switch unlocking the door to the priest-hole; he had also taken upon himself to have modified with a large steel blast door. Mark appeared at the door with his rifle already locked and loaded along with his other weapons from his room. He and El Toro ran to the window and, peering through the fire slats, spotted two helicopters flying low across the water directly towards them. Mark quickly slid his rifle through the firing hole and used his telescopic sight to scan the horizon. He cursed.

'Shit! Two fully armed, Black Hawk helicopters.'

'Armed?' El Toro questioned.

Mark could see the M134D-H rotating machine gun mounted on the sides of each of them, along with the thermal imaging camera mounted on the nose.

'Er, yeah, you could say that. M134D-H rotating machine gun mounted on the sides of each of them!'

El Toro and Mark started at each other. El Toro explained, 'There is no way they can access the castle. They need a really big gun!' Mark wasn't convinced. 'Doors are a blast proof!'

So he would just pick them off, one at a time. Mark rushed to another window.

'The first things to hit are the choppers!' Mark shouted.

They both chased up the winding stone staircase, which lead to the roof. On the way there, El Toro stopped at a wooden door and pushed it open; in the room was a wooden cupboard built into the wall with a control panel on it. El Toro punched four numbers into the control panel and his fingerprint and the door sprung open. He reached inside and pulled out probably the finest OICW (Objective Individual Combat Weapon) gun Mark had ever seen. El Toro loaded her up with ammo and grabbed the rest and put them in his pockets. Mark just stared as El Toro smiled.

'Señor?' he said calmly and matter-of-factly. 'If you are a, 'ow you say, kaboom with a 'elicoptere, you need a big a bombs right?'

Mark laughed out loud

'Haha yeah, a big a bombs.'

They both laughed and clinked gun barrels before both rushing to the roof. El Toro was first through the door and let of two or three grenades into the air. Two waiting choppers lowered ropes down to allow two men each to slide to the ground. Initially one missed, but the other caught the nose of a chopper and took out the thermal imaging camera mounted on the nose. The chopper beached sharply to the right sending the two men swinging on the rope before dropping them to their inevitable deaths on the rocks below. Mark's DAN .338 sniper rifle was already in the air as the two men clad in black were falling from the chopper's ropes. Mark, in a moment of mercy, fired off two shots and the flailing bodies now slumped as they fell. El Toro patted him on the back for his act of kindness, and to celebrate two of the most fantastic sniper shots he had ever seen. El Toro was breathless.

'Good man,' he huffed to Mark as he smiled, pleased with himself at his quick thinking.

They may have been out to kill them but that didn't mean they had to die a horrible grisly death on rocks.

El Toro was already on the other chopper, firing off shot after shot after shot of grenades which were bursting on impact but it didn't seem to do any good. They heard a loud explosion on the rocks and realised it must have been the first chopper eventually crash landing. Out of nowhere, a hail of bullets ripped the ground under Mark's and El Toro's feet as the inexperienced passenger of the chopper got the M134D-H rotating machine gun working and tried to fire it straight. As El Toro and Mark both ducked for cover, Mark realised that, if they were having trouble using this gun, they weren't perhaps as experienced as he had first thought and THIS was a weakness. The ropes descended and three men clad in black combat gear and helmets held their weapons up as they ran around the roof top. Mark was the first to reach one, kicking the weapon away and aiming a punch with a Kevlar glove to just under the chin guard of the helmet. The soldier let off a scream as blood shot out and onto Mark's black Kevlar vest. Mark landed a full weight kick to the soldier's knee, and he crumpled under the weight of the injury. Mark used the soldier's gun to smash him in the face whilst a shot rang out from Mark's left. He froze to the spot, moving only his head as he looked left and right. To his right he saw a dead armed soldier and to his left he saw El Toro standing with his OICW still aimed. Mark nodded to him in gratitude and El Toro raised his hand to his head in a salute of acknowledgement. Then he was gone and Mark realised he had seen no one vanish like that, but the rooftop was now crawling with bad guys in combat gear so he really didn't have time to stop and think about it. He dispatched the soldier he had fought with by a kick to the oesophagus, killing him instantly, and ran to the next one, this time with his weapon up, but it was too close quarters to use a sniper rifle for this style of fighting.

'Eh Señor,' El Toro cried.

Mark spun round just in time to catch El Toro's 9mm Uzi which had yet to be used. El Toro had figured out Mark didn't have the weapon for the fight, but he still had his OICW and was firing it off relentlessly while bad guys dropped all around him in splashes of blood and carnage. El Toro still had his cigar, and it was a real sight to behold watching him blasting away using this highly powered machine gun whilst laughing and taunting those he was killing AND sucking on a large cigar. For a large guy, he couldn't half move fast when he wanted to. Mark caught the Uzi and instantly spun round firing it as he did so, taking out at least four guys on the run towards him. A hail of bullets from above sent Mark scurrying for cover as the gun above them roared into action a second time.

The rapid thump, thump, thump of bullets hitting concrete, flesh, metal and whatever else was in its path was deafening and Mark sat behind a low wall panting for breath. Suddenly it was as if everything had gone into slow motion as Mark spotted a body of a bad guy lying near him. He hauled it up and over his shoulder, using it as cover as he walked across the body-strewn rooftop towards El Toro. He stopped in the middle and felt the thud of what seemed like a thousand bullets hitting the body he was holding. As he heard the whir of the gun's motor grind to a halt, he realised that was his moment; he dropped the body, took aim and emptied the entire Uzi's magazine into the chopper above.

Thomas Lundon was sitting at the control tower of this long abandoned military base which once belonged to the UN, anxiously awaiting news of the assault on Cabrera Castle. He had three or four radio and communications operatives around him and Roman Vose was forever at his side. He heard the crackle of the radio as he jumped forward to hear news of Mark King's death.

'Control, control, this is Black Widow,' the radio buzzed, 'Alpha and Bravo teams are down. Repeat. Alpha and Bravo teams ARE down. Reques... immedi... assist... ret... con.'

There was an explosion over the airwaves. The radio let out one long, high pitched 'beep', and then fell silent.

Everyone was speechless and silent. The colour dropped from Thomas Lundon's face as Roman Vose gripped his machine gun even tighter with rage. The radio operator tried repeatedly to get a response over the radio but it was no use. Lundon screamed and stormed out. It was now down to Charlie team to carry out what was left of their mission to kill Mark King.

'Charlie One, this is control, SITREP!'

Charlie One witnessed Bravo team's chopper crash into the rocks as they came ashore. Charlie One replied slowly, 'Roger that, control. Just come ashore from our amphibious assault. Bravo team is down. Repeat, Bravo team is down. Alpha team sustaining repeated heavy weapons fire. We are moving to assist.'

Roman Vose winced as he heard this, as there were only four men in Charlie team and it seemed like Lundon had seriously underestimated Mark King. He had worries of his own and decided now was the time to leave. He made his way to his locker where he kept his personal items and thought it was about time he made preparations for a swift exit, should the worst happen.

Mark's hand was sore from squeezing the trigger of El Toro's Uzi 9mm and the vibrations of what seemed like a constant supply of bullets. At one point, Mark thought the ammunition would never end. He turned his head skyward again toward his bullets and saw the underside of the chopper riddled with bullet holes. The bullets must have caught the fuel tank as smoke poured out of the side as it veered off to the right in the same direction as the first chopper. Mark watched it dip low over the water, and then its nose turned upwards as the pilot tried desperately hard to gain altitude to put out what was now the makings of a nice little fuel tank fire. There was a pause, and then it exploded, sending bodies and twisted burning metal down to the waves below. The rotors hit the water and there was another explosion which sent a massive plume of water and smoke towards the sky.

On the rocks below, Charlie team shielded themselves from flying debris, as they watched in horror as the second chopper was downed. The lead, Charlie One, was on his radio to relay the message back to base.

'Control, this is Charlie One. Both choppers are now down. Just Charlie team remaining.'

The other members of Charlie team looked helpless, wondering what to do. Once Charlie One had finished his desperate radio message, he waved them onwards and up the rocks towards the castle. Alpha team was down, now Bravo too, this really was turning into the mission they hoped it wouldn't. Just four people remaining; what were four men against whatever was inside that castle? They had no idea about what kind of hell they were just about to enter.

Back on the rooftop stood Mark and El Toro, cut, bruised, injured but alive, amongst all the other dead and unconscious. Not all of Lundon's soldiers were dead, some were injured and Mark made his way towards the survivors to question them. He held one at gunpoint and asked him repeatedly who sent them and where did they come from. This one spat at Mark as best he could so Mark took out his suppressed Glock and shot him in the chest before moving over to the next one.

'Eh señor. So mucha for the mercy eh!' El Toro commented.

Mark nodded and smiled, grabbing another by his throat. This one was slightly less injured and Mark shouted joyously to El Toro, 'Hey, I think we got ourselves a talker!'

Chapter Twenty-Eight

Williams was about to light his fifth cigarette of the day when the report came in. The admin assistant who came rushing toward him nearly tripped and fell in her rush to provide Williams with something which she thought would make his day. He looked up at her and smiled, almost laughing as she came tumbling towards him, her hands full of papers, trying desperately hard to stay upright in her heels.

'Agent Williams,' she puffed as she got closer to him.

'Careful there, Vanessa,' he warned, jumping to break her fall, 'what's the problem? I'm sure it's not worth breaking your neck over. Or preventing me from having a cigarette break, come to think about it.'

She tried a smile, unamused by his comment but determined to be the one to break the news. He helped her by taking the papers from her and looked inquisitively at her as she tried to speak.

'Agent Williams, we have the latest satellite imagery from our Algerian contact. Ain M'lila Airfield seems to be active and fortifying its position.'

'You what?' he exclaimed, looking stunned at her as she spoke. 'You're joking right, is this Rachel trying to take the piss?'

'I don't know what you mean sir, but these are the images just in,' she said sternly as she directed Williams to the relevant page.

'My god, what the hell are they doing?' he asked, shocked.

'We don't know yet.' Rachel's voice from behind them made them both turn to look. 'Looks like they are preparing for world war three from what we can gather. This place has been demilitarised for some time now so we're curious about what they're up to.'

Williams looked, horrified through the series of satellite images as he looked to Rachel for answers.

'Come on,' she said, grabbing the cigarette from him, 'I'll fill you in on the way.'

They both walked towards the ops room and Williams' eyes widened as she explained.

'Twelve hours ago, some heavy weapons were spotted by out Aerial Reconnaissance Drone after the locals complained of building noise coming from the airfield. Naturally this information reached our ears, and we conducted an over flight. Several armoured vehicles and a large number of troops were seen entering the base under cover of darkness. Intel suggests several large garrisons seem to be fortifying their positions.'

'Yeah, but fortifying them against what?' Williams asked.

'We don't know yet. We've checked with local intelligence and nothing seems out of place, no fall outs, no gang issues, and no political differences we know of.'

'You think this has something to do with Azidi?' he asked her, looking suddenly interested.

'Possibly. He was sighted in Algeria last year, in fact, he spent three days there before returning to Syria, and then we lost him for a while.'

'Well I have to get out there now, this could be our only chance to get him,' he insisted, making a move towards the direction of his office to pick up his weapon.

'Hold your horses, Nathan,' Rachel said, holding his arm, 'we have to wait for authorisation from the Algerians first. Until we know exactly what they are up to, our orders are to stand down and await further intel.'

Agent Williams was not a fan of 'waiting for authorisation'.

He was more swayed towards acting on information received, especially if time was a factor. And he WANTED Azidi, and he wanted him badly. He would not pass up an opportunity to take him out, even if it cost him his job.

'Listen, Rachel,' he placated, putting his hand on her shoulder patronisingly. 'I know you and I have had our differences, but I have been after this guy since before you came here, I KNOW him, I know how he thinks, how he acts, what he does, everything.'

She pushed his hand off her shoulder, glaring at him with a look that reminded him whatever had happened between them before this job meant nothing now, and she was still his superior.

'Agent Williams,' she said quietly but firmly, staring at him all the while, 'may I remind you I am your senior agent and superior; you will NOT try to undermine my authority!'

Williams gulped, realising he had pushed her too far. But he still would not back down.

'I want answers,' he hissed at her, his body language suddenly changing as he stood taller, shoulders back, back straight, almost in a defensive stance.

'I understand that,' she replied in a slightly more relaxed tone, 'but it won't get us anywhere If we burst in there, guns blazing and not asking questions.'

Williams sighed. He knew she was right, but it didn't make him feel any better.

'What did you have in mind?' he asked. She smiled as she motioned him to follow her.

The rooftop looked like a war-zone as Mark and El Toro wandered through the sprawl of bleeding, dead corpses. Smoke grenades that had been fired aimlessly at moving targets sat slowly smoking, the smoke blowing gently across towards Mark and El Toro, making it difficult for them to see. They both stood around staring at the carnage that lay before them. El Toro spoke.

'The massacre of Cabrera,' he sighed, almost weeping at the amount of death before them.

He'd left this life behind many years ago and had lived on this island in relative peace and quiet. Retired to a life of happiness, laughter and history, El Toro felt the familiar pain which always used to precede a firefight. Now it seemed this man, this friend of his closest friend and ally Nial Atkinson, had brought death and destruction to this once peaceful safe-haven. He didn't blame Mark though, he blamed his old enemy and shed a silent tear that someone he used to call 'brother' had still not learned from the mistakes of the past. Lundon still believed anything or anyone he couldn't control or understand had to be shot at, blown up, pursued across the world, and killed. It didn't bear thinking about.

Mark was breathing heavily and struggled to see through the plumes of smoke which almost engulfed him as he staggered to his feet, after dispatching the last of the dying men, with his Kadet knife. He was giving no mercy if someone tried to kill him or El Toro, especially as these soldiers, brave though they were and had put up an extraordinary fight, had been sent to kill and followed orders blindly, without thinking about the consequences of what they did, nor who or what the 'enemy' were and asking themselves if perhaps THEY were the bad guys. Mark felt like a bad guy as he stumbled over falling weapons, pools of blood and spent shell casings towards where he could make out the outline of El Toro. Once he reached him, he put a friendly and supportive hand on El Toro's shoulder and the two men gazed around them in silence at the scene of utter devastation.

The smoke grenades were dying down as Mark left El Toro to wander the bodies to see if anyone else was still alive, and to collect any ammunition, weapons, radios and anything else which could prove useful. These men had families and their loved ones deserved to know where they were. Mark was considering how best to pile the bodies up and how they would explain all this if the authorities came calling.

It was all too much for Mark to bear and he collapsed to his knees, head in his hands, trying to make sense of it all; all this needless killing and suffering, for what? For the good of mankind, to make Lundon feel better or to amuse those who pulled the strings, knowing they had conditioned these men, and probably thousands of others like them, to lay down their lives for a cause they didn't even fully understand. Lundon wasn't the master of some powerful organisation, and Invictus Advoca wasn't some shadow government with the weight of worldly decisions on their shoulders, they were a group of power-mad playground bullies, driven mad by the lust for control, dominance and perceived superiority over anyone who would serve them.

Mark wasn't mad anymore, or angry, or vengeful, he was sorry. Sorry for Lundon, sorry for Marie and the children, sorry for El Toro, dragging a war to his doorstep which had nothing to do with him, and above all, sorry for himself for believing he had no option other than to follow this path until he found Marie's killer. He didn't expect this feeling to suddenly overwhelm him and he was unprepared for it.

He looked up and El Toro was busy taking dog tags from around the necks of the dead and putting them in his top pocket. Now THERE was a man who had seen wars. Wars no one else should see and probably didn't even know about. Here was a man who had suffered and seen suffering at its most prominent, and yet he maintained a steely, cold silence as he stood, knee deep in blood, death and carnage, yet seemed to still stand tall and let it all wash over him. How he managed it, Mark thought to himself, he didn't know, as he searched around for dog tags and useful items. The smell of the smoke grenades caught the back of Mark's throat and he coughed, reaching for his cigarettes in his pocket and lighting one up. El Toro whistled at him and Mark looked up, just in time to catch El Toro's hip flask. Mark gratefully drank heavily from it, hoping it would numb him enough from the surrounding sights. It didn't, but it quickly made him feel less 'there' and slightly more spaced out.

Mark heard a noise a few feet in front of him. A cough mixed with a splutter; and he froze, looking around him to see where it was coming from. He saw movement and slowly moved over to where the noise had come from. As he crawled across the bullet-ridden concrete, he realised what it was, and suddenly hardened again; he slowly drew his weapon and released the safety catch with a 'click'. He found the soldier, wounded but alive, trying to get up and the soldier froze when he saw the barrel of Mark's suppressed pistol, right in his face, almost touching his nose. The soldier looked up and saw Mark's dirty, tear-soaked face with his bloodshot eyes from the smoke grenade and prepared himself for his imminent death.

It felt like a lifetime for Mark to reach the soldier, like time had slowed down and he was moving in slow motion. He thought it might have been the drink El Toro had given him, but his co-ordination seemed fine, it was just that everything else seemed to vanish into a white haze and all Mark could see was the soldier, staring at him in fright, his flak jacket torn and with several visible bullet holes punched into the chest protector. All Mark could think about was that someone who tried to kill him was still alive and Mark had to defend himself. Mark tried to stand up on his shaky, weakened legs, and they trembled as all he could do was lift himself up to his knees. He leaned back a little further and closed one eye, taking aim at the soldier who had propped himself up on the body of someone who had fallen next to him and probably saved his life by doing so.

The two men's eyes met and widened. Mark's were those of a possessed madman. The soldier thought Mark was suffering from being 'trigger happy'. He knew it was a form of hysteria when someone couldn't stop firing, even when everyone around them was dead. If this were the case, this man pointing a gun at him would likely kill him, so he propped himself up on his elbow and leant against the body behind him, ready to face his enemy. He watched as Mark's finger slowly moved towards the trigger and glared at Mark for all he was worth.

Chapter Twenty Nine

El Toro stumbled over the bodies to where Mark knelt and made eye contact with the soldier half lying, half sitting against the body of his dead comrade.

'Talk and I'll spare your life,' Mark promised.

The soldier nodded, having just witnessed Mark kill one other for not talking.

'We're based at an old UN fortified command centre – Ain M'lila Airfield in Algeria.'

'What is there? Co-ordinates and mission objective?' Mark questioned, taking a step towards him.

Mark realised Lundon being so near, made sense he could orchestrate an attack so quickly after Mark's arrival. The soldier continued.

'Ain M'lila airfield is an abandoned World War II military airfield in Algeria, located approximately seventeen kilometres north-northwest of Aïn Kercha in Oum el Bouaghi province, about fifty kilometres south-southeast of Constantine.'

The soldier coughed and spluttered so El Toro shook him vigorously, but it was no good; he was dead. Mark stood up and cursed and turned to El Toro for reassurance about their new intelligence. But El Toro's attention had moved to something which caught his eye on the rocks to the left of their rooftop position. He quickly called Mark over and the two of them spotted four figures moving silently through the rocks towards the main castle gate the same way Mark had climbed. The fading light meant that they stood out, dressed in black combat gear against the bluey grey rocks which guarded the castle against all but the most determined ground assault.

'This a guy, jeeze! Don't a know when to QUIT!' El Toro tutted impatiently.

He reloaded his weapons and made his way to the edge of the roof top to provide over watch. He gestured to Mark to take the left while he took the right and they took up their positions. El Toro held his hand to signal to Mark that he wanted to wait until they got to within a few feet of the gate before opening fire on them. The pair waited and, one by one, Charlie team walked towards the gate, looking confused that their entrance to join the battle above them seemed a little too late. Suddenly, El Toro jumped up onto the parapet, arms stretched upwards, holding his OICW in one hand and his bloodied Kadet knife in the other and screamed at the top of his voice some violent gargling battle cry.

'I, El Toro, commanda this a land and you, infidels, not wanted here!'

Mark stared at him, disturbed by this seemingly insane outburst. El Toro continued, 'Who shall a come in years gone a by and say, I was a there, with the El Toro. Who DARES trespass on a my land?'

Mark watched in amazement as Charlie team stood weapons down, motionless and terrified by this raving nut case shouting at them from the parapet above. They didn't fire at him, they didn't run, they stood motionless. El Toro reached in his pocket and pulled out a detonator.

'You scumbags have a choice. You are now surrounded by a mines, no? Run or we kill you dead!' he shouted.

Mark smiled, realising what El Toro had done. He had mined the main entrance with radio control mines. Not 'usual' landmines, these were different. They were only operated by a remote control which armed them. Once armed, they would act as normal mines but if they were not armed, they posed no threat to anyone. Charlie team stood still as each man in the team put his arms out to ensure no one else moved. There was silence and no movement for about a minute or two before one of Charlie team couldn't resist the temptation any longer and turned tail and ran in the direction they came, thinking somehow he might make it to the rocks before he stepped on a mine.

Sadly, he was wrong and was blown to pieces one step before the edge of the minefield. Seeing him nearly make it, the others were tempted and shot the ground to set the surrounding mines off. This seemed to work and two of them made it forward and out of the mines at the loss of just two of their team. El Toro laughed but then cursed at the fact that two were still alive. He signalled to Mark, who had his rifle trained downwards on the other two Charlie team members. They were busy trying to lace the door with explosives and counting their lucky stars they were still alive. Mark popped an armour piercing round through the first guy who was holding the detonator and he fell, staggering backwards back into the minefield, onto one of the few remaining mines, which promptly exploded. Three down, one to go. Mark trained his sights on the other guy who had his arms up in surrender. Mark was just about to move as his target was neutralised when the last remaining Charlie team member put his hand behind his back and pulled his revolver and pointed it at Mark. As quick as a flash, Mark spotted it and spun his rifle round, had his eye on his sights and found the soldier's forehead, letting two bullets go in quick succession. Mark watched in horror as the grass around the soldier flew up and he realised he missed. There was no third shot from the soldier however, as repeated shots rang out from the bushes behind him. He dropped to the floor. Mark looked stunned by this, as out of the bushes walked Pablo with his M16 and a flak vest on.

'Hey señores, you'll be requiring a boat man no?' he shouted, waving at Mark and El Toro.

Mark smiled and waved as Pablo turned and made his way back into the bushes towards the cove where his boat was moored. Obviously Charlie team had not seen it when they launched their amphibious assault on the island. Mark let out a relieved deep breath.

El Toro checked the perimeter from the rooftop and both men were satisfied no one else was following Charlie team.

Thomas Lundon was furious and worried. He'd sent his best men after Mark King and they were all dead. There was no word from Charlie team so he could safely assume they were dead too and if he knew Mark King correctly, it's possible he would have kept at least one of them alive to tell him where he was hiding out. So he had to prepare, for Mark King *WOULD* come to him.

'No matter,' he thought to himself. The area was covered by armed guards and he wasn't about to let someone as insignificant as Mark King get the better of him. Lundon reached into the drawer of the grand desk he was sat at in his secure room and pulled out his old revolver.

He caressed it menacingly and checked the clip: fully loaded. He put it in his inside jacket holster and felt much more protected now he was armed. What was he thinking? He was sat in a fortified ex-UN airbase which had bunkers capable of withstanding a nuclear blast and a fully stocked weapons room and at least a dozen armed guards, what the hell did HE have to be worried about? He laughed out loud as Roman Vose stood at the crack in the open door, watching his boss.

Vose concluded his boss had lost the plot and had worked out how best to get out when the slaughter began. There was no way Mark King would stop, not until he put a bullet in Thomas Lundon's skull and once he'd done that, he would come looking for Vose as he was a loose end to be tied up. Vose would not stand about and wait for that to happen. As time went on, Vose had time to sympathise with Mark King about why he was on this mission to avenge his wife's death. Vose had initially wanted no part in it but revelled in killing just the same. For all his faults, he wasn't as evil and twisted as many of the others thought he was. All the same, it was time to put his plan into action and he made his way down to the electricity room deep under the ground. He needed to have the strength to pull the plug when the time came so he could get out using Lundon's car. It was the only way out.

A few hours later, once they had collected all the bodies and put them in the castle grounds incinerator, collected what weapons were still of use and stored them away, mopped the blood up and put things back the way they were before the assault on the castle, Mark and El Toro were nursing their wounds in the main dining area. El Toro had radioed the coastguard to tell them about the two downed choppers and advised them he saw them go down but didn't know what caused it. There were a few coastguard vessels floating about around the areas in which the choppers met their grisly end. Mark was looking at one of the computer monitors and had found information about Ain M'lila airfield in Algeria. He read aloud to El Toro, who was downing a whiskey and staggering about clearing up.

'It was built by the Army Corps of Engineers on a flat, dry lakebed at an altitude of 2,580 feet, designed for heavy bomber use by the United States Army Air Force's Twelfth Air Force during the North African Campaign,' he read, 'with concrete runways, hardstands and taxiways. Billeting and support facilities consisted of tents. Due to its high altitude, the days are hot and the nights cold.'

El Toro stared at Mark and raised his eyebrows.

'You a want another dose of what we just a had?'

Mark didn't fancy that, but he fancied even less not moving on Lundon before he got word his attack had failed and either moved locations, or sent another team or three in to finish the job. El Toro nodded understandingly.

'We need to sort ourselves out first before walking into another fire-fight!'

They both looked back at the computer monitor at the same time, which was showing a map and satellite image of Ain M'lila airfield.

The barbed and electrified fence loomed up at Mark as he skirted around the perimeter of the airfield for a weakness. There wasn't one and he couldn't locate another way in. He decided the best way was to go under the fence and wondered how far under the ground it went. He took out his folding shovel and dug. He had spent the best part of two hours prior to this in a tree high up, scanning the base for guards and anyone else who would pose a problem to him. He spoke into a small headset mic.

'Eight wooden and metal watch towers with searchlights, which cover the perimeter, complete with armed guards, concrete bunkers looking out towards the open areas and what looks like it used to be a parade or training ground.'

He continued to scan the landscape.

'Control tower mounted on a large concrete structure with large blast doors at the centre of the complex and some smaller buildings scattered around. Look like barracks or huts of some sort.'

Finally, his eyes came to rest on tarmac.

'There's also what looks like the remains of an air strip which has seen its fair share of aircraft, both big and small.'

Mark also spotted a large raised helipad at the end of a narrow concreted road.

'Guards on the roof, snipers probably, and some patrolling the grounds, some with dogs, some others guarding the smaller buildings.'

He could see floodlight posts every seven feet around the perimeter fence. The whole complex was built in between two huge hillsides with flat ground ahead of it where the runway was situated. He noted that there was an entrance gate at that end with two guard huts and barriers and one further to the rear of the complex. Both entrances were covered by machine guns with sandbag walls. Lundon had *really* thought this one through before shutting himself away deep within the centre of the complex.

There would inevitably be a series of tunnels underneath the entire complex with potentially a tunnel leading out somewhere, but he had to find it first. He gave up on digging and instead, planted one of his remote detonated mines under the fence and quickly covered over the hole. Looking at it, anyone would think it was a badger or fox hole, at least he *hoped* they would. He decided again to search for a tunnel entrance and backtracked through the woods, searching for an entrance or anything that looked like it could serve as a tunnel entrance.

Mark had been walking for a while when he came across what he thought was an anti-tank defence block. He skirted round it and realised it was a hatch entrance. The bolts, as he had not expected, were not rusted or welded shut, but instead they were new and polished. Lundon was expecting to flee if the situation arose. He cleared away some of the foliage and tugged for a few minutes on the hatch handle before it squeaked open. He paused and winced at the sound, hoping it had not given his position away. He looked around and nothing happened.

He waited a further few minutes just to be certain before climbing into the hatch and shining his Maglite down the shaft. There was a ladder which, again, was new and he descended into the darkness holding his torch in his mouth. Eventually he stepped down onto the floor about twenty feet below ground and faced a tunnel. He peered into the darkness and listened intently for the sound of approaching boots. He heard nothing except the dripping of water and the occasional rat squeak. He wasn't worried about the rats as they seemed more afraid of him and concerned with where they heading to worry about nipping him or getting under his feet. He continued on through the darkness until he reached a small, steel door. He tried the door and realised it was bolted shut, but the control panel on the wall proved he was close to something that whoever owned the land didn't want people to see or get too close. He smiled and lined the panel with plastic explosives.

He wired the detonator up and walked back down the tunnel to escape being injured by fragments. He waited and pressed the detonator. There was a muffled thud as the control panel exploded, revealing bare wires behind it. He knew it wouldn't be long before the main system detected an intruder, so he worked fast on the wires, reconnecting the door which then released its bolts and he could pull it open.

He faced another long passage and noticed cameras mounted on the walls, luckily facing the opposite way. This meant the system hadn't detected a malfunction on the door yet so he reached into his equipment vest and took out the small can of black spray paint. As he approached each camera, he sprayed the lens from behind and made sure he waited for it to dry before proceeding to the next camera. He reached a metal staircase which ascended, he guessed, to the upper levels. By his predictions and from what he remembered from the plans he and El Toro found, he was now at the centre of the complex.

As he went upwards, the light grew brighter, and he found rooms off corridors to the left and right along a metal gangway. It looked like plant rooms and water and air treatment rooms, probably so that in the event of a nuclear attack, they could be fully self-sufficient. The sound of approaching footsteps forced Mark to flatten himself against one of the steel doors as the sound grew louder. He un-holstered his suppressed Glock and flicked off the safety catch. Holding it up to his right ear, he held his nerve until they were almost next to him. Mark saw the barrel of a semi-automatic machine gun pass him and threw himself towards it, grabbing at the barrel and forcing it up towards the ceiling. While he did this, he fired one shot at the other guard, square in the forehead. He didn't have time to react and hit the floor, while Mark elbowed the guard whose gun he was holding, and knocked him off balance before shooting him twice in the chest. Mark stood between the other two, careful not to get blood on the soles of his boots.

'Radios and weapons,' he demanded. Reluctantly, they handed them over.

Hauling them into a room next to him, Mark carried on his way. As he ran silently through the maze of steel corridors, he realised they must have been on their way to investigate the malfunctioning door he blew up and knew his time was limited.

He checked his watch and set the timer on a countdown. By El Toro's calculations, he had approximately thirty minutes to reach the top of the complex before all hell rained down on top of him and he was at a strategic disadvantage in these corridors as there was nowhere to hide if someone came up behind or in front of him. He reloaded his suppressed Glock and regulated his breathing, now regretting every cigarette he ever had.

Mark stopped running sharply as he came to a wider corridor with huge glass windows to the right. He stopped and looked through them and stared at the rows of tanks, guns and ammunition which spread out in a warehouse sized chamber behind the glass. This was someone preparing for something huge and it was much bigger than he thought.

'If this lot get free,' he said out loud, 'I'm up shit creek without a paddle!'

Another twenty minutes of more metal staircases and rooms and Mark reached a steel door with a circular glass hole of reinforced glass. He peered through and saw several guards on the other side guarding a door to another part of the complex.

'Two on the left, and two on the right, damn!' he said to himself.

He ducked away out of sight and wondered what the hell he would do next. Suddenly, he realised he had his repelling belt on, the same one he used in Holtenau to spy on Azidi's meeting of terrorists. He detached it from its belt fastener and used some of the plastic explosive to 'glue' it either side of the door at ankle level. He looked around and found a fire extinguisher hooked to a wall and took it, setting it down facing the door. Next he wired a plastic explosive to the fire extinguisher and to the door and set the trigger, which was the wire from his repelling belt. Finding a sufficient hiding place behind some old office tables stacked in a corner, he tapped the glass with his torch and ran to hide behind the stacks of tables.

He waited and a few seconds later saw the door open. When it did, the guards tripped the wire from Mark's belt, setting off the explosives. The explosion took the first two guards out at once. The next two and two more who had shown up were met with a whack from a flying fire extinguisher, which hit them in the chest as part of it ruptured. Mark quickly stepped out of his hiding place and dispatched the remaining guard, who was lying injured on the floor. The fire extinguisher was still going down the corridor beyond the door Mark had just stepped through, streaming foam and smoke as it went: the perfect cover, he thought as he stopped to hear screams from up ahead of him.

The fire extinguisher, still under its own power, had ricocheted off the walls and hit the guard's commander as he ran down the bend in the corridor ahead of Mark. Mark reached him a few seconds after he died and noted his rank from the insignia on his jacket; he must be close to Lundon's location. Suddenly a Tannoy announcement almost defended him as the voice of Thomas Lundon addressed him.

'Welcome Mr King. I'm so glad you could join us. I see you have found our escape route. Pity but no matter, I should imagine you will be dead before you reach me. Oh, and you are not the only one armed!'

Mark searched anxiously around until he found the reasons he was being addressed. There were small, rounded black CCTV cameras embedded outside every steel door in the corridors Mark had passed and he was being watched. Lundon advised that Mark give himself up but congratulated and baited him for coming this far undetected. Mark's response to this was quick. With a blast of the guard's sub-machine gun, he obliterated all the CCTV cameras he saw back down the corridor and those further ahead as he came to them. Now they were blind!

Chapter Thirty

Thomas Lundon had the head of the technical assistant and was throwing him into the control panels repeatedly as the poor assistant pleaded with Lundon that if the cameras were down, there was little he could do. Lundon, however, wasn't convinced and was enraged that they now could not track the person coming to kill them all because he had shot out all the cameras. The technical assistant fell against the long array of computer terminals built into the desk and hit his head on the edge of the terminal. He fell unconscious to the floor. Lundon was struggling to catch his breath and other assistants in the room stared in horror as he flung himself around the room in rage.

He grabbed his radio and desperately radioed for back up.

'Vose! Get up here!'

He got increasingly irritated and panicked when there was no response. Lundon threw himself towards the intruder tracking system and relaxed. They may not see Mark King on camera, but they could follow his movements on the intruder map. Lundon pulled himself into the desk, red faced and flushed, while he caught his breath. He had no Roman Vose and one less assistant to run the computer terminal but he suddenly became relaxed and contented as he leaned back in the leather lab chair and held his hands, fingers to fingers and smiled to himself.

Mark came to a sharp left turn in the corridor. It all seemed to happen in slow motion as he came face to face with a guard coming in the opposite direction. The guard looked just as shocked to see Mark as Mark was. They were both running when they realised they were facing one another. The guard raised his gun towards Mark and pulled back the loading mechanism. Mark pulled his Glock up to the guard's head level. Both fired but Mark's reactions were marginally quicker and the fact that the guard had an automatic weapon meant that his aim was hampered and the gun barrel flew in an upwards motion, catching the shoulder pad of Mark's flak vest as he flew out of the line of fire. The guard's face dropped and his finger continued to fire the remains of his clip into the ceiling as he fell slowly backwards. Mark's landing against the wall was heavy and knocked the wind out of him. He thought he had broken a rib but was glad to be alive as he checked his shoulder. The Kevlar shoulder plate had absorbed the impact of the bullet, but not before it had thrown Mark towards the wall and seriously bruised his shoulder. That, coupled with having the wind knocked out of him, had caused him to lose consciousness momentarily. By the time the high pitched tinnitus sound had abated and the mist in his eyes had cleared, Mark realised he was still alive and tried to get up but the pain in his ribs prevented him from a quick get up. He pointed his Glock towards the body of the dead guard before sweeping in front and behind him to check for reinforcements. He was clear, and the guard was dead. Mark felt his head thump as the impact continued to make its way up his body. This was no time for nausea and Mark shook his head to clear it. It seemed to work temporarily, enough for him to see straight to continue.

Mark was now entering the level below ground level of the bunker and his head still hurt as he looked around, surrounded by brighter lights, cleaner air and a buzzing sound. At first he thought it was due to the headache but realised it must be a plant room, which might house the main generators. He spotted a brown door with a hazard sign and kicked it open, clearing the room with his Glock before entering fully. He followed the sound of the buzzing toward a mains generator and had a quick look around it. It was at this point he realised his skills and experience were not enough to work out how to use it or to shut it down. He figured out that if he cut the main supply line, it should shut down the entire facility, providing him with the cover of darkness and unlock any secure doors. This came as a double-edged sword: he could enter any level, at will, with only the push of a door AND it would eliminate any further CCTV or Tannoy announcements. It also meant all doors were released for floods of guards and troops to overwhelm him from every direction. At least with a locked door, they would lose the element of surprise.

'Screw it,' he said determinedly as he smashed the control dial with the guard's automatic machine gun, before turning the gun to the mains wires and giving of three short sharp blasts, sending metal and sparks everywhere.

The generator made a whooshing sound and then a descending beep as it powered down and exploded. Mark ran to escape the shrapnel of nuts, bolts, sparks and machinery which flew in every direction. He was suddenly in total darkness as he made his way back out into the corridor. He could now hear voices getting closer, the shouts of armed guards and panic which had now set in. One thing that worked in his favour was the darkness. The guards had to use torches to find their way around, which meant that he could see them coming far more in advance than if he had to rely on his hearing alone. He opened the remaining magazine of the guard's machine gun onto the sprawl of guards who marched around the corner to face him, temporarily blinded by their torch light. They fell all over the place, wounded, as Mark stepped over them. As he went, he shot each one with his suppressed Glock, killing those who were still alive, instantly. He was NOT taking any chances and headed to the large set of glass double doors which led into a control room.

Assistants lay dead against the control monitors dressed in white technicians' coats all around him. Computers, riddled with bullet holes, sparked and the screens were shattered. Lundon had shot anyone he no longer needed or who was surplus to requirements once the power went down and he was now making his escape. A helicopter had since landed on the helipad but its rotors were stationary, so at least it wasn't about to take off. Mark was concerned more reinforcements had been called in before the power went down. The broken window which led out onto the metal platform that surrounded the tower looked like a tempting place to run, so Mark jumped up onto the computer terminal desks and out through the broken window. He shielded his eyes from the fading daylight as he got his bearings. He realised no one could have come out that way and turned back the way he had come. Edging silently through the corridor, he came to stairs going down to a garage.

If it wasn't for the sound of very expensive leather shoes behind him, Mark might have ventured down there and come face to face with Roman Vose, who was in the middle of executing his escape plan. There would be time for him later and Mark followed the sound of the shoes as they pattered their way out of sight. Then a door slammed and Mark faced more guards. He passed a small window and flinched as a sniper bullet shattered the pane just past his head. With one movement, he un-shouldered his rifle and found his target, one of the guard towers. He hit the sniper in the face and he fell backwards out of the tower. He quickly swivelled to the second tower, then the third, then the fourth, scoring a direct headshot with each movement. He'd taken fifty percent of the threat out quickly and he was counting his blessings. He then saw a door to one of the concrete buildings burst open and five guards come running out. He picked off whoever he could with his rifle before he had to resort to the machine gun, and the last magazine he had taken from a dead guard.

The five were now dead and strewn over the parade ground. Mark found the window of a concrete building a few yards away. He aimed a shot through the window and hit a guard in the side of the head. With that, the others flung open the door and used it for cover whilst returning fire to Mark's position. He ducked, ran along the wall and found another window where he sent two more shots from his machine gun through the door. The magazine had been filled with armour piercing bullets as the guards hiding behind the door fell after the first few shots.

'Keep moving,' he said to himself aloud as he moved along the wall.

He found a door and kicked it open only to be on a steel walkway which faced the last few guard towers he had not hit yet. Mark jumped back in the doorway and set his rifle up against the wall, pointing to the sixth and seventh towers. He took one guard as he was climbing the ladder and another as he was about to shine the searchlight to illuminate Mark's position. Mark counted.

'One, two, three, six, and seven. That means three towers left behind me.'

He heard Lundon shouting at him from the corridor and spun round to follow the sound. He stopped before turning the corner, flat against the wall, as he realised he was only a few feet from Lundon. He spun round to see Thomas Theodore Lundon, flanked by six heavily armed guards stood at the end of the corridor, baiting him to come out so they could fill him full of bullets. Mark narrowly dodged the hail of gunfire which preceded him revealing his position. His shoulder slammed against the wall and the sting of the injured shoulder made him dizzy.

He straightened himself out and held his ground, trying desperately to work out how to get them all out in one shot without hitting Lundon straight away. He looked about and saw that a guard had dropped a smoke grenade in the rush to locate him. He grabbed it, waiting before he pulled the pin, paused, and threw it round the corner, filling the entire corridor with smoke. He made his way tentatively through the smoke and caught sight of the guard's green laser sights on their weapons. He used his Glock to shoot four of the six, at point blank range. For the others he used the machine gun sideways, knocking them both against the wall. On the rebound, he punched one in the face and the crunch told Mark he had done some serious damage. The last one was retreating from Mark to cover Lundon's exit, facing Mark all the time.

Mark took two steps forward and heard the click of the guard's gun misfire. The guard cursed as he tried again and again to fire but to no avail. His last mistake was that he tried to reload his weapon, buying Mark precious seconds to intercept and shoot him in the head with his Glock. The smoke was clearing and Mark could see a lot more clearly. Lundon had backed into a room and out of the fire escape, down a metal staircase and was walking towards the waiting helicopter, its rotors now spinning at full speed about to take off.

Mark sprinted after him and onto the flat solid ground in pursuit. Suddenly and without warning, a Desert Chameleon six-wheeled armoured vehicle, followed by a dozen armed guards, edged out from Mark's left-hand side. He ground to a halt, seeking cover wherever he could. He stopped, rooted to the spot, watching Lundon mocking him as he stood in front of the group of armed guards. The turret on the armoured car spun slowly and deliberately anti-clockwise towards Mark and he waited for it to home in on his position, its terrifying bullets ripping him to shreds as Thomas Lundon, the architect for all Mark's pain, walk away unharmed and Marie, unavenged. Mark waited for his fate, somehow contented with the fact that this would be the end of the line, and knowing, beyond everything, he had tried his best to find his wife's killer. Suddenly Mark remembered the land mine he had planted earlier and felt the detonator in his pocket. He reached for it and clicked the small metal trigger. The fence behind the helipad exploded and Mark took the opportunity to gain ground, running towards the helicopter, determined to get at least one shot off at Lundon before he got away.

At that moment, an earth shattering explosion happened at the same point where Mark's landmine had gone off, and it wasn't his. Then Mark heard the deafening repeated thud of a large machine gun and looked on, stunned, as men from Lundon's protective garrison fell in a bloody, bullet ridden mess on the floor in the wake of the hell unleashed by the FNHFN Mark 46 M249 SAW Machine Gun. Next was the helicopter, exploding in such a massive explosion, its shock wave knocked Mark off his feet and onto his back. As he went down, he saw Lundon heading off on foot, in the direction the armoured car had come from but when the dust settled, Mark could see a combat clad figure stood in the wreckage and massacre. Mark smiled as a hand went up in acknowledgement. Mark clambered to his feet and saw a familiar figure stood holding an empty Saw machine gun: El Toro, 'The Bull'. He looked quite the part wearing his ammunition around his neck like Rambo, cigar in his mouth, laughing. Mark made an 'OK' symbol with his fingers as El Toro took a bow and waved Mark toward where Lundon had run. Mark saluted El Toro and ran for it in time to see Lundon climb another metal staircase up to the control tower.

Mark beat him to it and got ahead of him and took aim. El Toro was now behind Lundon but was letting Mark have this kill. Mark took his rifle and called to Lundon who stopped and turned, a face of horror seeing Mark stood there in front of him with his sights trained firmly on Lundon's forehead.

'Thomas Lundon!!!' Mark screamed at him. 'Why did Marie have to die?'

Lundon laughed as he swallowed two Topiramate, anti-epilepsy tablets, wincing as he swallowed. His hands shook and his vision became distorted.

'Why did the world have to turn on me for a condition that wasn't my fault?' he scorned, pointing at Mark.

Mark looked confused as he stood staring at Lundon.

'Oh yes, the world was kind when it suited it, the rest of the time it berated me and mocked me!' he hissed.

'No one's mocked you, Lundon. You're just insane,' Mark replied, lifting his weapon.

'See!' shouted Lundon stepping towards Mark, 'that's exactly what HE did too. The apple, Mark, doesn't fall very far from the tree!'

Mark stopped and thought for a second, before looking back up at Lundon, who was turning red and breathing heavily.

'HE?' Mark questioned, not sure what he was being told.

'Yes!' replied Lundon, satisfied they were getting closer to the truth, 'HE was YOUR FATHER!'

Chapter Thirty-One

Mark's body went rigid. His father? How could Lundon know his father?

'What do you mean?' Mark hissed back at Lundon, not convinced Lundon was telling the truth.

'Oh, the boy doesn't know the truth. Well my boy, let me fill you in.' He laughed manically. 'Yes, I knew your father. In fact, we were close, long before YOU were born. We were close, right until I was diagnosed with epilepsy, and then it became a different story.'

Mark shook his head in confusion.

'You LIE!' he shouted, pointing the gun at Lundon.

Lundon wasn't scared. He was far too angry to worry about someone pointing a gun at him.

'Oh, his "friendship" wasn't so strong then was it? He, just like the rest of them, laughed at me, especially when it came to making new friends, because the stress of interacting with new people used to bring on a seizure. Oh yes, they all thought it was hilarious, look at him, they used to cry, the madman. People can be cruel, Mr King, and so I learned that I could be cruel too!'

'Even if this is true, what did it have to do with Marie?' Mark cried.

'I wanted you to feel the way your father made me feel.

286

When you were born and grew up to become a successful lawyer, I thought you would work for me, but then Azidi was caught and guess who was prosecuting him!'

Mark's arm loosened as he remembered back to the trial.

'Naturally I thought you could work for me, but then I saw the man you had become, and that you would never abandon that ridiculous sense of "justice" you hold onto so tightly. This, what we do here, THIS Mr King, is justice!'

Mark stared at the madman who stood before him, arms outstretched, eyes bulging almost out of their sockets, sweating and red in the face, and, for a while, Mark pitied him.

'What kind of a life have you known?' he said sympathetically in a low voice, lowering his weapon and walking towards Lundon. 'How has the world treated you?'

'The world hated me!' Lundon screeched. Mark stepped towards him again. 'Just like the way you used to mock that journalist, the same way your father mocked me.'

Mark remembered Ian Hawking and how even Marie had scorned him for the way he spoke to him. He instantly felt regret at having been so cruel to Hawking. Lundon calmed down, thinking maybe Mark wasn't as much like his father as he first thought.

'I don't "hate" you. Not even for killing Marie. Hate destroys people, like it has destroyed you. You're not dangerous,' he explained.

Lundon almost smiled as the tone of the conversation dropped into one of pity and sympathy.

'It's purely "business",' he replied, putting his hands in the air casually.

Mark moved closer and Lundon's face changed into one pleading for his life.

'What business?' Mark questioned.

'The weapons for Azidi were to instigate a terror attack from Germany to the west so the west would retaliate, forcing them to upgrade their weaponry. As I own a weapon supply company which sold to world governments, the west would have no choice but to buy from my company, as would other countries that would be drawn into the war.'

The way Lundon saw it, he was the one to benefit.

'Marie was just a way to get to you and force you to run,' he said, half smiling at his accomplishment.

'Why?' Mark spat at Lundon.

'You are part of a world you do not understand, Mr King,' Lundon smiled softly.

Mark gritted his teeth angrily.

'With too much of an inquisitive mind, just like your father's, you had inadvertently uncovered the first parts of this during the Azidi trial but you were never in one place or predictable long enough to pin down,' Lundon explained in a trembled voice. Mark gritted his teeth and stroked the trigger gently. 'You were at the shooting club and Roman Vose and Hix Lomas only had a narrow window to eliminate you. On my orders, Hix killed Marie to make it look like you killed her, getting you permanently out of the way.'

'You're just mad,' Mark said calmly.

Lundon's face turned from calmness to anger as he screamed out loud at Mark and ran at him. Mark looked at El Toro, then at Lundon and saw Marie's face. He knew the only way to end this was for Lundon to die. He gripped the rifle with sweaty hands, steadied his breathing and, just as Thomas Lundon moved closer to him, he squeezed the trigger.

Thomas Lundon fell backwards. A look of confusion and shock contorted his face as the blood ran down the side of his head. He stumbled backwards and fell over the edge of the barrier holding the staircase up and dropped. Instead of a thud as his body hit the dust and dirt below, he heard a smash. El Toro and Mark ran to the edge to see the body of Thomas Lundon, smashed, half in and half out of the roof of a Lincoln limousine, windscreen smashed and alarm sounding. Mark could make out the body of Roman Vose, bloodied and eyes closed, in the driver's seat.

'Eh, er, Señor. It's a time for a 'oliday, no?' El Toro shouted to Mark.

Mark nodded and made his way toward El Toro, who put his arm around Mark and led him back out of the mangled perimeter fence which was still sparking from the explosion, and into the woods, to El Toro's waiting four-by-four.

Chapter Thirty-Two

New York. One month later

Mark pulled up in his rental car at the address his mother-in-law had given him before she took the children to New York. It was just after three forty in the afternoon and the sun was bright. He could hear laughter coming from inside the house and his heart was in his throat as he got out of the car. He grabbed his crutches and winced as he put pressure on his broken ribs. They were still sore, as were the cuts on his face, and his broken arm rested in a sling. He leaned on the car door as a voice came from the passenger side of the car.

'Eh Señor, you are a supposed to be letting me 'elp YOU!' El Toro pleaded.

He raised his eyebrows at Mark disapprovingly as he tried to be independent. He never had been a good patient. He smiled at remembering the way Marie tried to look after him when he had flu. Mark smiled at El Toro's attempt at a caring nature as he reluctantly agreed. Mark limped up the small steps to the front door and, looking at El Toro for encouragement, knocked on the door.

Benjamin opened it and turned to see his father stood there. He shouted for Hope and his grandmother, who came running to the front door to see what all the fuss was about. The three of them embraced Mark, who shouted in pain as his mother-in-law looked at him and burst into tears at the state of his shattered body.

The children squealed with delight and relief as they danced round and round their father shouting and hugging him. 'Daddy, daddy you're back, you're back!'

'Ready to be a father again?' asked Wendy, smiling. Mark nodded and smiled.

'Is he… I mean… are they…?' Wendy stumbled, almost too afraid to ask.

'Yes,' he said sharply, 'all of them.'

Then they noticed El Toro and Mark beckoned him in. Hope looked at her father.

'Daddy, who is this?' she asked, holding Mark's hand and pointing to El Toro. Mark replied, smiling at El Toro.

'This is a friend. Uncle Toro.'

El Toro smiled at Mark and put his arm round them all as they all walked into the house, shutting the door.

Monitors beeped and nurses came and went, monitoring their patient intensively. The patient had sustained massive internal injuries and the hospital were not sure if he would make it through the night. Wherever he had been, whatever he had been involved in, these injuries were life-threatening. He was intubated and on dozens of monitors and machines and the injuries spoke for themselves. Outside the theatre doors, two men in suits and earpieces stood watching half a dozen staff treat this injured man, waiting for a verdict on what the prognosis was.

One lead nurse spotted them and went to address them. They explained who they were and why they were there and she turned to go back into the theatre. One of the two men in suits left to make a phone call, while the other stared into the theatre, wondering if this guy would survive.

'We'll know more in the morning. He's been in surgery for hours and this isn't his first operation. We're trying to save his legs but it's touch and go. We'll do what we can,' a nurse said to the man in the suit as she left the theatres.

The man nodded and looked grim-faced.

'How long before we can officially question him?' he asked. The nurse looked regretfully at him.

'Another twelve hours at the least,' she replied, 'he fell from quite a height. If it hadn't been for his car breaking his fall, you would have been looking at him in a body bag. I don't know how he managed it, but he has lasted this long.'

The monitors continued to bleep and buzz as the patient laid in a medically induced coma, face slightly contorted and looking old. His old eyes were darting backwards and forwards inside their lids, looking like he was dreaming or in some torturous nightmare from which he could not wake.

The men stood around the bed, watching, as this man defied the odds and continued to live. With the sound of the monitors echoing around the room, they looked at each other gravely. Outside, a nurse stood watching through the side room window, wondering would happen to the patient and who he was. Whoever it was, many people were interested in his recovery and he had a large group of bodyguards, all armed.

Epilogue

Paris, France

The weather was warm, and the sun beat down from a pure blue cloudless sky as the black stretched Lincoln limousine with private plates pulled up outside the Hotel Plaza Athenee in Paris, getting lots of attention from onlookers and people milling about the rows of cafes and restaurants which lined both sides of the road. A young girl stepped out in black heels and walked towards the hotel entrance, putting on her sunglasses as she did so. She was clutching a small black handbag, and she paused for a moment, turning around to see the beautiful sunshine. She had heavy make-up and her hair had been cut short.

She entered the lobby area, checking her surroundings carefully. A man sat in reception reading a newspaper, pulling the paper away from his face and looking up at her as she walked towards the lifts, the sound of her heels echoing around the marble floors. He nodded at her and got up to follow. They waited at the lifts for several moments before the ping of the lift reaching ground level sounded. They walked into the lift and turned around to see the hotel reception staff looking at them expectantly. Their faces remained motionless as the lift doors closed.

Once they were at their designated floor, the doors opened and they strode out into a carpeted hallway. A man with an earpiece and suit was waiting by one of the open room doors. The woman was joined by yet another bodyguard as they walked towards the hotel room. Inside, a dead man lay on the floor, a bullet hole in his skull, photographs scattered all over the bed. The woman bent down to pick up some of the scattered photos from the floor. They had been scattered during the fight which had taken place the night before. The door was closed behind her, leaving her alone with just the body and the pictures.

As she slowly lowered herself down onto the edge of the large king sized double bed of the bridal suite, she collected the photographs of a man in uniform strewn all over the bed. A tear rolled down her face as she looked at the images. Her hands shook, as she clutched an image to her face, allowing the tears to flow.

There was a knock at the room door and she took her M24 suppressed pistol from her small handbag, put it in her belt behind her back, checked the spy-hole and opened the door tentatively.

'Elena Koskova?' a voice asked her carefully.

She nodded, opening the door. The suited man strode into the room clutching the evidence file which contained CCTV images of an obliterated UN airfield in Algeria. The young woman sat back down on the bed, putting the safety catch back on her pistol. The suited man stood over her, emotionless, and passed her the file. She opened it and immediately thumbed through the still images. Then the suited man spoke.

'Mademoiselle,' he said in a gentle, caring voice as she got up to walk out onto the large balcony which faced the Eiffel Tower.

'I am sorry for your loss. He was a brave soldier. He loved you very much.'

She smiled briefly and looked up at him.

'Who was this man here to meet?' she asked, pointing at the bloodied body on the carpet next to the bed.

'We think there was a meeting set up with someone within an organisation based at the airfield. Our sources are checking this out now,' he replied, still maintaining the emotionless expression.

The woman had a distant look in her eye as she imagined the firefight that would have happened at the airfield. It must have been terrifying. She imagined the explosions, the gun fire, the smoke grenades and the rush of armed soldiers as they attempted to defend themselves against the attack. She closed her eyes and she could almost hear the sound of shouting and screams of pain as bullets ripped apart the walls and flew in all directions.

She imagined the smell of the gases produced by the multitude of weapons being fired. She also imagined the pain and suffering that many of the men killed, would have felt, and the merciless way in which they were butchered, not offered any opportunity of surrender, just mercilessly gunned down, some at point blank range, some from a distance.

The sounds that echoed through her ears were of the man she loved, the man in the photograph, as she envisaged his final moments at the hands of the cold-blooded killer who had rampaged through the facility to murder everyone inside. She imagined it in slow motion; the bullet flying towards him from a heavily armed, combat ready figure hidden partially in shadow in her mind as her face wrinkled up, somehow bracing herself for impact as the imaginary bullet hit the soldier and he fell, a look of shock and fear on his face, to the ground.

She got angry as she pictured a man stood over his body laughing at the soldier as his last breath left his body. She also pictured the figure brutally murdering others, firing round after round at people running for cover and trying to get away. The tears rolled down her cheeks again and her heart pounded.

Two knocks on the door brought her back to the present and her eyes opened suddenly.

'Madame Koskova, Your father's car is waiting for you outside. Will that be all?' asked a voice from outside the room.

'Yes,' she replied coldly, standing up and collecting the photographs. 'You will pay for what you have done,' she spat angrily, taking one last look at the file, 'Mark Lucas King.'

COMING SOON!

Mark King returns in...

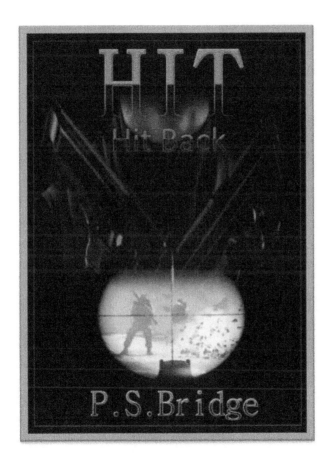

Lightning Source UK Ltd.
Milton Keynes UK
UKOW05f1909300617

304440UK00001B/47/P